The Author

ETHEL WILSON was born in Port Elizabeth, South Africa, in 1888. She was taken to England at the age of two after her mother died. Seven years later her father died, and in 1898 she came to Vancouver to live with her maternal grandmother. She received her teacher's certificate from the Vancouver Normal School in 1907 and taught in many local elementary schools until her marriage in 1921.

In the 1930s Wilson published a few short stories and began a series of family reminiscences which were later transformed into *The Innocent Traveller*. Her first published novel, *Hetty Dorval*, appeared in 1947, and her fiction career ended fourteen years later with the publication of her story collection, *Mrs. Golightly and Other Stories*. Through her compassionate and often ironic narration, Wilson explores in her fiction the moral lives of her characters.

For her contribution to Canadian literature, Wilson was awarded the Canada Council Medal in 1961 and the Lorne Pierce Medal of the Royal Society of Canada in 1964. Her husband died in 1966, and she spent her later years in seclusion and ill-health.

Ethel Wilson died in Vancouver in 1980.

ETHEL WILSON

The Innocent Traveller

With an Afterword by P.K. Page

"And as if on a stream I fixe mine eye,
That drop, which I looked on, is presently
Pusht with more waters from my sight, and gone."

JOHN DONNE

M&S

The following dedication appeared in the first edition:

TO
WALLACE
MY DEAR HUSBAND

Copyright © 1990 by University of British Columbia, by arrangement
with Macmillian of Canada
Afterword copyright © 1990 by P.K. Page

This book was first published in 1949 by The Macmillan Company of
Canada Limited

Reprinted 1990

Canadian Cataloguing in Publication Data

Wilson, Ethel, 1888-1980
The innocent traveller

(New Canadian library)
Includes bibliographical references.
ISBN 0-7710-8955-4

I. Title.   II. Series.

PS8545.I62I5 1990   C813'.54   C90-093955-9
PR9199.3.W5I5 1990

Typesetting by Tony Gordon Ltd.

Printed and bound in Canada

Published by arrangement with Macmillan of Canada

McClelland & Stewart Inc.
The Canadian Publishers
481 University Avenue
Toronto, Ontario
M5G 2E9

Author's Note

This is the story – part truth and part invention – of a lively woman who lived for a hundred years and died triumphant in Vancouver and is nearly forgotten after all her commotion of living.

The metaphors are not mixed. The drop of water, the bird, the water-glider, the dancer, the wind on the canal, and Topaz, are all different and all the same.

"I have a Father in the Promised Land" originally appeared in the *New Statesman and Nation*, and "The Innumerable Laughter" in *Orion IV*. I am indebted to the editors for their kind permission to republish them here.

E.W.

Vancouver
British Columbia
1947

Contents

ONE

Dinner at Noon

FAR AWAY at the end of the table sat Father, the kind, handsome and provident man. At this end sat Mother, her crinoline spread abroad. On Mother's right was Mr. Matthew Arnold. On each side of the table the warned children ate their food gravely, all except Topaz on Mother's left. Topaz, who could not be squelched, was perched there on the top of two cushions, as innocent as a poached egg. Mother sat gracious, fatigued, heavy behind the majestic crinoline with the last and fatal child.

Said Mr. Matthew Arnold in large and musical tones, speaking across the children and three jellied fowls to Father who with divided attention carved, "It is now my hope to make a survey of the educational systems of France and Germany with a view to the establishment in this country of reasonable educational facilities for every child, rich or poor. You will agree with me, Mr. Edgeworth, that a modicum of education, given under healthy and happy conditions, is the right of every boy. This I would extend to girls also." Thus spoke Mr. Matthew Arnold.

Father, as he carved for ten people, made encouraging sounds, although he had not yet considered this novel idea. He was, however, prepared to do so. He looked forward to a pleasant afternoon with this agreeable and enlightened person who was a coming Inspector of Schools, a present poet, and a son of Arnold of Rugby.

Mother's quiet sombre gaze swept round the table, dwelt

for a moment thoughtfully on the poet, rested on Father busy with the jellied fowls, rested on the two young grown-up daughters, on the four sons, on the little Topaz at her side, and on the ministering Cook and Emma.

Topaz was anxious to be noticed. But nobody was noticed today except Mr. Matthew Arnold. Not Annie, Mary, Blakey, George, John, nor Joe. She determined to be noticed immediately, so she spoke across the table to the guest.

As she was so unimportant no one paid her any attention at first until she was heard to say, " . . . and it's got a lovely yellow glass handle and you pull it and it goes woosh! Woosh, woosh!" she trumpeted, and smiled happily at Mr. Matthew Arnold.

"What goes woosh, my child?" he asked.

"Our new –"

"TOPAZ!" thundered Father, and Mother put out a grieved and loving hand. The outraged brothers and sisters looked across and downwards. Only Mr. Matthew Arnold regarded Topaz without horror.

"Topaz, eat your bread and butter," commanded Mother. But Topaz had succeeded. She had been noticed, although she had failed to tell Mr. Matthew Arnold about their new plumbing. All ordinary friends and relatives had witnessed the behaviour of the Edgeworth's revolutionary plumbing, which was the first of its kind to be installed in the town of Ware in North Staffordshire. Its fame had spread, and even strangers accosted Father in the street and asked him if it really worked. It was the joy of Topaz and the pride of the Edgeworths. It took the family a few moments to recover from the near-horror of the indelicate child.

The desire of Topaz to be noticed intoxicated her, and she went on. She looked only at the kind and unshocked face of Mr. Matthew Arnold, and she desired ardently to impress him now, at this very moment, while she still had the chance.

"Would you like me to say some poetry?" she asked.

"Topaz," said Mother half rising, "Emma shall take you upstairs to your room."

"Please, Mrs. Edgeworth," said Mr. Matthew Arnold, "let

the child say her poetry, and I will then, if I may, expound a favourite theory of mine."

Topaz sparkled and began:

> "Two are better far than one
>   For comfort or for fight.
>   How can one keep warm alone,
>   Or serve his God aright?" [1]

"And I'll say you another," she said quickly, "'How doth the little busy –'"

"TOPAZ – THAT – WILL – DO," said Father in a terrible tone. Topaz looked at Father. His eyes and his whiskers looked larger and darker than usual. She hung her head. Dear Father was angry. She slithered down from her cushions, down from her chair, and vanished under the table. The outraged brothers and sisters waited.

Mr. Matthew Arnold took things in hand and addressed both Father and Mother. "This is an interesting little child of yours. Will you, as a favour to me, let her stay under the table? She has not really offended. She is young, and she wishes to entertain. Don't make her shy. Leave her to herself. She knows in her heart that she has been rather forward. Let her think about it. Now, on the subject of coercion, I feel strongly that . . ."

Father listened. The children watched the good guest and the good food. Mother rested her graceful head on her hand. She gazed attentively and sweetly on the expounding Mr. Matthew Arnold, and did not hear a word that he was saying. Upstairs with the nurse was Hannah, the youngest, labouring with croup. Within Mother the last and fatal babe moved and moved. "It will be tonight," thought Mother, "I feel it will be tonight, and Joseph will be greatly disturbed. Dear Father. But I . . ." She turned her troubled look on Father and on the food. Swish went the white cap-streamers as Emma set down the sweet. "Cream pudding," murmured Blakey, looking with greedy eyes across to George, unchecked. Mother looked

[1] From an old Methodist hymnal.

upon George, upon all her brood. "Now, according to Rousseau . . ." said Mr. Matthew Arnold.

Underneath the heavy mahogany table sat Topaz in a world of shoes. She had recovered from fear and shame. Now she crawled from shoe to shoe. Each pair of shoes told Topaz a story. Mother had no shoes, no feet at all, just a beautiful rustling spread of purple silk. Topaz studied the silk without touching. Then she crawled to the large visiting boots of Mr. Matthew Arnold. Mr. Arnold wore elegant old-fashioned trousers which had straps under the feet. His feet were large, impeccable, neatly placed together. Topaz touched a leg with a friendly tickling finger. Above the table the great man checked his speech, smiled to himself, and continued. Topaz in the pleasing gloom of tablecloth, legs, and feet, crawled on.

Next to Mr. Arnold sat her nearest and favourite brother Joe. Joe's slippered feet curled round his chair legs. He listened, understanding a little, to the great man. Joe, gentle and frail, destined for early death, was never impatient with the chattering Topaz. Topaz dared to stroke Joe's ankle softly. Pussy pussy pussy. He gave no sign. She crawled on.

She put her head on one side and looked at Blakey's clodhoppers. What a smell! Blakey smelled of the stable and Father's horse. Topaz regarded Blakey and his boots coldly. He, the sharp-nosed boy, was already the farmer, the jockey. He was to sail cheerfully across an ocean and a half to Australia. Yes, Blakey said goodbye to the narrow streets of Ware and lived to be a happy horsey patriarch in a wide world of his own choosing. Happy Blakey. Topaz crawled on.

Here were the good shoes of Mary. Out she went to India, poor Mary, to marry a missionary. Glory surrounded the absent Mary who soon bore two little spinsters in the heat and died. Poor Mary, buried almost as her eyes closed, in that distant consuming heat. Topaz passed from Mary's shoes without interest and crawled on.

Here was Father. Two well-shod feet rested side by side on the thick carpet. Topaz looked at Father's boots with respect.

Father never buttoned his own boots. Godlike he extended a foot, and his boot was put on and fastened by a reverent son, or daughter, or Emma, or Nurse, or Cook, or sometimes by Mother. Topaz dared not touch these hallowed and angry feet. She crawled on.

Oh, the beautiful slippers of Annie. Topaz made little passes with her hands over Annie's tiny feet. Annie was as pious as beautiful. She was eighteen and modestly in love. She was to marry James Hastings, Father's brilliant young man at the Works. She was to be the gentle and obeyed mother of nine. She was, in her charming matriarchal old age, to go far away across sea and land to join distant sons yet unborn. She was yet in mildness and in formidable and unquestioned piety to infuse the lives of her sons, of her daughters Laura and Rachel, of her orphaned granddaughter Rose, of a wicked Chinaman, of more, of more, unborn, unknown. She was to be the refuge and comfort of her bereft young sister Topaz. She was to die in Vancouver (yet undreamed of), tiny, ancient, beautiful, gently amused, pure in heart, greatly beloved. Here she sat, as yet the young and filial daughter, neat feet, tender eyes, unknown thoughts, and ringlets of brown. Topaz looked long at the slippers of Annie. She fingered Annie's grey silk dress with pleasure, and then she crawled on.

She did not stop at the plain and lumpish shoes of George. George was red of face, genial, soon to be ardent, to be much wived. George was kindly, lazy, earthy, petted, and at last to be tamed. Topaz was never to be tamed, never. She crawled on.

Here were the neat and respectable feet of John. John was pretty. When Topaz called John "pretty," Blakey and George were rude. But so he was. He grew more elegant and fastidious as years increased. It became inevitable that John should be called Giovanni, that he should marry an heiress, that he should mingle with lords, that he should move with conscious distinction through several decades of public service. These neat feet of John's globe-trotted. They carried him busily among the great and the near-great with correctness. These quiet feet will hasten to many a directors' meeting.

("Hear-hear. Hear-hear.") John, the correct one, who could make you feel sneaped.[2] John never felt sneaped. If you were a dog, being sneaped would be the same as going off with your tail between your legs. If you were Topaz, people tried to sneap you, but you were hard to sneap. Even the proud gentle Annie, the eldest, could be sneaped by a look, but never John. Those who cause others to feel sneaped are vulnerable. Brother John, your day will come. Topaz pondered the neatness of John's feet and then curled up and fell asleep.

Above the table the future hung implicit, almost palpable, around the family. Above the table Mother sighed, caught the adult eyes, smiled her sad smile, and arose.

It was the next night that Mother died.

---

[2] Sneaped – a good Staffordshire word. Used by William Shakespeare too.

TWO

Mother, Mother!

THE DAY of Mother's funeral was long remembered in Ware. It was so sad that people almost enjoyed it. The chapel was "Packed! Packed!" as Great-Aunt Topaz used to say enthusiastically nearly a century later with her special genius for repetition. She remembered this funeral, with Father leading her by the hand, the youngest walker of the family, down the aisle, and all the other boys and girls following after. This dark pageant and slow procession of the black-clothed and bereft father and children smote with pity and tears those who were gathered to do honour to Mrs. Edgeworth. A hushed warfare had raged amongst Aunts and other next-of-kin during the days intervening between Mother's death and burial. Should Hannah, still almost a babe in arms, go to the funeral? If so, the nurse must carry her. If so, Hannah should be dressed in black. "A baby in black! What a dreadful idea, Aunt! Better keep her at home!" whispered an innovator. "White at a funeral! Certainly not. If Hannah goes – and she *must* go – the nurse must carry her and she *must* wear black. It would be an insult to her Mother's memory to allow her to appear in white. A blot!" (of white!) trumpeted Aunt Chalk lifting her high nose. "Merriman can run up a nice cap and cape of this good black very quickly, can't you, Merriman?" Such a snipping and cutting out and running up as there was now for this large family. Mother was badly needed to administer her own funeral. Decorum,

15

decoum, sorrow and decorum. Hannah solved the whole question by having the sniffles before the cape was cut out.

"Aunt Chalk," said Mary, coming in timidly, "Nurse says that little Hannah's running at the nose again and should on no account go out." The disputants looked at each other across the cutting-out table and nodded. Heaven had decided, and Hannah stayed at home in white where only Heaven and Nurse could see her, neither of whose feelings would be hurt by this unsuitable child.

"See *me*, look at *me*, Mary!" said Topaz importantly, revolving in black on the cutting-out table where she stood because it was more convenient to fit one so doll-like there. "I'm all in black, you see! I'm all in black! I'm going to the funeral tomorrow!" as the dressmaker tried a nice bit of crape on the body of her dress ("the scraps will do for that, Merriman"). There was silence. Topaz hearing the silence, glanced from face to face, and saw the looks. Her features puckered, she opened her mouth wide and wept loudly. "Mother, Mother!" she cried out loud in face of these looks. But Mother was not there. Sister Annie's arms went round her.

Father had the kind of handsomeness of a happy dignified extrovert inspired by a strong and simple faith and the equanimity that shone from his fine eyes. If Father had ever faltered in his faith, how deep would have been the crack, the fissure, the ultimate chasm into which he would have fallen. You and I, who pick our way unsurely amongst the appalling wreckage of our time, patching the crack here, avoiding the split there, anticipating the unsure footing, rejoicing in a bit of solid ground and going ahead until we again trip and fall on our noses – we can take our troubles much more easily than Father could have done. But Father never tumbled down. Both he and his partner Mr. Cork walked along with a grave and simple integrity that was neither smug nor proud.

Father had a fine nose with generous nostrils, the kind of nose which, when surrounded by other suitable features, causes more trouble among females who are responsive to a bit of trouble than people suspect. He was tall, with good strongly-growing hair and whiskers. All these attributes, together with his deep sorrow and helplessness, touched the heart of every woman in the Chapel and of every man too. Each woman knew in her heart that Mr. Edgeworth, with all those children and bereft of his wife, was, for all his vigour, ability, and good looks, much more vulnerable than Mrs. Edgeworth would have been if her Joseph had been taken from her. Every wife and mother yearned over him, and so did others who were neither wife nor mother.

At home things were rudderless and difficult. There were times when the gentle Annie and the young Mary were taxed too much, and when the inroads of Aunt Chalk made for dispute and confusion. Each night Father knelt for guidance beside the silent bed that gaped for his Mary who had never failed him before, and when he got into the abominable bed where she was not, his spiritual loneliness exacerbated his physical loss. It was all bad and sad for the children – Father's heaviness of spirit and the vacancy where Mother had been. As for Father, he had done with Love.

It is all very well to say that Father had done with Love, but there remained the need for companionship and a sharing of the household's cares which were inescapable. Hannah's intermittent croup, the broken nose of Blakey caused in a fight whose fame and shame defaced the name of Edgeworth, the finickyness and indifferent progress at school of John, Annie's projected marriage, the flightiness of Topaz, the fragility of Joe – all these things, combined with new activity at the Works, an unexpected extension of the American china market, and a sudden large irrational order for earthenware poes (said Great-Aunt Topaz with authority, nearly one hundred years later) for an African tribe (these articles were prized as hats by the savages, it was said at the time, although this seemed unlikely) – all these things drove Father into a second marriage, whether he would or no. The foundations of this marriage were respect and integrity.

It seemed to Father (who within two years became Grandfather Edgeworth and within a twinkling of the century's eye became Great-Grandfather Edgeworth) that beyond his personal preference and delight was his need for a house partner who would maintain the standards by which he wished his children to grow up, and could run smoothly and easily his pleasant home and keep it happy. With all the propriety that was observed in such a home as this, we know that there was also fun of a fairly robust kind. There must have been fun. For from this sober home there bubbled up the sparkling volatile Topaz, the pleasant and tittering John, the guffawing George, and the crackling laughter of Blakey. You couldn't down these people. There was not much humour, but a good deal of fun.

Let us look at noses. Most people do not pay enough attention to noses. Noses are significant features and should be regarded more carefully by those about to marry and bequeath. Take Aunt Chalk, for example, Mother's eldest sister. She had a nose like the august beak of the great Duke of Wellington soon to be lamented by the nation ("Pull down the blinds, Topaz. The Great Duke has died.") and she walked in an unpleasant aura of command. When Aunt Chalk's nose was seen coming up the driveway, the young Annie and Mary gazed stricken at each other and felt guilty in advance, the poor little housekeepers. Mother's nose had been a pleasant enough nose to live with, neither here nor there. The nose of Jane, Mother's younger sister, was a perfect pug, like THIS – as Great-Aunt Topaz used to recall, suddenly flattening her own mobile and rather boneless feature up against her face, with her hand. But Father saw past the pug nose into the kind heart and sound judgment of his majestic spinster sister-in-law, and it was revealed to him that here, in his Deceased Wife's Sister, was the stepmother that his children needed. But the Law was not, up till then, on his side.

At this moment of Father's dilemma Fate took a timely hand and beat the Law, since a Peer of the Realm found himself in much the same boat as Father, and the Law was revoked for a while to oblige this exalted man. Democracy was then only in bud, and Justice and Privilege were still related, and although the unfairness of the whole thing was noticed by a good many Radicals who made it their business to notice everything, the Repeal of the Act was welcomed by many more in the same plight as Father. There was a temporary rush to the altar of Deceased Wives's Sisters. For some reason often explained by Great-Aunt Topaz to her Great-Niece Rose three or four generations later (but not understood), Father went to Switzerland to be married. He travelled alone to Switzerland, and after two weeks, which seemed to be a chaste and fairly safe interval, Jane followed him, pug nose and all, chaperoned by Aunt Chalk. After a suitable honeymoon among the surprising mountains, Mr. and Mrs. Joseph Edgeworth returned home.

"Did you know," said George, "that Father is going to Grindel*wawld*?" The Edgeworth family took no notice of that silly foreign habit of pronouncing w like v.

"Where's Grindelwawld?" asked Topaz and no one paid any attention.

"On business?" asked Blakey.

"What's Grindelwawld?" asked Topaz.

"What for?" asked Joe.

"I don't know. I think there's Something Up," said George.

"What's Grindelwawld?" implored Topaz. "John, *what's* Grindelwawld, is it that sweety shop?"

"That's Grimble's, Topaz," said Mary.

"What . . .?" began Topaz.

"Look at the map," said Blakey shortly.

"What's a map? Show me a map. *Show* me," said the aggravating Topaz.

"*Be* quiet!" said Blakey. "Little girls should be seen and not heard."

"Come, dear," said Annie, "we will look at the map. See, there is Switzerland, and look – that's Grindelwawld."

"Oh . . . well, what is it?" asked Topaz, who couldn't see anything that looked like anything. "Why is it pink? What is it? What do you do with it? Why is it pink?"

"It isn't pink."

"Well, it looks pink."

"Hold your peace," roared George.

"See, Hannah, look," said Topaz to her little playmate

Hannah, and pointing at the globe, "Father's going to Grindel-wawld and it's pink and if we're good he'll bring us a piece back."

Father did not bring back whatever it was that Topaz expected, but their stately Aunt Jane who was now their mother and their stepmother, and she began to live in Father's bedroom with Father. The household moved again into smooth accustomed gear.

The Stepmother's first achievement was the successful wedding party of Annie. Pretty Annie was now "our sister Mrs. Hastings," and after a year was out Annie's first baby, Laura, changed Father into Grandfather Edgeworth.

And while the years passed over Grandfather Edgeworth, Joe gently died; Blakey departed to Australia where he prac-tised the two R's of Rearing a family and Racehorses; and Mary, poor child, went to her distant land.

George married the first of his three diverse wives, the daughter of Father's partner Mr. Cork, and from the earthy ground of George sprang three strange flowers of tempera-ment. From the elegant and Italianate John, no children; but from the uninhibited George a poet, an artist, and a beauty of distinction. All these three had a splendour of du Maurier-esque beauty not again seen in the Edgeworth family.

All this time Topaz and little Hannah played together with a twin-like affection.

THREE

"By Our First Strange and Fatall Interview"

SOMEHOW the whole family was surprised when Edward Shaw wanted so much to marry their second sister Mary. If it had not been for young Edward Shaw's pertinacity in forcing a meeting with her when he did, Mary would have had a different life – and death – and would no doubt have followed what seemed to be her predestined uneventful course as her stepmother's helper. But Edward Shaw changed that in one single interview.

Across the Chapel Edward Shaw looked at Mary Edgeworth.

So strong was the woven fabric of their large domestic life that the Edgeworth family were first of all members one of another, and next, each became aware of his own individuality. They were sons, daughters, sisters, and brothers before they were people. They rapidly became cousins, nieces, and nephews. Also uncles and aunts. Quickly one child, slowly another, apprehended its own condition as a person. Only the small and irascible Topaz was an individual from the time she uttered her first sentence ("Oh, yes, I spoke clearly and fluently at the age of nine months; my Mother *was* surprised!" "Now, Aunty . . .!") until that day nearly a century later when, still speaking clearly, she died. But even she was bound for a hundred years and beyond to this powerful family. For, speaking clearly, the words she said as she died were, "Me, the youngest!" and although the last of her generation had twenty years ago departed, her life was still tied to her powerful

assembled family which had slipped one by one with accep-
tance or amazement through the strangely moving curtain of
Time into another place. But the docile Mary, who preceded
Topaz there by ninety years, had hardly discovered her own
identity, apart from being a daughter and a sister, by the time
that Edward Shaw looked at her and loved her.

Upon the plain and serious Mary the young man looked.
He had made up his mind. During the service he regarded with
apprehension the noble Mr. Edgeworth, as far removed from
him as Jove. Mr. Edgeworth had often nodded kindly, as
might Jove perhaps, at young Shaw. He had nodded kindly
because he felt kindly disposed towards a young man who,
having finished his term at the Theological College at Manchester, had come home for a furlough before sailing for the
Mission Field in India. Horizons of yellow grain floated
before the eyes of the young Edgeworths when they heard of
the preparations of Edward Shaw – Edward, with his young
and confidence-inspiring beard, waist deep in billowing
grain, from which appeared here and there black and easily
recognizable heathen. Edward was well thought of, and the
Edgeworth family regarded him warmly. Even his newly
developed beard was a suitable sign of responsibility and of
inner grace. So when young Edward Shaw, his youth
armoured by the deceiving beard, cleverly joined the spreading and multiple Edgeworths as they left the Chapel, nobody
was surprised, except young Edward Shaw. He, breathing
quickly, knew that not Chance but Edward Shaw was now
taking a hand with Fate. Edward was nearly sick with excitement.

At the Wesleyan Chapel at Ware, greetings did not begin
between Chapel-goers until they were free of the Chapel door.
Only the faintest and most religious of smiles might be
exchanged in the slow progress of the congregation towards
the Chapel door. This was well done. How should one spring
at once from the heights of spiritual contemplation down to
the level of the five senses and their curiosities? This was well
done, and a right recognition of things great and things small.
Do not mix them, do not admit the mundane. But outside the

Chapel door the House of God became the street of man. Edward, in the dark, beyond the chapel porch, successfully isolated the surprised Mary and walked home with her.

They walked slowly but without loitering along the narrow dark pavement where few lights shone. The large Edgeworth family walked ahead in twos and threes, their numbers augmented by friends and relatives. Edward had been adroit, for in the darkness of the ugly street, Who could see Who walked with Who, or that Edward Shaw walked alone with Mary Edgeworth.

As Edward walked with Mary on the narrow pavement, sleeve rubbed sleeve and arm touched arm. It was enough. For Edward it was almost too much.

"Miss Mary," said Edward in a low voice, grateful for the darkness which made him bold, "I am sailing for India in less than two weeks' time." (As Edward said these words he could hardly believe them. India. Staffordshire. India.) "I may not see you again. Do you mind if I walk home with you? I have longed to talk to you a little before I go. There is so little time left now and I must tell you Something. What you will say I don't know." The young man's voice shook and was husky. This agitation was something special and Mary in the darkness caught his agitation. "What is this? What can Edward Shaw have to say to me? I know what Edward Shaw is going to say to me. What shall I say to him? What would Father say? Well, I'm a woman." She asserted herself. "I'm a woman. Annie got married. But Annie is different. Oh, Annie, are you happy? I think you are. What is Edward Shaw going to say? Keep still. This is your life. Wait."

In the family, Mary was not important. She was not even the eldest. Annie was the eldest and the beautiful one. Annie was a wife, already the admired head of her small household, soon again to be a mother. Mary was the rather unregarded helper of the kind and important Stepmother. ("Oh yes," said Great-Aunt Topaz ninety years later, "very strict and important was our Stepmother, but a good mother to us children, with a little pug nose – like this!") Mary had never yet been Mary, a person in her own right. And here she was, a person, with Edward Shaw walking beside her in the dark and speaking to her in urgent husky tones, and a future coming quickly towards her. She was inexperienced, but she knew.

"Oh, Mr. Shaw, Father told us that you are going into the Mission Field. We do hope that you will be happy, and we do hope that God will bless you in your work," she said simply. She endeavoured to still her little trembling. "Aren't you excited at the prospect of going so far away to such a strange country? Ware, I know, is very quiet and dull." Mary was astonished to hear herself say this in the darkness. The life of her family in Ware, the catastrophic death of Mother, Father's marriage, the boys growing, the comings and goings of Father, the life of school, of Chapel, of relatives, of the busy home – all these things had not seemed quiet and dull. Mary was hardly prepared to see the future leap out into the open and transform her past into something which was not enough. But this was now achieved by the young man in black walking by her side.

He seized her arm, not roughly. "Mary," he said, speaking rapidly, "no, don't stop me. I've watched you every time I've been at home, and I've dared to think about you, but I've never dared to come nearer you – your family" – (the Edgeworth family, strong barrier against the young and uninvited) – "I love you and I want to marry you, Mary, and now time's going so quickly, and if I go away without some hope from you, the future – well, I can't bear it, not even to do God's work." The young man spoke unhappily, and while he spoke he felt his case suddenly become desperate. His hopes that this young girl so near him in the darkness would leave her home of comfort to join him whom she knew so little, in a land yet unknown – these hopes seemed preposterous.

To Mary these hopes were not preposterous, but she did not at once enquire of her heart. She relaxed her arm in his and experienced an unfamiliar confidence. She honoured him; she trusted him; she, the big sister of once motherless young boys, pitied him in his need of her. His nearness was welcome. She did not shrink and she controlled her little trembling.

"Stop, Mr. Shaw," she said gently, "let me be. Just for a

moment. Please. You've surprised me. I didn't think. This is such a big thing. No – don't talk to me for a minute." And they walked close and quietly, saying little until Edward again poured out his heart. ("And where can Mary be?" demanded the majestic Stepmother, far in front, of the dark.)

When Mary and Edward left the pavements and, walking slowly, reached the lane's end beside the gate of the house, Mary stood still. How displeased Father would be if his eyes could behold his daughter, Mary Edgeworth, standing in the shelter of the hedge in the arms of a young man in love, be he never so much a missionary! For that is where Mary was. "Edward, very well, dear Edward, I will, I will marry you if Father will let me, and if Mother can spare me. I will try to make you a good wife – no – not yet, not again. Let me go! I shall slip in at the side door. It's better that you should see Father alone."

As she left him Edward could have sung aloud. He was a King. He owned the world. A few minutes later he sat in Father's heavily curtained and lamplit study. He was no longer a King. He was a young and importunate theological student without proper means of support for a wife. Except for the importunity that shook him, he was nothing more than that.

One year later Mary sailed for India from Tilbury Dock, in the care of the Rev. Charles Pickering and Mrs. Pickering. All the family went to Tilbury with the travellers. "I'll tell you something," said Topaz to little Hannah in the corner of the railway carriage, "Mother said to Father, 'The girl's very innocent, Joseph. I do believe she's going to her first kiss.' What d'you think of that?" Hannah, aged five, did not know what she thought of that.

As the ship drew out they all waved. The departing Mary waved. "Can you see them now?" Topaz waved and waved. She jumped up and down flapping her white handkerchief. "Going to her first kiss," she chanted, "going to her first kiss." The family whirled round. "TOPAZ!"

But really, never since the time that young Edward Shaw

and Mary Edgeworth had walked home from Chapel and stood clasped in the shelter of the hedge had they been alone together. The Stepmother had not thought it fitting. But "Dear Mary," "Dear Edward," they wrote. People had said, "Mary Edgeworth is going out to India to marry a missionary. She'll be such a good suitable wife for him. Not pretty like Annie, but a very nice girl." The whole family from Father to Topaz, and even little Hannah, were proud of Mary now because she was going to the Mission Field. Mary had begun to feel that she was nothing but Mr. Edgeworth's good girl who was going to marry a missionary, no longer Mary who was going to marry Edward. On the ship, in the constant company of the reserved Mrs. Pickering, Mary began to feel frightened and homesick. She longed to return to the safety of the large family, but the disregarding days brought her nearer and nearer to India and to Edward from whom she sometimes fled.

After Mr. and Mrs. Pickering had seen Mary safely married to Edward Shaw, they departed at once to their mission station. Mary, dressed in the grey of a dove, found herself arrived at the inevitable moment. She stood alone facing this man who was Edward, but who was nearly a stranger. She was more alone that she had ever been in her whole life. She was in India. She had reached the Mission Field. She looked steadily, almost fearfully, at Edward and tried to smile. This little lonely smile smote Edward. He looked at his Mary and saw the frightened courage in her face. He took only one step towards her. He overflowed with tenderness, compassion, and his desire. Mary broke into weeping which she could not restrain, sprang forward and cast herself, more in homesickness than in love, upon Edward's beard.

On the scorching day that followed the suffocating night when the babies were born and Mary died, Edward buried the young girl his wife with violent and shocking haste.

He sat at his desk with the notepaper lying in front of him. He sat there suffering and helpless and blinded by his loss. Was it for this that he had brought Mary to the land that had killed her? He gazed unseeing through his desk and at last summoned and steadied himself and wrote slowly, "Dear Mr. and Mrs. Edgeworth. It has pleased God in His Infinite Wisdom to take from us my beloved Mary." He read, and tore up the paper savagely.

He wrote, "Dear Mr. and Mrs. Edgeworth. It has pleased God to take from me –" He stopped, read, tore the paper across and flung it down.

He wrote, "Dear Mr. and Mrs. Edgeworth. I regret to tell you that Mary died last night. Our two infant daughters are well. Accept my deep sympathy. Yours faithfully, Edward Shaw." He folded and sealed the letter. He bowed his head upon his empty arms in his anguish, and wept.

"A very strange letter indeed for that young man to write!" said the majestic Stepmother, turning the pages this way and that, seeking lamentation and finding none.

FOUR

Mr. and Mrs. Porter

IT WAS NOT long before the six Edgeworth children who remained at home became used to seeing the kind and portly Stepmother, who was Mother's sister, who had always been Aunt Jane, who was now "Mother," sitting in Mother's place at the head of the table. In orderly families, such as the Edgeworths', Father and Mother, flanked and separated down a fairly long table by a double row of children, might consider themselves to be practically alone. At the Edgeworth table no child, save one, raised his or her voice unless addressed. All, save one, behaved with astonishing decorum, while Father and Mother carried on their own Olympian conversations. The six remaining sons and daughters were as nearly inaudible as six normal children could be except for Topaz, who could not keep silent (how should she, who talked persistently for over ninety-seven years?), and was often admonished by both parents, and sometimes had to be sent from the table because she was too bumptious; and Topaz annoyed only in the same way that a fly annoys. Father and Mother, being alone then, except for at least eight other people in the room counting Emma and Cook or Betsy, spoke freely to each other and settled much of their domestic business at the table.

As Father dealt with his letters, he retailed them to Mother.

"Dear, dear, dear!" said Father one morning.

"What, Joseph?" asked Mother.

"Mrs. Porter."

"What about Mrs. Porter, Joseph?"

"Mr. Porter has left Mrs. Porter," said Father, forgetting his children who should not be aware that husbands left wives.

Topaz always followed these conversations closely, turning her head and her intelligent grey-green eyes towards each speaking parent. Images evoked by these adult conversations sprang at one to Topaz's mind, but they were often incorrect images as they were limited by her own experience, which was slight. Topaz took part at once.

"Where did Mr. Porter leave Mrs. Porter?" she asked. Never having heard of a Mr. and Mrs. Porter before, she pictured Mr. Porter in a peaked cap taking Mrs. Porter for a railway journey (a novelty) and leaving her in a strange Ladies' Waiting Room all alone, as Mother had left her and the alarmed Hannah, only a week ago, with instructions not to budge.

Her parents took no notice.

"Oh, Joseph, *poor* Mrs. Porter! Whatever will she do?" exclaimed the Stepmother, deeply shocked.

"Was it in the Ladies' Waiting Room?" persisted Topaz.

"Was what in the Ladies' Waiting Room, Topaz? Speak clearly, if you speak at all," said Father sharply.

"Where Mr. Porter left Mrs. Porter."

George choked on his guffaw.

"Be quiet, Topaz. This does not concern you."

"I cannot believe it, Joseph!" said the Stepmother, incredulous.

"Was she in the Waiting Room all night?" asked Topaz, sympathetic to the fate of Mrs. Porter.

The Stepmother gave Topaz her attention. "What are you talking about, Topaz? Tell me and then keep quiet."

"She meant like you left me and Topath at the thtation the time I cried," explained little Hannah.

"Mr. Porter did *not* leave Mrs. Porter in the Ladies' Waiting Room. Now that will do, Topaz. You must learn to hold your peace." Then to Father, "But I thought Mr. Porter was such a *nice* man, Joseph!"

"Porter always seemed a nice enough fellow, but I have reason to think that he has been given to fast friends," said Father.

"Who gave him? Who gave him? Did Mrs. Porter give him? Why did she give him to fast friends?" demanded Topaz, horrified at the thought of this nice fellow being given by his wife, like a bundle, to these fast friends who had galloped off with him, probably on horseback.

"*Silence!*" said Father, turning wrathful eyes on her. "Mother, either Topaz may have her meals in the kitchen or she may behave at table. I do not propose to spend my meals in disturbance!"

"You hear what Father says, Topaz!" said the Stepmother in awful tones. Topaz's pink and white face flushed, and she made no sound but applied herself to her porridge.

"And," continued Father, still holding the letter in his hand, "Mrs. Porter writes to say that she has decided to open a school for girls at Brighton, and she is writing to all her father's old friends . . . she has little Fanny to support . . . she will take about twenty boarders. It will soon be time for Topaz and Hannah to go to boarding-school, and I cannot think of anyone I would rather send them to than Emily Porter. She is quite a Blue Stocking." ("A blue stocking?" puzzled Topaz.) "What do you think, Mother? Pass your Mother this letter," and he handed the letter to John.

"Oh . . . to America! . . . well, no wonder! . . . I see she hopes to have Mrs. Pocock's girl Lily to help her," said the Stepmother, perusing. " . . . I gather that she prefers to board all her pupils." (Topaz and Hannah looked at each other; would they be strapped to it, the board? How would they stay on?) " . . . Yes, but that entails a deal of work! Ah, yes, she will not take day girls. All the pupils will have to board. But I do wonder why ever Mr. Porter did such a dreadful thing!"

And this was why.

FIVE

"The Dark House and the Detested Wife"

THE LAST term that Mary Davis (who became Mrs. Joseph Edgeworth) and Jane Davis (who also became Mrs. Joseph Edgeworth) were at school in York, there came a little beautiful motherless girl named Emily Fanshawe who was put, for a while, into Mary's charge. Shortly after Mary and Jane left school, the child returned home, and there she lived, cloistered in the country, with her father who was a Greek scholar. And so it was that the beautiful child, who was her father's most diligent student and devoted companion, became old for her years and a little too grave. About six years ago, so they had heard, Emily had made a journey with her father to Greece, and next they learned that Emily had married young Edmund Porter, whom Joseph Edgeworth knew, in Brighton. And then nothing more. And now "Mr. Porter has left Mrs. Porter." However could this be?

"The isles of Greece, the isles of Greece," murmured Emily, as the wind filled the sails and the small sailing ship beat slowly to the south of Cape Matapan. Many an evening she saw the Grecian islands melting away, mauve and pink and purple and a dying grey, into the darkening sea. "The wine-dark sea," thought Emily. What had she expected to see? Sea the colour of wine? No. At this moment the colours of the Mediterranean slid from steel-blue into sapphire into indigo into purple into bronze, and this, this was the sea which the

31

Hellenes had smitten with their oars and which Odysseus had sailed for adventure and for home. Emily was romantic. The death of Lord Byron in Greece, not two decades before, had warmed the hard-headed and romantic and freedom-loving English people to the land where he had died. Yet it was not because Lord Byron had lived rashly, and had been a poet, and had died in Greece for Greece that Mr. Fanshawe and his daughter Emily had sailed on this pilgrimage down the Adriatic Sea, past the shores where Nausicaa played and the shipwrecked Odysseus slept, round the tip of the Peloponnese and north to the Piraeus, but because Mr. Fanshawe was fulfilling his life's dream of seeing, together with his daughter, before he died, the height of human truth and beauty, the small hill of the Acropolis, in Athens, and upon it the ruined Parthenon.

Emily wrote in her diary, "Papa and I today ascended the Acropolis. It was very strange and it pleased Papa very greatly that our guide is called Socrates. 'Are you indeed Socrates?' enquired Papa smilingly. 'No,' replied the old man gravely, 'I am not Socrates himself but I am his favourite nephew.'

"Up the stony steps we went and over the flintstrewn hill and upon our left was the small temple of the Erechtheum with the tall maidens, standing there these twenty-three hundred years, and still as noble as ever. Oh, unconquerably noble! The full sight of the pale honey-coloured pillars of the Parthenon sent us into a dream that went back to Pericles and the great days of Athens, and to Socrates and to Plato who must have walked on this very hill and up the wide steps which look so level and yet have a hidden architectural perfection of curve. It seemed to me as Papa and I stood with the old man Socrates that there was something timeless in the air. All truth, all beauty, has blown about this place that Papa and I have so long desired to see. We looked across at Hymettus which was growing violet in the darkening rays of the sun. Papa and I will go there again and again, but today we just stood and looked and felt the thousands of years go by. As the violet glow touched Hymettus, Socrates drank the hemlock, and tonight the violet touched Hymettus again and I could not contain myself, but wept as I looked."

It will be seen that Emily was a learned and romantic young girl with a large share of what was called "sensibility," and that Joseph Edgeworth was not wrong when he called her a Blue Stocking. It was on the way home from this studious journey which crowned Mr. Fanshawe's life, and perhaps was the crown and sorrow of Emily's life too, that the travellers met young Edmund Porter who was carried away by Emily's beauty, fell in love with her, followed her back to England, and married her.

It was unfortunate for Edmund Porter that the studious and poetic girl with whom he fell in love had the beauty and gentleness that promised him everything that he wanted, but promised him in vain. He was not long married (and still under the spell of his infatuation for the girl) before he knew that Emily's large dark-fringed eyes, her creamy skin, her soft grace, meant nothing for him, nothing. "My God," he thought in anger with her, "how cold she is." Never once did Emily's soft limbs melt willingly into his arms. When he approached her she became sealed away from him. He grew diffident and morose with her. Emily herself was uncertain and unhappy. She knew that she had failed. She did not want to fail, but her new life was repugnant to her; she was helpless and she was proud. When, before a year was out, their only child, a daughter, was born, Edmund saw with bitterness that the child aroused in his wife a passion of tenderness that he could never evoke. He detested seeing Emily bending over the baby and lifting it to her breast. He absented himself from home whenever he could. He was an easy, natural, sensual man, and she an academic beauty who had better have married one of her father's old friends, and spent her life puttering about a library with a lot of bloodless old scholars with their academic jokes, thought Edmund bitterly. He knew by this time that she had begun to bore him. All her high-falutin ideas bored him to fury. He no longer noticed that she was beautiful.

One day he came into his wife's room. She was sitting in

front of her mirror, brushing her long hair with slow sweeping strokes. Edmund was impelled to go to her and place his hands upon her shoulders. Over her head he looked into the mirror and their eyes met there. His wife became motionless and in the mirror he saw the indifferent sweet expression of her face grow defensive and become almost the face of an enemy. He took his hands roughly from her shoulders and said angrily, still watching her immobile face in the mirror, "What made me fool enough to marry a woman like you! I'd as soon live with one of your damned Greek statues!"

Edmund took two steps to a bookshelf and lifted a small white sculptured goddess from the corner of the shelf. He dashed it to the ground where it broke into fragments. He looked at his wife and saw her involuntary gesture and her look of anger and distress. "That moves you, does it?" he said. Her face resumed its marble look. Edmund went out of the room. At the door he turned and said shortly, "I am going up to London," and he left her, hating her.

Emily was deeply humiliated, yet she was unable to do anything. She kept a silence which was both proud and stupid, because she did not know what to say, or what to do. When Edmund returned, as he did from time to time, a light in her room showed where Mrs. Porter was reading, and a light in Mr. Porter's study showed where he was. There were no bright lights or pleasant people in the young house when Edmund came home. Emily could not bear to show their estrangement to their acquaintance and he did not care. The house became dark and, except for the love of Emily for the child, sad and empty.

One day after a long interval, a man came to see Mrs. Porter. He was commissioned, he said, by Mr. Porter, to give some information to her. Edmund had left her, and he had left her destitute. She was now, in fact, a deserted wife.

When Mrs. Porter received the positive assurance that Mr. Porter had really left her and was on his way to America and would not come back, she walked to the fireplace and looked long into the fire, seeing not the fire but Edmund and his ways. "Please go and leave me alone," she said, without turning, to the quiet man standing behind her. The man standing behind her bowed gravely and went away.

Emily heard the door close behind her. She heard the house door close and knew that for a few minutes she would be alone. She was afraid. She was very much afraid of being afraid. "If I can prevent myself from being afraid," thought Emily, feeling very cold all of a sudden and shaking all over, "if I can stop myself from being afraid, I can manage, step by step. I think I will go out. I think perhaps if I walked . . ."

She went to the library door, opened it, and listened. There were only distant sounds from the kitchen. The child, Fanny, and her nurse had gone for their walk along the Front. Mrs. Porter walked upstairs disdaining the banister. She held herself rigid so as to stop shaking and went towards the wardrobe. She took out her bonnet and mantle. She rummaged blindly on her neat shelves and found gloves and a heavy veil. "Do things," something at the back of her mind told her, "don't think, yet. Especially don't think about Edmund and the future." She stood in front of the glass and with cold hands tied her bonnet-strings and put on her veil. She did not see what face looked from the glass. She felt very cold. She threw back the veil from her bonnet and walked downstairs. She would not go out from the house as a woman humiliated and concealed. At the front door she looked to the right and to the left, turned to the left, walked quickly towards the Front and took the direction to Rottingdean. The wind blew in from the sea and the waves assailed the shore with rhythm. The rhythm. Roar, crash, withdraw. Slowly. Roar, crash, withdraw. She dropped the veil over her face, slackened her steps, and with assurance of solitude within and without, felt herself relax. Roar went the waves, crash, withdraw. She walked on slowly and at last descended towards the beach. She found a low rock on the shingle and sat down. Her large skirts spread around her on the shingle.

"What a shipwreck it's been!" she said. And that was all she dared to think about Edmund. Thinking of Edmund would come later. That was a luxury she could not afford now. She took off her bonnet and veil and the wind blew her brown hair.

Solitude and the wind would free her thoughts. She must make a plan. What plan? She now forced herself painfully to think. What plan?

She sat, looking out to the grey sea, and sometimes looking down at the shingle, stooping and running the smooth pebbles slowly through her fingers. She found her thoughts straying and with great effort jerked them back. Her thoughts then went to Fanny and she became angry. "Don't waste your emotion. Don't let yourself suffer. Pull your thoughts back. What will you do? What can you do? What is there that you know how to do? What . . ."

A plan. What plan? Books. Her father's books. When Mrs. Porter had learned to read books with her father the whole world had opened before her. "A Blue Stocking," said Edmund's friends commiserating among themselves, "poor old Edmund!" "Let me see," thought Mrs. Porter astonished at her own boldness, "I can't teach them sums; I can't teach them to play the piano but I can teach them manners; I can teach them a little French and I can teach them to read and I can teach them the Classics. And I can get Lily Pocock to teach them sums and the piano and take them for walks. They shall read their History and Geography. They shall read quietly and they shall read out loud, and before they leave my school they shall be educated. And as for Edmund, he shall never come back and make me so unhappy. I must begin at once. I must waste no time. Here is my plan. I can do this. I shall be strong. I do not need Edmund. I don't want him. I can live without him very much better – if I can live."

At last she got up. She took a deep breath and smoothed back her blowing hair, pressing her hands firmly against her temples. She put on her bonnet and secured the fluttering veil. She walked slowly over the shingle and up the slope to the road leading to the promenade. "I am a strong woman," she told herself with satisfaction and surprise. "I can do this. I am not afraid. Fanny. Darling. You will have little girls to play with and learn with. We shall be more happy than we have been. I am not afraid any more. Yes – oh, I am afraid – no, no, I am not afraid . . ."

That was why in about 1853 Topaz and Hannah were sent to Mrs. Porter's School for Young Ladies at Brighton. And it explains why Topaz received there not a classical education but the English reflection of a classical education which tinctured her whole life, and particularly an unknown pagan part of her.

At Mrs. Porter's School Saturday night was homeletter night. All the pens were scratching. Topaz Edgeworth wrote:

My Dear Father and Mother

I hope you are very well. Thank you very much for the 2/6 for me and for Hannah. Hannah's cold is still bad so Mrs. Porter kept her in bed. I like it here. Every afternoon we have a walk. The waves are lovely. There are goat carriages drawn by goats and little Fanny Porter had a ride. She is an amewsing little child. It is sixpence and if I were not a great girl I should like to have a ride too. There is a place called the Pavilion that the Prince made for a friend of his. There is nothing like it in Ware. We do a deal of reading. Mrs. Porter made us copy out our timetable with black ink and red ink and we are to send a copy home. After Scripture we sing and Miss Pocock teaches us our sums. Miss Pocock is our pupil teacher I like her. Her mother brought her here. Her mother has big eyebrows. We think Miss Pocock is only 16. Her mother is a friend of Mrs. Porter and she is a friend of Miss Caroline Hershel the famous lady Astronomer and she is going to lecture to us next week about the Plannets. It is very nice to meet all these famous people. After dinner we read aloud a Leading Article from The Times and then we talk about it. Everything we read aloud we talk about after. Mrs. Porter reads about the Greeks and Pan and Midas and the Golden Fleas. For our Geography we are reading the Journeys of Marco Polo with a great big globe and then we talk about it. We are reading a play of Shakespeare's King John and I am the bastard Faulconbridge. I wanted to be King John too where he says his soul will not out at windows or at doors. But I like the bastard. Eliza Pinder is King John although she reads indifferently. Mrs. Porter says that Eliza Pinder and I are bound to confess to our Parents that we did not behave like a lady. Mrs. Porter reads our letters. I am going to cross my letter now and I will do it very carefully so that you can read it. Eliza Pinder said that Topaz Edgeworth was very fond of the sound of her own voice and I said I was thankful indeed that I hadn't a Yorkshire accent to listen to and she said I was a rude cow with no manners from Staffordshire and I said no one should say such a thing to me unscathed and I slapped Eliza Pinder and Mrs. Porter came in. And Eliza and I had to apologize in public to each other after prayers for not being a lady. I make my Confession and hope my Parents will forgive me as Mrs. Porter has told me too. That is my Confession and I will now resume. For Ancient History we shall read aloud some parts of Gibbon's Decline and Fall that Mrs. Porter has chosen. For Modern History we shall first read Mr. Charles Dickens' Child's History. For serious reading we shall have Mr. Pope's translation of Homer's Iliad for Profane and Milton's Paradise Lost for Sacred. I like reading aloud and saying poetry. When somebody reads the others sew. I hope little Tilly and Sassy are all right. Now that Miss Lizzie Shaw is looking after them I suppose Edward Shaw will not send them to England although we are their auntys too. Hannah is afraid Tilly and Sassy may be a little black after living in India so long. Mrs. Porter wishes to know if you have any objection to Hannah and me joining in a card game. It is called Old Maid and is very amewsing. And she says will you please send the red flannel for Hannah. Miss Pocock is teaching us to sing songs and take part songs. I am beginning to sing seconds very nicely in hymns. We are learning a beautiful song called "Star of the Evening Beautiful Beautiful Star." I like this school better than Miss Astys. Mrs. Porter is very kind and so is Miss Pocock though she is not very old. Adieu my dear Parents j'espère que vous allez très bien. Pray give my love to Blakey and George and John and to Sister Annie. How are her babys.

Pray accept my love my dear Parents. I beg to remain
  Your respectful and affectionate daughter
                                          Topaz Edgeworth

P.S. Miss Pocock is very jannock and she has cruley hair.

Topaz considered this for a moment. Then she stood up. "Please, Miss Pocock," she said, "do you spell curly with an 'e'?"

As the girls went upstairs to bed "Listen to the wind!" said Topaz, "And the sea how it's pounding tonight!" said Eliza Pinder.

"Yes, listen," said Mrs. Porter, "these are the Equinoctial Gales."

And the wind was blowing, too, among the great undiscovered pine trees in the yet unnamed place far away where some day Topaz Edgeworth would live and die. In this place Topaz would some day write and receive many letters, but no one could yet send letters there. This place was still silent and almost unknown.

SIX

In Elder House

FATHER and the ponderous Stepmother and Blakey and George and John and Joe and Topaz and little Hannah lived now in a large square house called Elder House. Elder House was set back by its "own grounds which surrounded it from the Waterloo Road which, as the main thoroughfare from Bloxum to Ware, bore most of the traffic between the two manufacturing towns and their small grim satellites, and was, owing to its general undeniable drabness, a depressing street. Yet it was an exciting street, too. The Waterloo Road was exciting to Topaz and to Hannah because it carried the daily life of the towns, and because it was important, and because of its multiplicity of small brick shops which contained people, sporadic genteel rows of brick houses which contained people, incroppings of residential brick splendour which contained magnates, brick public-houses radiating their own peculiar stale allure, posters advertising shockingly the dramas at the Bloxum Blood Tub, here a brick Chapel and there a brick Chapel, and, walking up and down the rather narrow pavements in front of all these bricks, the people of the towns with their own private stories. These people of the towns were mostly working people, factory hands. Many were poor, and they all possessed for the two young girls a strong and secret fascination. The poverty of many of these people exalted them in the apprehensions of the two girls. Topaz, for all that she was the child of a strong up-springing persistent breed and fed upon comfort, took for granted the formidable quality of the poorest people who, unlike her, ate the cheapest of food, lived in the meanest of dwellings, were clothed in the sorriest of garments, and yet walked with a dare, and talked and gesticulated with an economy of violence. The Waterloo Road was not *a* Waterloo Road. Its "the" was its distinction and its crown. "They say they're going to have trams in *the* Waterloo Road." "There is a funeral going down *the* Waterloo Road." "Where does Dr. Russell live?" "In that there big 'ouse in *the* Waterloo Road."

In Elder House, which had a comfortable Victorian splendour, Father and the Stepmother continued their long uninterrupted life with an eternalness which seemed to make them immortal to their children, who now had begun to demonstrate vicissitude and change.

Joe died of phthisis in Elder House. Blakey went to Shropshire to farm, and then had his trunks packed at Elder House and left rejoicing for Australia. Hannah, after a short lifetime of croup and coughs, sickened, rallied, sickened again, and died of phthisis. Topaz, white of skin, pink of cheek, and voluble, had things called sniffly colds and was dosed with ale and stout in Elder House (and lived to be a hundred). The elegant bronchitic John was packed off to Italy for a year, and for some time after his return to Elder House had to be called Giovanni. George, strong and noisy, left the family and went into Father's partner's brother's bank in London. Four miles away from Elder House Annie, a devoted wife and already a pretty pocket matriarch, administered with gentle rectitude her growing family. Mary, who had never seen Elder House, had long vanished into an Indian grave. Father and the Stepmother and their biddable lively daughter Topaz now lived together with serenity and much quiet dignity, comfortably served and attended, removed by trees and garden from the busy thoroughfare, and by lack of imagination from the bitter realities of their world, to which, however, Mr. Charles Dickens and others had begun to call their attention.

It is hard to fathom how so lively a person as Topaz spent her allotment of twenty-four hours in the day, month by month and year by year. Time slides into time, and the extroverted

Topaz did not consider that time, even one's own specific personal piece of Time, slides into eternity. After the death of Hannah, her dear companion, she turned to books, for which Mrs. Porter's School had well prepared her. She read every English and French book that was permitted her. She could write Greek, and wrote the enchanting characters with enthusiasm. She could not read much Greek and so she bought a Greek Testament of the parallel translation kind, and amidst fountains of ejaculations of surprise and pleasure ("Oh, what a pretty word, '*εἰρήνη*,' I do declare!") Topaz read the Greek Testament. At Mrs. Porter's School she had been nourished on the pagan deities. Mrs. Porter, that strange and beautiful Blue Stocking, with a passion for the classics and a fair knowledge of Greek, had sent her pupils back to their homes in Bradford, Middlesbrough, Birmingham, and Ware, fairly convinced, in secret, of the existence of the Greek gods – as far as Greece was concerned at all events. Pan in Bloxum? . . . Well . . . Topaz did not consider the Greek gods in connection with the Waterloo Road, although it was true that her own private god lived there.

"Come, Topaz," the pug-nosed imperious Stepmother would say as she sailed into the breakfast-room, her rotundity entering first, "put away your books now. I have ordered the brougham for eleven. We are going to Bloxum. We will see about your clothes for your London visit. And I hear that Huntbach's have some very handsome plush, old gold, the right shade, just what I need for draping the piano. And some Leek silks. I have an authentic Persian design on raw silk for the border, which I think you can embroider nicely." And Topaz, diverted and exclaiming, would hasten upstairs for her mantle, hat, and gloves.

"We are going to Bloxum, Cook!" she would exclaim on the stairs.

"We are going to Bloxum, Sarah!" she would announce to the parlourmaid on the landing.

"We are going to Bloxum, Austin!" she said delightedly to the housemaid upstairs.

And as she embroidered the elegant Persian design in the

faded yet permanent exquisite silks from the neighbouring town of Leek, and related and re-related to the Stepmother, majestically inattentive, the account of her visit to Annie and the children the day before, the Stepmother would interrupt her, saying, "Topaz, is there fresh frilling in the neck of your grey?" and Topaz knew that the Stepmother's mind was on the Book-Meeting-Party to which they would go that evening.

And as Topaz drove home from the Book-Meeting-Party that evening, sitting facing her Father – who nodded – and her resplendent Stepmother, and talked eagerly of Eliza Pinder's rendering of Guinevere, and hummed her own coo-ing melodious part of "We fell out, my wife and I," her Stepmother said suddenly, "Topaz, you may help Austin wash the chandeliers in the drawing-room tomorrow, or it will take her all day." Topaz fell for a moment silent, wondering if, the last time that she helped Austin wash the two great cut-glass chandeliers which reflected themselves interminably in the large end-mirrors of the room, she had detached and attached two hundred and sixty, or two hundred and sixty-four pointed lustres. It was a good thing that Father and the Stepmother did not listen to Topaz overly much, or they might have stilled her incessant happy talking – and one must do *some*thing. Now that Hannah was gone, her pleasantest listeners were Cook and Austin and Sarah and her friend Tottie Hay in London and a few school friends who were within driving distance; so she enjoyed helping Austin, in an inept fashion. When she was with any of these listeners she was fed with applause and enjoyment, and often became very funny. But it was a fact that although Father had a sense of fun, he had no sense of humour, and the Stepmother had neither the one nor the other. But Topaz, uncritical, did not notice this. Rocking home in the brougham she put the thought of the chandeliers aside and continued to recapitulate the party to the indulgent elderly smiles and yawns of her parents.

And as she stood on the step-ladder the next morning and detached each lustre and, talking, handed it down to Austin who washed it carefully in light suds and rinsed it, and when she helped to dry each lustre in turn, and then mounted the ladder again and, receiving each gleaming pointed piece of glass from Austin's careful hand, attached it in its place, still merrily talking, she did not think that her life was uneventful. Her life was happy and eventful. She had found her god in the Waterloo Road. She had fallen deeply in love with William Sandbach who lived there.

I suppose that when Topaz Edgeworth realized that she had fallen in love with William, Mr. Sandbach must have been about thirty-five. He was easily the most distinguished person in the Waterloo Road, which runs straight or slightly curving for some miles. He was a widower, and, as mortality among wives was high, this seemed almost according to nature. He was a tragic widower who had lost both wife and child together under shocking circumstances when he was a very young man, and had borne his sorrow with a proud silence that distinguished him. He lived in a small and admirable Georgian house a little way down the Waterloo Road, which, with its well-tended and hedged garden, was hidden from the dingy thoroughfare. He was the only man in the two towns who gave dinner-parties. His voice was not the voice of the two towns, but had a quality of beauty that was almost suspect. His natural courtesy was a thing apart. He showed some friendship and hospitality to the Italianate young John Edgeworth. He had a handsome presence, kindly eyes, and an admired beard. He was Member of Parliament for the Borough. He had for the first time invited both John Edgeworth and his sister Topaz to a dinner-party the following week, and Topaz adored him. How should she not adore such a man? She had idolized him from afar ever since her school-days. And yesterday he had stopped her and her Stepmother in the Waterloo Road and, taking Topaz by the hand and looking kindly and directly into her eyes with the charm that had won him many an honest vote, had expressed his pleasure that she and her brother were able to dine with him, and to meet the Prince and Princess Colonna. And when this first time he took her by the hand and looked at her, Topaz ceased chattering, and her long adoration turned to the love which she now recognized. An extraordinary sensation flooded her. As she looked up, rapt, plain, and silent, at the grey eyes and light brown beard of Mr. William Sandbach she felt within her the ancient disquieting question arise, "Is this indeed love?" And it was. It was the very passion of love.

There was a distinction in dining with Prince and Princess Colonna who, owing to an interest in Italian and English china, had come to visit some of the factories in the two towns. Because they could not dash from factory to factory in a motor car, since there were no motor cars in which to dash, but drove from factory to factory in a barouche, the day being fine, and because the Princess, instead of climbing rapidly and unimpeded up and down stairs, moved with the slowness of gracefully manipulated skirts, swaying, bending gracefully to examine, to exclaim, to compare, the whole leisurely performance took a long time, and the Prince and Princess spent the night in the pretty Georgian house of Mr. Sandbach. Young Giovanni Edgeworth with his easy Italian and his pretty manners, his rather tittering wit and his kissing of hands when required, so satisfied William Sandbach's need of a good dinner guest, that whenever Mr. Sandbach again entertained distinguished visitors, and he often did, John and Topaz Edgeworth – that pleasant and presentable young brother and sister who could carry their weight in conversation in two or three languages – were always included in the Sandbach parties. They became almost indispensable. Topaz loved the sound of music, and, twittering, flew as a bird to where the other thrushes were. She was not aware of the deep knowledge, the frustration, and the exultation of the conductor as he moulded the plastic impassioned air into sound. "*What* a good concert! The Mozart, beautiful!" She did not assess the sustained cry of violin and flute, or the controlled fury of brass and drum, but when she met the conductor the next evening at dinner at William Sandbach's, she rejoiced to cry, "Ah, Herr Stein! Your Beethoven, magnificent!" She enjoyed music as she enjoyed food, with pleasure, but without passion, like a warbling unimportant bird; and perhaps she was as musical as any other bird. John and Topaz were full of amusing talk following each party, and people said what lucky young things they were to have all this experience, which was ⎯ue. And after a time people said, too, "You'll see, Mr. Sandbach will marry Topaz Edgeworth one of these days. She's not pretty, and it's a pity she doesn't wear her clothes well, but she's entertaining, and, my word, she *can* talk! She'll be Mrs. William Sandbach, M.P., you mark my words, and she'll make a good wife for Holy Willie." People went on saying this for three or four years.

And the Stepmother said to Father, "Joseph, I hope William Sandbach intends to marry the girl. She's in love with him, I am convinced, and he is making her conspicuous. Couldn't you say something, Father?"

And William Sandbach said to himself, "Shall I marry again? . . . I wonder if Topaz Edgeworth . . . she's very good at a dinner-party . . . but I don't love her and I don't think I ever would love her, and I can*not* go through all that misery again. I'm free. And yet . . ."

And Austin said as she unhooked Miss Topaz's yellow moiré that was so good and so unflattering, "Cook said to me, Miss, only this very evening, 'Mr. Sandbach will pop the question any day now, see if he doesn't,' and Cook says that Mr. Sandbach's Mary said that the way Mr. Sandbach looked at Miss Topaz anyone could tell that there'll soon be a second Mrs. Sandbach. There then, you step out of it and I'll loosen the stays."

All these cruel things Austin said, and when Topaz was in bed, and the light was out, and the evening beat brightly about her brain, she said to herself, "Can it be possible that he could not love me when I love him so much? What do I do wrong that he does not love me? What will please him that I can do? I would lie down and let him tread upon me. When he is there, everyone else is just a shadow. Until he comes back into the room the room is empty. Just to touch his sleeve. Oh God, what shall I do? I cannot live like this."

And still Downs drove John and Topaz to Mr. Sandbach's evening parties and William Sandbach greeted them with the same urbane charm that he gave to each guest – or perhaps a little more. Topaz became rather more animated, a little more gay, but pale. Before she went into a room, now, she furtively pinched her cheeks that were so pale. ("Like this, you see? Like this . . ." she said fifty, sixty, and seventy years later, vigorously pinching her wrinkled but soft cheeks, "a great help to the complexion!")

Austin at last stopped her warm exciting welcome hints to Topaz as she undressed her after a party, although in the kitchen she (Austin) and Cook and the new Betsy talked commiseratingly.

"*I* could learn her how!" said young Betsy, boasting.

"You hold your tongue, miss," said Cook sharply, "our Miss Topaz needs no lessons from such as you!"

And upstairs Topaz wept alone. She really wept. Many a night she wept in the dark, and slept on a hateful moistened pillow.

And when three more years had passed, John made a runaway marriage, and this affected the happiness of Topaz a very great deal.

SEVEN

What a Delightful Evening!

WHEN, AT ELDER HOUSE, the letter arrived from John in London announcing his sudden marriage, Father faced Mother across the breakfast table, and Mother faced Father. They looked at each other and for some moments were unable to speak. It was nothing to them that in John's letter a general trembling could be discerned plainly. Let him tremble. So he should. But that John – the dilettante, the indolent, the elegant, the diner at good tables, the indifferent apprentice at Father's Works, without an income, with hardly a wage – should have slipped away to London and become a married man, and should have done it without their permission, shocked Father and Mother to their strong foundations. And that Mrs. Grimwade, the rich and miserly friend of their childhood, who each year entertained the young Topaz in a niggardly fashion, should, in her house in Lambeth, connive, and should abet this marriage, and should chaperon the bride, and should lend her an ancient silver bouquet-holder which appeared to be the only visible sign of celebration, was incomprehensible to them.

And Uncle Montague, at his breakfast table, glaring above his long beard – in which crumbs had lodged – at a letter from London, cursed so horribly that the parlourmaid went out to the kitchen door and beckoned Cook to listen. In Uncle Montague's letter, which was also tremulous in tone and matter, Anne Edgeworth informed her father, oh, so timidly, that she had married dear John, and that she hoped to be forgiven, and that she had slept at dear Mrs. Grimwade's as Mrs. Grimwade would testify, and that Mrs. Grimwade had lent her a silver bouquet-holder which Mrs. Grimwade had herself used at her own wedding – "the old bitch," said Uncle Montague. Anne hoped her dear Father would also forgive her dear John, and would receive them soon, and she remained his devoted daughter Anne Edgeworth.

When Uncle Montague had cursed as much as possible and had spilt his coffee which flew up and hit him as he banged the breakfast table, he went to his lawyer's where he revoked his allowance to his daughter and also changed his will; then he drove to the Works to roar at his brother Joseph. Joseph Edgeworth was not there, so Uncle Montague had himself driven to Elder House, where he found Father, Mother, and Topaz still in consternation. Topaz fled. Father had rallied, as he foresaw the coming of Uncle Montague with his rage upon him, and Father, a strong man of peace, had prepared himself for storm. Uncle Montague could not frighten the Stepmother, who drew herself up to the last proud and portly inch and at once took the part of Giovanni and of Anne, who thereafter became known in the family as Annie-John, or, sometimes, John's Annie.

Although Father and Mother were quite properly annoyed at the action of the preposterous young fellow John, they knew what circumstances had brought about this forbidden marriage. It had already been mooted, and John's parents and Anne's father had at once forbidden a marriage between the cousins. Having forbidden this marriage, these Olympians, accustomed to obedience, had dismissed so trivial a matter from their minds. Father did not propose to support John, and Uncle Montague had other plans for his daughter who was a bit of an heiress. Not only was Uncle Montague a wealthy and violent man, who blew where he listed, but he was a widower whose wife had gone to her peace, having made her own plans for her daughter's future beforehand. This rich and gentle woman, before she died, made her will, and left to her infant daughter Anne a pretty fortune, to be hers at the age of twenty-one. And here was Anne, a week after her twenty-first birthday, proceeding to London, and marrying her handsome and penniless young cousin, bringing with her a dowry which would support them both, very nicely indeed. True, John was a young man of integrity and he loved his cousin very much, but he was wise, and he and his bride chose this course which, although shocking even to themselves, was easier than facing the gales of family wrath wherein their little ship might founder.

Topaz, after much exclaiming and running about and relating the romantic news and writing on her own account an affectionate and welcoming letter to the culprits, was stricken with doubt. She withdrew to her bedroom to think, as the house seemed to be full of gasping exclaiming relatives.

Mr. Sandbach. John had been inconsiderate. Mr. Sandbach was entertaining the Baroness Burdett-Coutts at dinner on the following evening. Of course John and Topaz Edgeworth were both invited; and now John had gone off to London and got married without a word! Would Mr. Sandbach want her to come without John? Each evening with William Sandbach now filled her with misery, yet was her dearest joy. She would not relinquish this joy and this misery. She would not submit the problem to her Stepmother, who with dignity and spacious consideration was now deciding upon Stands to the taken in the future with John, with Anne, with Montague, with Mrs. Grimwade, with the daughters and sons, with the servants, with the aunts and uncles, with the cousins and with many other people. On the next evening Topaz, to the Stepmother's great surprise, ordered the brougham on her own account, put on her favourite green plaid taffeta with the many ruchings, and drove to Mr. Sandbach's house to dinner. During this very short journey she told herself again that the news of John's marriage must have spread quickly, that Mr. Sandbach would be prepared for John's absence and for her presence, since she had sent him no message. With a little apprehension she left the carriage, and rang the bell at Mr. Sandbach's well-known door, alone.

"Are you all right, Miss Topaz?" called Downs from the box. A maid took her mantle, and Topaz advanced smiling but uncertain into the drawing-room filled with talking people who immediately fell silent, and as immediately resumed talking with greater zest than ever.

"Yes, they do know. They are talking about John," she thought quickly and did not know how to proceed. But her host came up at once.

"Ah, Miss Topaz!" he said smiling (how often "Ah, Miss Topaz!"), "we were waiting for you impatiently! What is this we hear about your dashing young brother? But first let me take you to Baroness Burdett-Coutts, and then you must tell us . . ." and Topaz felt at home, and everyone turned their laughing friendly faces towards her.

There was in the mind of Topaz as she laughed and chattered and expatiated more and more lavishly an uneasy feeling of imminence. Imminence of what? Of something which would happen. Of a sign. This feeling grew throughout dinner-time, and afterwards became almost unbearable to her. "Yes, this evening will bring me a sign at last," she thought. Without looking, she watched William Sandbach. She saw – without seeming too much to observe – his every movement. She was not aware, then, that she, Topaz, was also observed. She, never self-conscious, did not feel that other guests watched with interest the possible crisis of a little play – a play of which they had grown, perhaps, after so long a time, rather tired. She saw Mr. Sandbach, with a gesture to the guest of honour, take her towards his little conservatory and his famous begonias. Then the Baroness led; he followed, impeccable, the host. *What happiness it might be, what unbelievable happiness!* Topaz renewed her animation and talked to Edmund Bond about the new Academy pictures which she intended to see when she visited Mrs. Grimwade in London – the same Mrs. Grimwade who so naughtily had contrived to help John. Edmund teased her.

"A very dangerous house to visit, Topaz, for your family," laughed little Edmund Bond, "you had better beware . . ."

"They are magnificent," said the Baroness, near at hand. "What richness of colour! So perfectly fringed! Have you seen them?"

"Would *you* like to see my begonias, Miss Topaz? They are at their best. May I take you?"

I must not show how I care. I must smile. No one shall see. And with her hasty eager tread which not even Mrs. Porter had been able to tame to the desired grace, Topaz stepped forward and laid her hand on Mr. Sandbach's sleeve. *Oh, I cannot come here again unless I come to stay!*

They went into the gloom, or it seemed at first to Topaz that it was gloom, of the little conservatory where light from the drawing-room showed the pink, the rose, the crimson, the white, the primrose of the great begonias. William stopped. Topaz stood facing him and fidgeted nervously with the ruching of her basque. They did not look at the begonias. It was evident that Mr. Sandbach had something to say. He looked down at her with the kind look that was to her so personal and tender. ("Oh, look at Holy Willie!")

"I hope, Miss Topaz," he said seriously, "that this sudden marriage of John's has not caused your parents real concern. I think, if I may say so, that it is a good marriage for John. His wife is a most estimable young lady and will, I feel, be a steadying and sensible influence on our young friend, on whom, so far, responsibility has sat lightly. You do not mind my saying this? I wished you to know how fully I sympathize with your parents – and yet I understand, believe me, and congratulate John heartily." He paused. Something in Topaz's uplifted face smote him, and caused him to be uncomfortable, and sorry, and ruthless.

"Oh," she thought, "he only wants to speak about John. It is only of John he is thinking, not of me."

"Thank you," she said at last. "I will tell John. Yes, I will tell him."

"Thank you . . . and I will write to him," said William. "And now . . . But Miss Topaz," he turned to her again and she stood and watched the shadows on his face, "I trust that when John and his wife return, and dine with me, as I hope they will often do, you will not neglect us altogether? Such a charming and lively young lady as you . . . we should miss you . . . I hope that . . ." He cursed himself. *How cold and*

*clumsy I am! What am I saying? Yet I cannot speak otherwise.
What am I trying to tell her?*

"Oh, he is too courteous, too cold!" thought Topaz despairingly. "He does not care whether I stay or whether I go. He doesn't care whether I live or die. This is plain to me now. This has been waiting for me. I need not deceive myself and put myself in this ridiculous position any longer. This is the sign. This is what was waiting for me." And she knew beyond any doubt that William Sandbach did not love her – not if she dined there for years and years and years would he ever love her. Her nervous fingers still played with the silk ruching and the frill of her bodice. She was glad that in the half-light he could not see her face clearly. She said with a pitiful dignity, with a little toss and agitation of her head, and with an unsure laugh, "I wanted to have this opportunity of telling you, Mr. Sandbach, that my Mother persuaded me to come tonight for fear lest I should disarrange your party, and that in future John's wife will, of course, accompany him – an extra woman does so much complicate your numbers. You see? You see? I understand these things," said poor Topaz. "This has been a very delightful evening," and the tears were near her eyes, "but I must keep my promise to my Mother, and go back to her, early. The event has been very trying for her. You understand? You will excuse me, I am sure. I will go, before Mrs. Beardmore begins to sing." She turned towards the door and stepped forwards with her swaying hasty tread.

I cannot stay and finish this evening. How best can I leave this place. I must go home. I must go home. There is no other sign. I know that I shall never come here again, for I cannot bear it any more. And she moved busily across the room towards the guest of honour. The faces of her friends were no longer the faces of friends. They were only talking, grimacing people. She had to be alone.

"Baroness," she said smiling, with death in her heart, "this has been charming, so charming! but my Mother is tired tonight, and I promised her that after I had filled my place at the table I would go home. You will forgive me if I leave before you? Goodbye. Goodbye . . . and Mrs. Beardmore, I

am so sorry I shall not hear you sing!" *Is everything said? Can
I escape without betraying myself?* And Topaz nodded and
smiled and nodded, and made her exit, pale and smiling.

When Austin opened the door of Elder House, Topaz
passed her headlong without word or sign. She hurried up the
stairs, her long green skirt with its ruched frills trailing behind
her. Half-way up the stairs she turned. "You need not come,
Austin," she said in a choking voice, and proceeded hastily
to her room. "I shall undress myself."

"Eh, what *has* happened to Miss Topaz! Not even going
near the Master and Mistress, not to tell them about the party!"
Austin said, and stood looking up the stairs. "It's all over
then. . . . Nothing else could ever make her look like that. . . ."
And, still looking up, she heard Topaz's door shut. And the
silence.

In the great four-poster with its ocean of feather bed, Father
and Mother lay comfortable in its billows and waited for their
daughter to come in as usual, full of talk. They heard her at
the front door, so early. The Stepmother raised herself slowly
in the bed and lighted a candle. Topaz would come in and sit
down and talk, and a candle would do. Some light shone in
through the open door from the landing. But Topaz did not
come. They heard her rapid tread. They heard the rustle of her
silk. They heard her pass their door. They heard her own door
close. Louder than words could tell, they heard that something
was wrong.

"Why hasn't the girl come in to see us? I want to settle,"
said Father at last. "Is something the matter? Hadn't you
better go?"

"Nay, Joseph, not yet," said Mother, and lay down again.

Inside Topaz's room the lamp was lighted. Topaz stood in
the middle of the floor. So the impossible and outrageous had
happened to her, Topaz Edgeworth. She had spent seven years
of her life in the preoccupation of love, and there was no
return but this emptiness. The placid bearded figure passed
and repassed smiling before her eyes and she whispered "I
hate him."

"Go, Jane, do," urged Father in the feather bed. The mountainous woman got up slowly, and silently and slowly passed through the door. She stood, holding her breath, outside Topaz's room. There was no sound. What was the girl doing in there. (She was still standing there, rigid, her hands clenched at her sides.) The Stepmother raised her hand to knock, and held it raised. She heard in a cold strong voice unknown before to her the fearful words "*Curse him!* I call Heaven to witness that I curse William Sandbach!"

Fear and compassion smote the Stepmother standing there. "Oh," she thought, "is that our Topaz? Our poor Topaz? I cannot help her now. I will let her be. She wouldn't want me to know." And she turned and went back to her bedroom.

She closed the door. She blew out the candle and mounted heavily into the bed and pulled on the covers and lay there looking into the dark.

"Well, Mother?" asked Father beside her.

"Oh, Joseph," said the big kind woman, "she cursed him!"

"Cursed who?"

"Cursed William Sandbach."

"Cursed William Sandbach? Our Topaz cursed William Sandbach?" Father repeated in amazement, while William Sandbach flitted past him and past again, the suitably bearded William in a frock-coat, William in a Prince Albert and striped trousers, William Sandbach, M.P., Holy Willie.

"What will you do, Jane?" he asked at last in dismay.

"I don't know," said Mother miserably.

There was a long heavy silence in the feather bed.

"Take the girl to Bloxum tomorrow and buy her a good mantle," suggested Father at a loss.

"A mantle! Oh, Joseph, sometimes you're very stupid," and Mother began to cry.

Joseph lay aghast. His enormous wife had never wept before. He reached out his hand and patted her great arm.

"Come, come, Mother. There then . . ." he said helplessly.

EIGHT

Recurring Pleasures

OF ALL THE inventions human or divine which have been bestowed upon civilized peoples the one most taken for granted, yet the one most practical, is the division of Eternity – or is it of Time – into seven days of the week. Uncivilized persons, one supposes, do not feel the lack of this arbitrary division. The passage of Time is marked for them by such signs as the seasons if any, by day and night if any, by the lunar and solar changes at all events, and by the occurrence and duration of other physical phenomena such as hunger and gestation. These changes are enough; and to some indolent civilized people that is a very enviable kind of existence which they would willingly exchange for their own. For our existence which we call civilized becomes increasingly complex; so that 3 P.M. next Wednesday week has an entity and form and prognosis before ever it arrives; and instead of living in polar time and space like free Eskimos, we make prisoners of ourselves by appointments which we arrange for ourselves for 10 A.M. on Tuesday week and 5 P.M. on Thursday fortnight, and the first two weeks in July, and thus, between us, we murder our peace. The only thing in our changing world that we can now regard as being safe and sure is that next Monday will certainly be Monday, next Tuesday will be Tuesday and nothing else, and that Saturday afternoon will always be Saturday afternoon; and for this much stability we should be thankful.

Topaz was what might be called a civilized although not a

conventional being. She was not indolent but she was idle. She seemed very busy, and for the most part she was busy in useless matters and recurring pleasures, so that if the book of her life had been shut up bang at an early age, history would have gone on much the same.

Between the time of her slow but complete and lively recovery from her one-sided love affair with William Sandbach and the time of her going to live in Canada as she ultimately did, there was a long stretch of years which had every right to be unbearably dull. Instead of being unbearably dull, these years were educative, amusing, and profitable, and this is a tribute to people who like Topaz are not particularly useful but are unquenchably gay.

While it is true that each year was very much like the last and the next and therefore the years slipped away uncounted and unmarked except by births, marriages, and deaths from old age, for no one was ever ill, the set and recurring pleasures of these years kept memory and anticipation alive.

During the winter months Topaz, since the age of seventeen, had met with other pleasant and knowledgeable people of the Pottery Towns at what were called the Book Meetings. Evening lectures were held at the grimy Bloxum Institute; but the evening journey was long for the family broughams, and so, among the Edgeworths and their friends, the Book Meetings were born. These continued for years to be among her recurring pleasures. I was never at a Book Meeting, because I was not alive and had not then been thought of, but I have heard so much about them that I am there with Topaz. There we sat, rising to greet with delight the Arkwrights, the Huntbachs, the Stocker girls, the Stalker boys, old Mr. Saddleback, the Greens, all the large Edgeworth family, and visitors. People came in their carriages, unless they lived very near at hand. The Book Meetings were held only once a month, because much real work had to be done beforehand. The standard of discussion of books, or of the performance of music, was good. Lecturers did not in those days rush about the country by plane and train and lecture at great pains and expense for half an hour after lunch to the time-driven citizens

about Poland, Canadian Art, the University as I See It, and
Political Changes in Our Time; nevertheless we are fortunate
that they do this for us now, as thus we know more about more
subjects, although less about less. The Book Meeting members did this for themselves, and they did it very well; so well
that such early temporary members as young Mr. Kipling
(later to be the surprised father of a poet), and the other lively
and amusing in-laws of young Mr. Edward Burne-Jones were
noticed to be bright, but not unusually bright nor potentially
famous.

Topaz had a sweet singing voice, only moderately pleasing, because it was not so much like a singing voice as like a
flute's note, or the notes of a thrush. She shone in the duet,
because her voice was true; and she had absorbed on her way
so much musical knowledge that she was able to harmonize
nice airs which occurred to her or to other people, and to set
them to music and to play the music too, while she warbled a
flute-like true soprano and her younger sister Hannah (or after
Hannah died Miss Arkwright or Mrs. Tennant) took a melodious contralto.

There was, of course, the busy and spreading family,
political, and Chapel life which went on continuously, and
which composed the background of the Book Meetings of the
winter months, of Topaz's annual visits to old Mrs. Grimwade
in London, of a short visit annually to the seaside which was
held in only moderate esteem, and of an occasional journey
to the continent of Europe. This sufficed for Topaz since she
was congenitally lacking in any private or inner life and did
not seem to miss or need it.

Father – who on account of James and Annie Hastings'
growing young family was now established as Grandfather
Edgeworth and was slipping almost unaware into being
Great-Grandfather Edgeworth – had an esteem for Exhibi-
tions. This dated from a visit to the Exhibition held in the new
Crystal Palace in 1851. Father was a progressive manufac-
turer and had sent some teapots – brown teapots – to the
section of the Exhibition devoted to china and pottery. His

children's future as travellers on the continent of Europe was sealed at the moment when Father, standing aside with his two young sons, beheld the small Queen of England, escorted by her tall consort and the immensely popular Duke of Wellington and an entourage of ladies and gentlemen, advance to the stand on which were Father's teapots. Queen Victoria picked up each teapot and handled it. She almost caressed its rotundity as she discussed its merits with Prince Albert and the Duke who presumably were interested in brown teapots; she laid it down; and then amidst the hush of her subjects, she passed on. Father's business received a notable stimulus from this experience. The French next had an exhibition in Paris which they perversely insisted on calling an Exposition. Thither went Father and his sons. Next thing, Father was exhibiting in Amsterdam and in Rome; and next thing he had an agency in Naples.

As time went on and Father's sons grew up, it was obvious that John was the one for European travel, and so it was John who with a weak chest spent a year in Naples and developed a culture of Europe which blended very nicely with the natural charm which he possessed, which was English. It was John who was sent hither and yon to exhibit and report on each new Exposition and to develop business connections on the Continent. As a business man John was only fair; but since he spoke foreign languages easily and his manners were good, he made a worthy representative of his father, who was very able and much more useful at home. An odd but lucky thing was that Father could trust John completely and had no reason to feel uneasy about the debasing of the handsome young man's morals in the notoriously easygoing continent. John was a mirror of convention as he knew it; moral lapses were almost as serious to him as were lapses of good manners; so Father had no worries about John.

In the late summer of the year 1889, Topaz was in London. One day towards the end of her customary stay with Mrs. Grimwade, her brother John called and was admitted.

"Oh, here you are, John!" exclaimed Topaz, entering the

drawing-room with a rush and finding her good-looking brother there. "What brings you to London?" and her brother told her.

Father had directed John to go to Naples to visit the factory's agent there, and had suggested that John should take with him his sister Topaz, as, although she had been to Switzerland, to Holland, and to France, she had never yet been to Italy. John had agreed, adding, "And I think it would do Topaz good, sir. I have noticed that she is in danger of becoming provincial."

"Is she indeed?" said Father indifferently; "well, I hadn't noticed it." And that was probable, because Father himself was incurably and proudly a provincial of the finest kind.

"But Annie! Annie-John!" cried the delighted Topaz, when she heard the news, speaking not of her eldest sister Annie Hastings, who was far too busy with her own family of nine children to think of going to Europe, but of John's own wife, Annie-John. "How is it, John, that you are taking me, and are not taking Annie-John?"

John looked down his nose which was well modelled. He said, speaking with some importance, "A reconciliation has taken place between Annie and her father" ("Oh!" breathed Topaz with two round eyes and a round mouth), "and it seemed timely, as he wished Annie to accompany him on a visit to the Lakes, that she should go with him. I do not, however, feel that Uncle Montague" (his terrifying and reluctant father-in-law) "is yet completely resigned to me as Annie's husband, so I am taking this opportunity to go to the continent on business."

It would be a dull dog indeed who could call a life dull in which there suddenly occurred an unexpected visit to the Continent. Topaz, full of joy and anticipation, set out with brother John.

She exclaimed all the way across the Channel and in the train which puffed across the fair land of France, until they reached Paris. She exclaimed all day every day in Paris, and often John had to restrain and correct her. He became increasingly aware that ordinary convention which he so sin-

cerely worshipped had no meaning for his sister. This placed
John in many uncomfortable situations in which he felt that
he was conspicuous not as the lordly and distinguished En-
glishman which he liked to be, but as the brother of an
irreverent and carefree youthfully middle-aged sister from the
Midlands; and before he arrived in Italy he often wished that
he had left her at home to deteriorate.

The brother and sister began the ascent of the new and
amazing Eiffel Tower. How delightful! What a wind! The
skirts of Topaz whirled around her head obscuring her view,
but she did not mind. John did. "We will descend, Topaz!" he
said, tapping his cane sternly on the hand-rail.

"No, no, John!"

"Yes, yes!"

"No, no!"

"Yes, yes! This is no place for an Englishwoman of modesty with all these Frenchmen about. Descend! Descend!" he
cried. With Topaz expostulating and backing down all the
way, skirts whirling, they descended. Frenchmen watched
with pleasure. This kind of thing happened continually.

John became more pallidly handsome and anxious as he
escorted his sister about the continent of Europe. Topaz
rejoiced too openly, she had no reticence; she did not seem to
know the right people from the wrong people; she made
friends with the wrong people without patronizing them
suitably; she was openly entertained by the frank private
habits of the wrong people. "Thank God," thought John, "that
my sister is not physically attractive to men, or my position
would be worse still; she is disgracefully natural." And Topaz
thought – when she thought about it at all – "Really, how
easily shocked John is! He does look silly with that martyred
expression on! Oh dear, dear, John, I've put on odd boots, I
do declare!"

And then, when they had reached Lyons, and John had
decided that his sister was not physically attractive and that
her particular kind of artlessness did not arouse the baser
passions of men – especially of Frenchmen – he had a nasty
jar, and resumed his anxious watchdoggery. Their plan in each

new hotel in each new town was that John's room should adjoin the room of Topaz – an arrangement well suited to a brother chaperoning his unmarried sister through Europe. But in the thrifty little hotel found by John in Lyons there were no such rooms available. John could sleep just above Topaz, but not beside her. "Oh, I will, John. No, I won't, John. You see, Madame has given me a key! Yes indeed. If anything happens in the night, I shall stand on my bed at once and pound with my umbrella!" promised Topaz hopefully, and she slept soundly each night with her umbrella beside her in the bed, in case ("*Such* a comfort!"). But one day John, descending, paused aghast at the head of the narrow flight of stairs. There, outside his sister's half-open bedroom door, stood a man in earnest low conversation with the attentive Topaz. Out flew the Frenchman's hands, persuasive, this way, that way, flic-flac; out rushed the words; he paused for a moment and laid a hand upon Topaz's arm. Topaz dusted him off. She did not attempt to go away, but listened and interrupted with her usual eager vivacity. As John gathered himself together and bounded down the stairs like an avenging mountain goat he heard his sister say, "Mais, Monsieur, attendez un moment! Non, non, nous ne sommes pas froides, nous Anglaises! Pas du tout! Au contraire, je vous assure que . . ."

"An assignation!" roared John.

"Oh, is that you, John?" said Topaz, turning to her brother. "This gentleman . . . no, I never saw him before . . . oh, where can he have gone? . . . tells me he finds the English cold, and I was only trying to reassure him that so far from that being the case we . . ." John stood silent, furious.

Then, "Into your room at once!" he hissed between neat teeth.

"Well I never, what a fuss to be sure! He was a very interesting young man . . . parted his beard in the middle in flourishes . . . east and west . . . like this . . ." twiddling her fingers each side of her face, "very peculiar!"

"And did he accost you?" asked John severely.

"Accost? Oh yes indeed he *did* accost! Never had such an accosting in my life! On the stairs! But I wouldn't have let him in, whatever he did, I do assure you, John, oh dear me, no!" said Topaz, delighted to be accosted, yet armed with all her gay purity.

"But you must have encouraged him!"

"*Me!* Encourage him! I did no such thing! I only greeted him politely as we met!"

"*Greeted* him . . .! It's evident you don't know Frenchmen, Topaz!"

"Well, John," said Topaz shrewdly, "you don't give me much of a chance, do you?" which was true.

At dinner-times, John marked his sister as she drank the pleasant and sometimes unpleasant wines of France and Italy. He would lay his hand upon her glass.

"One glass is enough for you, Topaz; you are sufficiently intoxicated by nature without drinking wine."

"*Me!* Intoxicated by nature!" But so she was, like many another much more famous lady.

It was when Topaz lay flat on her back on the floor of the empty Sistine Chapel, better to observe the wonderful ceiling, in an attitude that John's idol, Ruskin, would have comprehended, that John nearly started back home in a fury. Topaz had to do a little cajoling, at which she was not very good, to restrain him; she had to point out, for example, that Michael Angelo himself had had to take up unorthodox attitudes and had thereby actually developed a goitre while painting the great frescoes, until at last John spoke to her again and there was peace between them.

In the end they both went home as culprits. John had been unable to resist the opportunity of an audience with the Pope.

"Get Signora Castellani to give you a bit of black lace for your head, Topaz, and we will join the throng." And they did.

The pilgrims flocked in thousands. Every mind, every heart was high uplifted. The great spiritual and temporal power of the Church of Rome seized the imagination of these two intelligent English provincials, and in excitement and fervour they moved with the great throng. Gone were the scruples of John. Topaz had none. ("It is of course true, Topaz, that people died that England might become a Protestant country, and let us not forget that; and you know perfectly well also that our great-grandfather was made a class-leader by John Wesley. It is true, too, that Father and Mother will not be pleased. But in view of the opportunity to join in the service of this great historic church I prefer to become a casuist, and I shall not conceal it from my parents." "Oh do, John. Oh don't, John. Oh do, John!" cried Topaz, ready for everything. That is actually the way that John and Topaz talked to each other.)

It was fine to see John standing proud and erect in the presence of his parents when the travellers returned to England. Father did not seem to mind very much about the audience with the Pope, but the Stepmother was displeased. So Father spoke.

"And did you – bow the knee to the Pope of Rome, John?"

"I did, sir. To a great Prince of an historic Church." The green eyes of Topaz glanced quickly from parents to son.

"And did you commit yourself with any . . . remarks . . . or ritual during the ceremony?" asked the Stepmother, portentous with her girth and her black satin and her pug nose.

"I instructed my sister to repeat *sotto voce* the Apostles' Creed, and I did so myself," said John nobly.

The Stepmother raised her chin and looked down her proud pug nose across at her husband. She deferred, as always, to her mild lord. She trumpeted melodiously (as she so often did), "then Lay your Commands upon them, Joseph!"

But Father laid no Commands upon them. He only said, "Let them be, Mother. I hope when I die that I shall have friends in the many mansions and they won't all think like me. Let them be."

All the journeys of Topaz, whether great or small, were packed with adventure and reminiscence. The world blossomed daily into incident; and so the years passed too quickly. Then suddenly, in all her opinion, rotundity, dignity, and integrity, the Stepmother died.

NINE

Nuts and Figs

UNTIL THE death of the Stepmother, the private life of Topaz, if life must be compared to a journey, had been like travelling on a canal. Topaz had never said to herself, "My private life is like a canal" ("A canal indeed! Whatever are they talking about!"), but nevertheless when for purposes of recollection or recapitulation she regarded her past and passing life, it was as a canal that she saw it. This canal had been soundly constructed by her progenitors, and was well administered by those now in charge. The banks of this smooth canal were pleasant, and presented much variety to her, not in scenery, but in people who were seen in passing – to whom Topaz eagerly spoke, nodded, or waved when possible, whatever their station or occupation – and objects, which she pointed out with many lively comments. Except for a period when she passed through a long and dark tunnel, when, distraught, she did not know where to turn (but the way led straight on regardless of her despair), her journey was comfortable and well-conditioned. Sometimes Topaz alighted and made an agreeable excursion. She went with Father to the Lake District ("Ah, Keswick, Keswick! Poor dear Ruskin!"), and she and Mother went to Manchester when Mother was very old (" . . . and we took her to the Art Gallery, Austin and I, in the bath-chair, she would go! And Ellen Terry running like a girl from room to room, and coming in and meeting Mother again on purpose, and studying her, and laughing and saying, 'Oh, look, isn't she *perfect*!'

And Austin *was* cross at anyone for laughing about Mother, Ellen Terry or no. Because Mother looked just as important as Queen Victoria in the bath-chair, you know, and far better dressed, and, of course, she had a pug nose, but Mother never noticed . . ." – just the same blessed obliviousness that preserved Topaz for a century). And a journey to France (" . . . and we climbed the Eiffel Tower, and *such* a wind, oh, *such* a wind! And my skirts blowing above my head – such skirts! And John said, 'Topaz, turn and descend this instant! This is no place for a young Englishwoman with all these Frenchmen about!'"). And a journey to Italy (" . . . the ceiling of the Sistine Chapel! Wonderful! And there was hardly anyone there, so I lay down flat on my back to see better. And John hissed, 'Topaz, get up at once, I disown you completely!' and he walked away. Oh, John *was* annoyed! I thought he'd never get over it, but he did, he did . . ."). And a visit to Dartmoor (" . . . and away went horse and trap down the hill, and over it spilled and when I came to, the horse and I were lying in each other's arms. Oh, Father *was* surprised!"). And a visit to Switzerland (" . . . ah . . . Lucerne . . . beautiful . . . and the Prisoner of Chillon, Byron, you know, and *such* good cheese!"). And the annual visit to Old Mrs. Grimwade in London (" . . . a very miserly woman indeed, but kind; but I took good care to have a tin of biscuits with me, *I* can tell you, and I always saw the Academy, and I saw Gladstone!").

After these journeys by the way, the leisurely travel down the canal was resumed once more under the general direction of the Stepmother, until Nature perversely had caused the Stepmother to die, and Topaz was left in a position for which, to tell the truth, she was not by experience prepared.

Topaz did not know that it was not an evil thing that her Stepmother should die in the ripeness of her age, for she loved her. What talk, now, of giving us twenty-five more years of life! Who would wish to live, Methuselah among a multitude of Methuselahs? Let us find another star. For unless aged persons have the very wisdom of God, if their authority has been exerted unquestioned upon adult younger persons, they may at last die, and leave those younger persons too old to have any youth, too young to have any age. And so it almost was with Topaz. It was perhaps as well, then, for her that her Stepmother at last left Topaz, still in her light-hearted minority at forty-five.

For the strange thing was that Topaz had never bought an essential thing for herself in her life. Ends of lace she had bought ("so pretty!"), and pictures of scenes which she had visited and enjoyed. She acquired boxes, and fans, and other pictures, too, when painted by cousins or friends, or by some artist whose nephew she had met at Torquay. She bought books, good and bad, although she preferred good ones. She bought china and glass, and sometimes extra chairs and tables. She bought "goodies." She bought, not from discrimination, but by reason of association, or, best of all, because she liked the looks of something.

But her mantles and dresses had been selected and paid for by the Stepmother, who was guided in choice not by beauty, nor by taste (of which she had none), nor by fashion (to which she was indifferent), but by "handsomeness," and by generosity, and by the time of day. Wool or alpaca for the morning; cloth (braided or bebuttoned) for the afternoon; silk, satin or velvet lavishly trimmed for the evening. Without regard for the face or figure of Topaz, but with the agreement of Topaz, the Stepmother bought The Best. Food, also, had appeared upon the table as by the Stepmother's well-ordered magic, but Topaz knew little of the mechanics of ordering, marketing, selecting, planning, cooking, or serving. She saw food upon the table, she ate it, she loved it, she praised it, she digested it. Such things as railway tickets were obtained by brothers, or by such practical young women as Rachel, Annie's second daughter, or Elise, George's only girl, an effulgent beauty who feared neither man nor devil and captivated both – the only dazzling beauty in the family. Topaz had already become Aunt Topaz, and was now on her way to being Great-Aunt Topaz, without noticing it at all.

After the bewilderment of Mother's death Topaz cared for Father will all the love and inefficiency of which she was capable. The results were excellent. Austin became the housekeeper, and took over where Mother had left off, and Topaz became her Father's loving, constant, and talkative companion. Father was now a very old man. Now that Annie's eldest daughter Laura had given birth in South Africa to a child, he was always Great-Grandfather Edgeworth. Annie had in her turn become a Grandmother.

Great-Grandfather Edgeworth sat in the garden in the sunshine. A white handkerchief covered his face. Puff in, puff out, puff in, puff out. The white handkerchief, neatly secured under his round black skull-cap, rose and fell with the blasts from his wide ingenuous nostrils. Behind the concealing and expressionless handkerchief was the noble face of the sleeping old man. Happy, happy old man. He sat there, sleeping in security in the sunshine. His world was a good world. His Queen was a good Queen. His country was a good country. His business was good. His health was good. His family was a good family and God was good. All this goodness flowed together in this strong and gentle old man. He had served his community well. He had never turned aside from recognized Duty. He had known consolable grief and inevitable worry, but not much grief and not much worry, and no doubts. None. God? God, invisible but real, was obscured from him only by the lofty and so often clouded English skies, but with spiritual eyes Great-Grandfather Edgeworth beheld his Maker. He even knew just what God looked like. He, like and yet how unlike Blake, beheld the Ancient of Days, bearded with majesty. How surprised Great-Grandfather Edgeworth would be if Death, the incalculable stranger, disclosed a different Being. Though God was ageless, God was old. For in the world in which lived Great-Grandfather Edgeworth and his daughter Topaz and his friends and his neighbours, wisdom was synonymous with bearded age, and the opinions of a beardless man were not worth attention, any more than the vague sweet songs of birds or the lashing of the wind in the trees. Great-Grandfather Edgeworth and his neighbours, practical bearded men though they were, lived deeply the life of the spirit. But they did not wander in uncharted spiritual ways. The great John Wesley remained their guide. He led them past the wayward phenomena of birds, winds, and stars, the calamitous inequalities of life, and the strange plaguings of beauty, to hard facts and spiritual certainties. Great-Grandfather Edgeworth was a kind and just employer, but he accepted without question what he saw, and he saw a world become at last static. His imagination, which flew beyond the bright blue sky to the invisible, did not pierce the squalor of the Poor so near at hand in the grim town. The Poor took their familiar deplorable place in squalor, and it would have seemed a novel and disturbing idea to Great-Grandfather Edgeworth that the Poor should reasonably aspire to eat well, drink well, live well, and die well. Not wrong, of course, but chimerical. Each age, like our own, has its large blind spots. The social conscience was stirring but not awake. Great-Grandfather Edgeworth was a product of the ages which preceded the young Victoria. Here he was, sleeping in the garden, ninety years old, an upright old man in a world which he really thought was upright.

Austin the old housemaid crept out to see if the master was asleep. The handkerchief puffed out and in rather uncertainly. The master stirred. He was waking. Where was he? Oh, in the garden. After lunch. *Such* a good lunch. But where was Topaz? Topaz! Topaz! Where are you? Oh yes. Topaz was coming home this afternoon from her visit in London to Mrs. Grimwade, bringing with her Mrs. Grimwade and bringing little old Miss Raphael too. Each year Topaz still spent a fortnight in London with Mrs. Grimwade. This austere and miserly lady did not offer to provide entertainment for the young girl of forty-eight, but at least Topaz could leave the narrow house in Lambeth and with her friend Tottie Hay visit the Academy, chatter in Piccadilly, whisper in St. Paul's, and return to the wiry grey curls of Mrs. Grimwade and the soft white curls of her little sister Miss Raphael and vivaciously recount and re-recount her day.

Great-Grandfather Edgeworth missed Topaz. She was his loving daughter and his comfort. A man needs comfort when he is ninety. She talked continuously. If no human ears were within range, she talked to animals or to birds. "Whee-whoo, whee-whoo," she called to the birds. "There, you see, it answered me, whee-whoo, whee-whoo!" She disliked silence. Silence existed only to be broken. If nothing new presented itself to be said, she said what she had been saying all over again. To Great-Grandfather Edgeworth Topaz's talking was an accompaniment of life like his skull-cap. He did not often notice it, but he was used to it, and he missed it when it was not there. He liked Topaz near him, or some woman. Austin the housemaid had been very good, very good. When one became old, women were really better to have near one than men. More comfortable. Men had been part of his responsible daily life, of course. But now women for comfort. Women in the house. A woman in the bedroom, and within the bond prescribed, a woman in the bed, as was natural. His mind turned slowly back to his first wife. He thought without surprise but with tenderness of Mary's death at the age of forty-two at the birth of their tenth child. He felt tenderness for Mary, and for himself, left with so many babes, immense pity. How lost he had been. But soft hands had been held out to help, and soft voices had said to the handsome man, "Oh, *poor* Mr. Edgeworth!" Not "Poor Mrs. Edgeworth!" but "*Poor* Mr. Edgeworth!" And he had turned to his stately Jane, and Jane had helped him, and he had become again strong, no longer poor Mr. Edgeworth with all those children. And now, after a lifetime together, Jane too had died and left him, an aged and lovable patriarch, to the care of the young Topaz. And the young Topaz whose bonnets and mantles had been bought by Jane, and whose chest had been rubbed by Jane, was at the age of forty-eight the astonished and inexperienced young mistress of this orderly household which still ran on the momentum generated by Jane. But now Jane the autocrat was only a silent name in the cemetery. And on the upper half of the stone was the word Mary. Poor Mr. Edgeworth.

Great-Grandfather Edgeworth tugged the handkerchief from his skull-cap and rang the bell on a little table beside him. Obscurely the phantom thought passed, Topaz really needs a mother. She has been used all her life to a mother. She is very inexperienced. And it would be nice, very nice. "Eh," he sighed puffingly, "it would be nice to have a woman near me." This he said disregarding the proximity of Topaz and the constant nearness of Austin, Cook, and Betsy. A household of women, but lacking its head. "Aus*tin*, Aus*tin*!" he called with rising voice. "Oh, here you are. Scratch me back." Beside the bell on the little table lay a long slim ebony rod, and at the end of the rod was a small carved ivory hand, a little concave hand with fingers bent scratchingly inwards. This was The Backscratcher. Confiding as a child, Great-Grandfather Edgeworth leaned forwards and Austin loosened the back of his collar with her fingers. She slid the back-scratcher down Great-Grandfather's back and drew it up and down discriminatingly. Austin was a good back-scratcher, she was. She knew just where. Scratch here, scratch there. Great-Grandfather Edgeworth shut his eyes in bliss and drew his breath inwards through his excellent old teeth. "Oh, nuts and figs," he murmured. And then "Nuts and figs, nuts and figs." "*There* then," said Austin. Great-Grandfather Edgeworth sighed comfortably. "Is Miss Topaz come yet?" he asked. "In about half an hour now, sir," said Austin. "Well, then, I'll go in. Help me up," said Great-Grandfather Edgeworth. "Eh, I'm stiff."

The evening was cold. Great-Grandfather and Mrs. Grimwade sat by the fire while Topaz helped little Miss Raphael to bed. As Topaz's rôle was that of young daughter, so little Miss Raphael's rôle was that of young sister. She was younger sister to the formidable Mrs. Grimwade who now sat erect by the fire, her feet on a hassock, her black silk skirt lifted a little, disclosing a phalanx of petticoats above her slippers. Mrs. Grimwade always raised her skirt as she sat by the fire, which at home was always a very small fire, believing that heat was bad for silk. So severe were Mrs. Grimwade's cerements of black, and so forbidding and lined and yellow was her face, that the grey and wiry ringlets that hung down each side of her face seemed to mock the aged features they adorned. They bristled and mocked. Mrs. Grimwade was an exceptionally ugly old lady, but to Great-Grandfather Edgeworth sitting opposite her in the firelight she was neither ugly nor forbidding. She was just his old friend Maria Grimwade come to pay him a visit. She was Jane's old friend, and the annual protectress of his giddy Topaz. The same firelight that deepened Mrs. Grimwade's wrinkles and could not soften her features, illumined the majesty and repose of Great-Grandfather's handsome old face. The two old people spoke little. The fire, the comfort, and the companionship were enough. At last Great-Grandfather said, "I've been thinking, Maria. I've been thinking, Topaz needs a mother."

Mrs. Grimwade turned sharply and her ringlets swung.

"A mother? Don't be silly, Joseph. The girl's nearly fifty. She doesn't need a mother, she needs a husband. If she needs a mother at *her* age, she'll still be needing one when she's ninety!"

"Well, perhaps she will, Maria," agreed Great-Grandfather equably.

Silence while the coals glowed and shifted.

"I've been thinking, too, Maria," said the old man simply, pursuing his thoughts, "I miss Jane. I miss Jane very much. Topaz is a good girl, but it's not the same thing. Someone me own age. There's nothing much left now, Maria, but to talk of old times and just to sit together like you and I are sitting now. You have Sarah and I have Topaz, but – well, I do miss Jane. I suppose you wouldn't marry me, would you, Maria? Just marry me and stay on. There'd be you and me, and Topaz and Sarah." (They could chatter together, the two girls, thought Great-Grandfather Edgeworth.) "There's plenty of room."

Never before had the imperturbable Mrs. Grimwade received such a shock, certainly not when Ebenezer Grimwade proposed to her, not when her brougham turned over at the foot of the hill, nor when her cook fell all the way down the stairs and broke her neck. But her lined yellow face showed no surprise. She gave Great-Grandfather Edgeworth a quick look. He gazed peacefully at the fire; his comfortable thoughts, the pleasant glow, the comfy chair, his good dinner, his old friend, all blended very well indeed.

"Joseph," said the old woman with sound sense, "you don't really mean this. You think you do because you see me sitting here and I'm your old friend. But you don't realize that you're over ninety and I'm eighty-seven and we'd be the laughing-stock of our families or at least upset them very much. You've got Topaz to look after you, and I've got Sarah to look after and we do very well as we are, you here and me in London, just the way we are. No, I won't marry you, Joseph." Through her clear mind passed quickly her gratification that Joseph Edgeworth, the man she had always admired above all men, should, even almost in his dotage, wish to marry her. There passed also the thought of her Will so carefully made, leaving her fortune in Consols to the Missions and leaving small bequests to the young Raphael nephews and their wives. What complications would ensue! There passed the thought of the genial comfort of this house, butter with bacon and no remarks passed, fires in your bedroom, little luxuries that her niggardly management could not endure, and so she spoke again emphatically, "No, Joseph, nonsense, Jane wouldn't like it, and it would never do. Put it out of your head."

"What did you say?" enquired Great-Grandfather Edgeworth, who had been nodding to the warmth of the fire. "Oh yes, yes. You really think it wouldn't do? Well, perhaps you're right, my dear, you always were a sensible woman. But it would have been very nice and comfortable." "*That* it wouldn't," thought Mrs. Grimwade.

The coals glowed and Great-Grandfather's eyelids began to close on the soft light. The two sat again in silence looking at the fire until Great-Grandfather slept in his chair. Mrs. Grimwade's tight mouth moved in speculation, her lips invisible. She almost smiled as her thoughts turned over and over and settled themselves down again. To think of it. She, Maria Grimwade, the third Mrs. Joseph Edgeworth. What a to-do there'd be! Nay, she'd keep it to herself. But what a triumph! Upstairs, Topaz and little Miss Raphael still chattered and laughed as Miss Raphael went to bed.

When on a bright late summer morning Mrs. Grimwade and Topaz went for a drive in the brougham, little old Miss Raphael and Great-Grandfather Edgeworth stood in the garden sunshine well muffled up.

"Shall we take a turn down the path, Miss Sarah?" suggested Great-Grandfather.

"Oh, that would be very nice, Mr. Joseph," said Miss Raphael. So Great-Grandfather, leaning on his stick, and the fragile little old Miss Raphael took a turn down the path. They walked slowly to the end of the path without speaking, little Miss Raphael's white silky curls bobbing as she walked. Then they walked back. Miss Raphael, who knew that gentlemen like to be entertained, searched her mind for something to say. Her old friend seemed content not to be entertained, but Miss Raphael had been brought up in the ladies-must-talk school, so she began in her gentle way. She admired the petunias, she admired the roses, and she greatly admired Great-Grandfather Edgeworth's gold-headed cane and "Oh, what a pretty butterfly!" "She is a dear little creature," thought the old man, but he was feeling rather tottery. "Let us sit down, my dear," he said, and reaching the two garden seats they carefully sat down. Miss Raphael sat opposite Great-Grandfather Edgeworth, and as he looked at her it seemed that for the first time he saw how gentle was her look, and how pretty were the white curls that framed her sweet old face. "Sarah, me dear," he said, "how is it you never married?" Little Miss Raphael was not used to direct questions like this, especially from gentlemen. No one had ever before asked her why she had not married. What could she say? She could not tell the truth, that no one had ever asked her in marriage. "Oh, Mr. Joseph," she fluttered. "I've been so much with Maria, and I have never seen many gentlemen, and, as a matter of fact, Mr. Joseph, I'm very shy with gentlemen." And indeed she was, even with old Mr. Edgeworth whom she enshrined as the perfect man. An idea floated again to the surface of Great-Grandfather

Edgeworth's mind. His rebuff from Maria Grimwade, which was no rebuff at all but the friendly statement of an old friend, had gone from his memory. He looked kindly at Miss Raphael. A glow of discovery warmed him. Here in Sarah Raphael was a sweet companion, really the suitable companion for his closing days. He saw no difficulties in the way and came straight to the point.

"Every woman should marry, my dear, especially a pretty woman like yourself. You are much too charming, my dear Miss Sarah, to continue in single blessedness."

Miss Raphael nearly suffocated. Never before had a gentleman, sitting alone with her, said such exquisite and provocative things to her. And this from the perfect Mr. Edgeworth! She was fascinated but frightened. But Great-Grandfather continued.

"You see how alone I am, Sarah. My dear Jane has left me and I am a lonely old man –"

"Oh, Mr. Joseph, *surrounded* by Loved Ones!" murmured Miss Raphael.

"What is a daughter, what can children ever be, compared to a wife?" Great-Grandfather Edgeworth's face glowed as he looked upon the waste of sweet womanhood before him. "You should marry, Sarah," he said. "You should marry. Why not stay here and marry me and let us be old together? There's nothing much left now, Miss Sarah, me dear, for old people, except to sit together as we are sitting now, and talk over old times. To be companions, that's it, companions."

"But Maria . . ." said Miss Raphael faintly.

"Maria can look after herself very well," said Great-Grandfather Edgeworth. "Maria's a strong sensible woman."

"But Topaz . . ." faltered Miss Raphael.

"Topaz is a good girl, a very good girl, but it's time she got married herself." He had forgotten that Topaz needed a mother. "And Topaz is fond of you. Many's the time she's said to me . . ." and, using up far too much energy, he continued warmly his address to Miss Raphael.

While Great-Grandfather Edgeworth continued his speech to Miss Raphael, light steps came up the gravel walk. Into the garden came and out of the garden went a radiant young creature dressed in faded blue cotton. Pretty Milly, the dressmaker's daughter, brought Miss Topaz's jacket in a parcel to the side door. Milly's feet lightly crushed the gravel and she walked quickly to the door and away again out of the garden. She wore no hat and her fair hair shone in the sunshine. Because the sun shone and she was young, and because she was happy and beautiful, sparkling smiles came to Milly's lovely face. And as she walked away from the house she looked carelessly at the two old people wrapped up and sitting in the sun, and to Milly they were hardly people. "Look at them two old mummies lapped oop like tha'. Eh, I'd as lief be dead as look like tha'." Her gay glance only touched them as she sped down the path, and as lightly out of the garden she went, shining.

But the two old people had not discovered that they were mummies. Great-Grandfather Edgeworth's long speech, which rather tired him, gave Miss Raphael a little time in which to collect herself. The moment of her life had arrived, and she must meet it suitably. Phrases heard, read, echoed in her head. She adored Mr. Edgeworth. Whether she loved him or not she did not know. Only one thing she knew, she could not marry, and only one thought confronted her – how to make a suitable refusal. This was unexampled. She was unprepared and alarmed. Absurd, at seventy-nine, still to feel inadequate. She wished Maria could do this for her but she had to do it for herself.

Great-Grandfather Edgeworth ceased speaking. He had said what he wanted to say, and to tell the truth he did not much mind what Miss Raphael decided, but he would abide by her decision and he was feeling a bit hungry.

Miss Raphael began, "Oh, dear Mr. Joseph, I cannot tell you how grateful, how honoured – I hardly know what to say – by you of all men. I cannot truly say, Mr. Joseph, that I do not requite your passion – that is, your feeling so kindly expressed – but I'm sure I should never enjoy being married to any gentleman, even – if I may say so – to you, dear Mr. Edgeworth, whom of all men I – well, Maria has always felt

that I was too young for marriage and I think perhaps I am."
(Mr. Edgeworth received this statement without surprise from
the aged maiden.) "I hope you won't think, dear Mr. Joseph,
that I – oh, I beg of you, *do* understand that I appreciate – that
I am fully aware of the honour you have done me – but I think
that under the circumstances I would rather not – that is, I
must regretfully beg to decline . . ."

She trembled. Her curls danced and trembled.

"All right, all right, me dear," said Great-Grandfather, who
had made his little effort and was content, "there's no need to
get excited; either you do or you don't, you know. Well, well,
there's the brougham and I'm ready for me lunch *I* am."

But Miss Raphael put her hands to her breast. Her heart
fluttered so.

The visit of the two sisters came to an end early as little
Miss Raphael was not well, and Maria determined to get her
home and into her own bed. The two ladies sat opposite each
other in the train to London and had the carriage to themselves. Mrs. Grimwade's moment of human weakness came
upon her. She became feminine and confiding. She could not
resist telling her secret to her little sister now that they were
safely alone together. She tasted her enjoyment. "*Won't* Sarah
be surprised!" thought Mrs. Grimwade agreeably as she prepared to tell her tale.

"I do not usually discuss such matters with you, Sarah,"
she announced in her severe manner as though proposals were
a daily occurrence to her, "and I trust you to regard with
secrecy what I am about to tell you."

"Yes, Maria," promised Sarah, her soft look fixed on
Maria's wrinkled yellow face.

"As things have turned out, we are travelling back to
Lambeth together, but this might not have been the case."

"Oh?"

"I came to a very important decision last week, partly on
your account, and partly for other reasons."

"Yes, Maria?"

"It may surprise you to learn that Mr. Joseph Edgeworth
asked my hand in marriage but I declined."

Sarah's world spun round her. "Asked your hand in marriage, Maria?" she faltered.

"Yes, Sarah."

"Asked your hand in marriage?"

"That's what I said," snapped Maria.

"Are you sure it was *your* hand that Mr. Joseph asked in marriage, Maria?" timidly.

"Don't be ridiculous, Sarah. Why shouldn't he ask my hand in marriage? Don't act like a simpleton." Maria was annoyed. Sarah's surprise had the wrong sound.

"You're quite sure you didn't misunderstand Mr. Joseph?" persisted Sarah.

"Do I ever make mistakes?" said Maria quite furious.

"No, Maria," said Sarah simply. Poor Maria, so she had thought Mr. Joseph was asking for *her* hand, while, of course, it was her young sister's hand that he had demanded in marriage! Sarah had just been about to take her sister into her confidence, but now she could not disillusion her. Maria seemed so complacent about it. Poor Maria. And besides, weak as Sarah felt, she was unequal to facing Maria's anger on discovery of her mistake. Some other time perhaps, when she felt stronger. Not now. What could she say?

"Well, that was very kind of Mr. Joseph," she said at last placidly.

Maria looked sharply at her. What was wrong with Sarah? Where was the amazement, the admiration, the envy? Maria was displeased. She looked out of the window. Sarah looked out of the window too.

"May I ask, Maria, just when this occurred?" asked Sarah, turning again.

"I am not prepared to discuss the matter further," said Maria huffily.

"Very well, Maria," and they finished the journey in silence.

Sarah was very tired when they reached the narrow house in Lambeth. "I feel poorly, Maria," she said. Into bed she went, and the next day Maria looked at her little sister and saw that she was ill.

On the day that Sarah died, Maria stood beside the bed. "Sit down, please, Maria," said Sarah weakly. Mrs. Grim- wade sat down.

Sarah waited for a moment, collecting her little strength that was slipping from her. Then she spoke.

"Maria," she said clearly and sweetly, "I think that you should know that you are in error. It was not you, my dear sister, whom Mr. Joseph Edgeworth desired to marry. Your mistake was natural, that when he mentioned marriage you thought he referred to yourself. But dear Maria, it was I who had the great, great happiness of being desired in marriage by Mr. Joseph. I declined in spite of his protests, partly on account . . ." and she died.

"Well!!!" said Mrs. Grimwade. But it was too late. She could not put Sarah in her place. Lost satisfaction. Lost joy. Sarah was gently, irrevocably removed. Oh my little sister Sarah, what have you unaided done? You have died.

TEN

The Majority

WHEN FATHER died, Topaz attained her undesired majority and independence at the age of fifty. But she was only a girl grown old, however much strangers might take her for a woman. Life with her father had promised to be permanent, but the promise was broken. When Topaz, drying her reddened eyes, looked about her and found that decisions had now to be made by herself, and that people regarded her as an adult who should herself define her next move, she felt her weakness. Her spirit sought Father and the Stepmother in vain. They were not there any more. She no longer sat in their shadow.

John's Annie said to John in a melancholic voice, "Jee, dear" (Jee for Giovanni), "of course I should be *delighted* for Topaz to come and live with us."

John's distinguished face became clouded, and he said in an extremely religious tone, "That is very good of you, Annie, most kind indeed. I appreciate it. There is nothing I should like better than to give a home to my sister. But the fact is that she talks too much. I cannot *endure* to be out-talked at my own table."

John's Annie's face cleared. "Then she must come and stay with us for six months."

"Yes, or for one month at least," said John. "I will speak to George about Topaz." If John needed to atone for his natural reluctance to be out-talked at his own table, he atoned

80

a hundredfold. He became for thirty years Topaz's faithful and valued correspondent while six thousand miles divided them. His letters were her tie with all that she had known and loved before. ("Look!" triumphantly waving an envelope, "another letter from John! Now, let me see!") For thirty years he gave her deep satisfaction and lasting pleasure, and thirty years is a long time.

And George said to his handsome wife Eleanor, "Hrrumph. What about Topaz coming to live with us? Uh? Mm? What?"

And Eleanor said, "Nothing would please me more than to have Topaz here. But I believe that Mrs. Williamson in the village has some very nice rooms that would suit Topaz well, and wishes to let. She could have her own furniture there, and Mrs. Williamson could Do for her. She would be near us all, and much more independent. I can think of nothing nicer."

George's worried look brightened and he said, "Hrrumph. Splendid! I will speak to John about it. Hum!"

But Annie, the eldest sister, came back post-haste from Llandudno, where in her new sad widowhood she had gone with her daughter Rachel, and came straight to Elder House. She entered the house in the dignity of her sorrow and of her black mantle and widow's weeds. "Where is Miss Topaz?" she enquired, and went swiftly to find her, calling "Topaz, where are you?" Annie tossed her black veil back over her little bonnet, and with all love and goodness in her face she looked at her grief-stricken sister. She ran up to her, and reached up – Annie was smaller than Topaz – and put her arms around her, saying in her gentle voice of comfort, "My dear sister. My dear dear sister. You will come to me, won't you? I need you."

And some months later a letter came from Blakey in Australia. It was not very well written and not very well spelled, but it shouted a welcome. "You must come and live with us, Topaz," it shouted. "We will get you a horse. How you and John and the rest of you can live in England when you could come to Australia I can't conceive. The children all

want to see their English aunty and Maudie sends her love."
Topaz looked sideways at this invitation (a horse?), but its
kindness warmed her now established heart.

Rachel helped her to close up Elder House (a factory stands
there now). And Annie said, "If we decide to go and join Frank
and Stephen and Andrew in Vancouver – we can try it for a
year – you will come with Rachel and me, won't you, Topaz?
Now that the three boys here are settled, I feel I should go –
for a while."

"Where thou goest, Annie . . ." said Topaz, with a tremulous laugh, and Rachel set about moving three women, instead of two, on the long journey.

Into her majority and for ever, Topaz took her three loyalties. Not religion, although she had an indigenous faith in
God, for Topaz might well have been (and perhaps she had
been) a heavy-footed Bacchante, a milder Maenad with satin
white skin, dancing heavily and happily, excited before the
flickering shrine, carefree among the olive trees, calling to the
other boys and girls; not patriotism, although she loved her
country; not love for a man – William Sandbach had become
only a still interesting object seen from afar. But the Royal
Family moved through her life with banners streaming. Mr.
Gladstone stood for ever four-square in his integrity ("Yes, I
shook his hand, I heard his wonderful voice – like an organ it
was . . .") and through his spell she adhered in a wishy-washy
way to the Liberal Party. And now her loyalty to her father
lived as a loving memory – or perhaps it expanded, to include
the person of her little eldest sister.

It was soon plain, however, that Topaz's majority was
virtual, not real. Rachel slid by nature and unaware into the
Stepmother's place. "Shall I take Mother's good black with
me, Rachel, in case? And shall I take the little Portland Vase
that Mr. Wedgwood gave Father? And, oh, shall I take John
Lockwood Kipling's pen-and-ink sketch that he gave me?"
The niece was fifteen years younger than the aunt, but Rachel
was a woman grown, and older than Topaz in wisdom, and
now took upon herself another care.

ELEVEN

The Journey

WHEN MISS Topaz Edgeworth, and her eldest sister Annie who was now several times the Grandmother, and the Grandmother's unmarried daughter Rachel left their homes in England, they embarked at Liverpool and crossed the Atlantic Ocean to a new home prepared for them in Canada. It was courageous of three women whose years added up to over one hundred and fifty, because, although they were going to make this new home with the Grandmother's welcoming sons in British Columbia, they were leaving behind them all the familiar safe things that had for so long composed their lives.

The Grandmother left behind her the happiness of familiar loves, dear places, and ordered days. She left bereavements, her great and only sorrows. But wherever she might go, in all circumstances and places, the Grandmother was at home, because she carried heaven in her heart and in her face.

Her daughter Rachel left nothing behind her, not even an unhappy love affair. Marriage? Not Rachel. Rachel, laughing and smug, used to say:

> "Whene'er I take my walks abroad,
> How many babes I see!
> When I get home I thank the Lord
> They don't belong to me."

And she meant it. She turned rejoicing towards Canada.

Rachel's Aunt Topaz left behind her much joy and most of the sorrow she would ever know. She left there the mordant years of unfulfilled love. They were finished. It was done. It was almost as if it had never been. And now she turned readily to the West and faced a fresh free life which she was eager to enjoy.

Aunt Topaz now looked forward with rising infectious spirits to every minute on this precious ship. She at once enjoyed talking to the exciting people who walked up and down and round and round the deck on the first day out, wearing important hats. It was exciting and unexpected also on the second day to meet a completely different lot of people walking about, facing the breeze in completely different hats. Some of these hats were humbler, some were more rakish, and their wearers were not identifiable. It was exciting on the third and subsequent days to totter in perfect health around the reeling windy deck, and stumble, laughing and apologizing, against passengers who with bowed heads charged into you, or against the protruding deck-chairs of passengers with only one eye partly open. Aunt Topaz got to know a great many people in this way and also at meals. Life extended immeasurably and intoxicatingly.

News about passengers was disclosed from hour to hour. It was said that there was an actor on board. His name was Mr. Otis Skinner. The fame of Mr. Otis Skinner sped round and round the ship. People tried to identify him. There was also a Lord. People tried to get into conversation with single men, so as to discover if they were the Lord. The determined Lord was never found throughout the voyage, and was probably one of two indistinguishable morose men who read books all day long. There was an English Admiral and an American Lecturer. They were soon discovered. Besides all these famous individuals, there were enough pleasant people to keep Aunt Topaz going for the rest of her life. Aunt Topaz spoke to everyone who could possibly be spoken to. She would hurry back with face alight to Sister Annie who was well tucked up on the breezy deck. "Annie! Just imagine!

There's a Mr. and Mrs. Palfrey from St. Louis on board who know the Davises in Torquay!" How wonderful! The little Grandmother seldom spoke first to people, but people often spoke to her, and then she responded cordially.

One day the Grandmother leaned upon the rail of the ship with some other passengers and looked out to sea. Someone had seen a whale. She longed to see a whale. The passengers lingered at the side of the ship hoping that this phenomenon would graciously appear again. And oh, look, there was a ship against the horizon! Yes, look, a ship! The black veil of the Grandmother's widow's bonnet whipped about her in the wind.

"Would you please be so good as to tell me," she enquired of her next-door neighbour with circumlocution, "if that is what is generally known as 'the bulge'?"

The person at the Grandmother's right hand said disagreeably, "If what is what is generally known as the bulge?"

"That," said the Grandmother pointing with a small gloved hand at some dirty water that issued from the ship's side.

"What?" asked the disagreeable man.

"That dirty-looking water," explained the Grandmother.

"I don't know what in the world you're talking about," said the disagreeable passenger shortly and moved away.

The Grandmother was stricken. No one had ever been rude to her before. Really, for about fifty years, no one had ever been rude. She had seen and heard other people being rude to other people and she had deplored this. She had trained a large family in the practice of politeness. No wonder she looked stricken. She had seldom felt so exposed.

Her strickenness was written all over her. A passenger on her left hand (oh, such a nice man) had seen and heard all this, and said with a smile, "You are quite right, Madam. That, I believe, is the bulge, very frequently called the bilge. In fact it's nearly always called the bilge in seafaring language, but how could you be expected to know that!" The kind man smiled down at her with all the protection of a son. Grannie looked up prettily at him. "How kind of you! I was afraid perhaps I'd said something very stupid. But still I don't think I deserved to be spoken to like that, do you? I don't think anyone ever spoke to me quite like that before!"

The kind passenger with the nice voice told her soothingly No, that it was quite inexcusable. He took the affronted one by the arm, led her to her deck-chair, tucked her rug around her, said "Comfortable?" just like a nice son, and left her. "What a charming man!" thought the restored Grandmother, "I believe he's an American. How truly kind! What a delightful nation indeed!" The whole American nation had tucked her up.

On Saturday night the word went round that Mr. Otis Skinner was going to read the Lesson at the Church Service on Sunday morning. A great many people who had intended to stay in bed or out on deck joined the congregation shamelessly and sat there in solemn rows. Grannie sat there too, but, of course, she would have gone to Church whoever had read the Lesson. It grieved her that so many people seemed anxious to hear the Lesson only if it were read by Mr. Otis Skinner. And an actor! She did not feel sure about the rightness of this. When the time came for the reading of the Lesson, there was the kind passenger who had tucked up the Grandmother on the day before. So this was Mr. Otis Skinner! There he stood, grave of face, what a surprise. Otis Skinner then read the Sermon on the Mount. "Blessed are the pure in heart," he read gravely and the people listened. The Grandmother listened, luminous. People forgot the reader in the noble Word so nobly read. The Grandmother went quietly to her cabin after the service, spiritually refreshed but a little shaken too. A crack had appeared in one of her tiny strong bastions. Some stones had fallen out and a fresh air was blowing in. Through the aperture Grannie saw a disturbing view that she had not seen before. Her so-sure condemnation of the Stage was now not so sure.

Unknown to himself Mr. Otis Skinner forever shed a radiance on the Stage which to Grannie had hitherto been dark, and on the whole American nation which to Grannie had hitherto been unknown. Years afterwards she would say, "Yes, indeed. Americans are most charming. The very first

American I ever met (not counting that very disagreeable person, of course) was an actor, Mr. Otis Skinner. So kind and, one felt, so good." This encounter with the Stage had a far-reaching determining effect. Ten years later, long after a young granddaughter Rose had joined this family in Vancouver, "some Shakespeare plays" came to the new Opera House. Polite and fashionable Vancouver attended, flattering William Shakespeare by evening dress or at least by a "fascinator" over the head, and even by a sprinkling of tiaras and pearl dog-collars (we have grown plainer since then). Of course, Rose wanted to go to a play. In spite of the hallowing influence of William Shakespeare, her Grandmother was mistrustful lest Rose, a girl so young, might through these delights "learn to get a taste for the theatre." Grannie, Great-Aunt Topaz, and Aunt Rachel debated, while the eager yet despairing girl prayed to each of them in turn. The die was really cast by the memories of Mr. Otis Skinner, "so kind, and, one felt, so truly good." Rose went to the Opera House and saw the play. She saw, too, the legendary beauty of Mrs. MacJames of the Klondike, sitting in her box, gleaming with white shoulders and diamonds, brilliant against the black coats and white shirt-fronts ranged behind her; sitting there dazzling and still, with her beauty shining across the sibilant Opera House; sitting there, accustomed to homage and to her own loveliness. Rose at once got a taste for theatre and the deceits of beauty. And all this miracle was being prepared unaware for the yet almost non-existent Rose by Mr. Otis Skinner, reading the Lesson on board ship to the Grandmother, to Topaz, to Rachel, and to all the other passengers.

On the last day of open ocean the seeming and delusive eternity of the voyage vanished. "Tomorrow we enter the St. Lawrence River!" Friendships suddenly ceased to have validity, or developed with ardour; flirtations became cool or poignant. Even the Grandmother, who lived neither in the present nor the past nor the future, not in Time at all but in a constant moment of Eternity, felt the approaching change.

Her sister Topaz, taking down addresses, promising visits, recklessly giving invitations, running round to people's cabins, lending books, returning scarves, impeding stewards, collecting autographs at parties, hardly had time to regret the end of the journey across the famous Atlantic Ocean, in the anticipation of something imminent, new, and rare.

That night the sky was lit from zenith to horizon by Northern Lights. Rachel and Topaz, niece and aunt, leaning at the ship's rail, saw a long and wavering luminous plume of pale-golden colour ascend in the north. The light fanned out and raced to the midmost topmost sky where a black whorl took shape and poured forth a cataract of glowing green. Successive cataracts of light issued from the whorl and became banners which flapped in silence across half the sky made vaster by the antics of the unexplained and ungovernable heavens. From the left of the spreading whorl, which changed shape and character as the onlookers gazed upon it, came a glow of dull crimson. The crimson ran rapidly down to meet the black ocean, changing and doubling and spreading as it ran. The colossal performance of the Northern Lights was exaggerated up up up, on and on, down down and across; and beyond and behind the zenith it encroached upon the southern sky. For time immeasurable and lost the heavens continued to ripple and wave with light, sometimes ghastly, always incomparable, filling the diminutive travellers beside the ship's railing with unprecedented awe.

"Can we hear them?" marvelled Rachel to herself. "I can't believe that they don't crackle and bang, but with the noise of the waves . . ."

"A portent!" trumpeted Topaz happily. Rachel moved away. She wanted to contemplate the Northern Lights in silence, and to prolong this memorable moment of curious time alone.

Aunt Topaz looked round. Rachel had gone.

"A portent!" she said happily to an old man beside her. "We are coming to Canada for the first time, you know," she informed this listener, "and I certainly regard this as most favourable, an indication, I would say, that my sister and my niece and I have made the right decision in coming. A welcome indeed! Yes, I would call it a portent."

"A what?" asked the muffled-up old man.

"A portent, an omen," explained Aunty, waving her arm at the phenomenal heavens. "What the Greeks would regard as a sign. The Greeks watched the heavens very closely, you know, the stars and the planets, you know, and the flights of birds, geese for example – oh, very sensible – and I'm sure such a spectacle as this" – she again waved her arm at the resplendent and changing sky – "would have impressed them very deeply. I'm very fond of the Greeks myself. In fact I've read the Odyssey and the Iliad more than once, not in the original, you understand," she continued truthfully, developing a favourite theme to the muffled-up old man and the Northern Lights.

"I knoo a Greek," said the old man simply, willing to oblige. "He lived just a little ways down from our place when we was on the prairie and he kept a fish shop. Yes *sir*, he sure had good fish, that fellow. But he had a very bad nose and it got worse and they couldn't operate. It got to look like one of them lobsters. I sure felt sorry for that man."

As that was not the kind of Greek that Topaz had in mind she returned to the contemplation of the sky whose light now began to show a lessening and tremulous vitality, yet withal a threat or a promise. "I can do this again any minute that I want to. I can do more than this. I am independent of you, uncontrolled by you, indifferent to you, and you know nothing at all about Me. Behold!" said the mighty heavens rolling up like a scroll. The Grandmother went to bed, feeling with awe and rapture that she had had a foretaste of Heaven and Hell out of her own port-hole, which perhaps she had.

In the fresh morning the ship followed her course smoothly up the river, looking large in relation to the sometimes near banks as she had appeared small upon the wide ocean. On the banks of the St. Lawrence River were green trees, red trees, yellow trees, blazing signs of autumn. Everybody, homecoming Canadians and newcomers alike, exclaimed at the gorgeousness of hardwood maples set against the sombre utility of dark fir trees, and at the white villages which had grouped themselves cosily around the spires of churches. The river was immense, a prince among rivers. When at last the ship moving with stately slowness approached the city of Quebec, Mr. Otis Skinner stretched out his hand. "See!" he said, pointing, "over there are the Heights of Abraham." In Aunt Topaz, as in Mr. Otis Skinner, the spirit of History began to swell.

Mr. Otis Skinner spoke again. His voice was lower, and he spoke as it were unaware, to his own breast. "*There*," he said, "Wolfe fell." And he added, still more low, "And Montcalm." There was a moment of silence. Everybody looked respectfully and with deep interest at the steep Heights of Abraham.

The spirit of History swelled in the bosom of the well-informed Topaz, rose into her throat and nearly suffocated her. She gobbled a little and cried, "See, Rachel, see! The Heights of Abraham! That is where Wolfe fell!"

"Well, well, well," said a fat man, "so *that's* where Wolfe fell! Well, I don't blame him! I don't mind saying I'd a fallen there myself!" And he looked round laughing, courting applause, his shoulders shaking as he laughed.

Aunt Topaz glared at him, astonished. The hound! The base fellow! To jest at death and history! Her eyes flashed a dangerous green; she opened her mouth wide and held it open as Rachel turned quickly and with a bright anxious look stilled her. Then she remembered to close her mouth, and swallowed back some of the most enjoyable things she would ever have said in her whole life.

The ship resumed her lordly passage up the stream, and at Montreal, among the bedlam of landing and leave-taking, travelling companion cast off travelling companion and the unity of the ship was gone. The last friend waved and was gone. Gone. Oriented to his home or journey, each traveller moved away. Here the three ladies, a little experienced in European travel but novices in the New World, were met by a friend of the Grandmother's sons in Vancouver. Away went

Rachel with this helpful Mr. Jackson and returned, saying, "Well, Mother, the Boys were able to get a drawing-room for us on the train."

"Did you say 'a drawing-room,' love?" enquired the Grandmother with surprise.

"Yes, Mother, a drawing-room."

"I wonder why the Boys got a drawing-room?" queried the Grandmother. "A bedroom would be quite enough. I think it would be more convenient and more generally useful. We could, I think, dispense with a drawing-room."

"I think a drawing-room *is* a bedroom, Mother," explained Rachel.

"Then why is it called a drawing-room, I wonder! Indeed," continued her mother, "I would really have preferred a bathroom. On so long a journey I feel sure I shall often feel the need of a bathroom, dear, but I suppose the Boys know best."

"But I understand the drawing-room *is* a bathroom, Annie," said Topaz pounding up hastily from the book-stall, magazines under her arm. "I have had *such* an interesting time! The man at the book-stall speaks French! Imagine! I said to him, 'Parlez-vous français alors?' and he said, 'Mais naturellement, Madame!' What could be more delightful?"

"Then," said her Sister Annie, with her luminous and guileless smile, "if the drawing-room is not a drawing-room, but is a bedroom and a bathroom, I foresee a good deal of confusion. We shall have to try and learn new ways, dear, and I for one am quite ready." And she walked away, and stood, a small cone-shaped figure in black, alone and minute in the now empty centre of the big station. With her gentle enquiring gaze she looked around her at the new scene which was indisputably Canada, where a drawing-room was not a drawing-room, but a bathroom and a bedroom. She would accept it.

As the Grandmother walked, her long black circular skirt, topped by her black mantle, concealed the fact that she had feet. Since her steps were small and level, it appeared that the Grandmother moved smoothly upon wheels like a toy mouse. Her foot-work, unlike that of her sister Topaz, was imperceptible. She returned, composed, to her family and Mr. Jackson who now escorted them along the platform to the train.

"Ah! Negroes!" exclaimed Aunt Topaz with delight, hastening ahead. "How do you do! How do you do! I'm sure I'm very glad to see you! Have you a wife, yes? And family? This is a charming surprise!"

"Yassum," said the porter, presenting to Aunt Topaz his unusually wide swelling nostrils and a preposterously fine set of dazzling white teeth. Aunty gazed at them, admiring. "Splendid!" she said. "Magnificent! Much better than ours! What do you use? I understand that in Africa they use a stick! It is very efficacious! Or is it diet?"

"Oh, Anty, get on, *do*!" begged Rachel. Aunty clambered up and they made their way to the drawing-room. "Well, this *is* nice, I do declare!" said Aunt Topaz, looking around her. Assisted by Mr. Jackson and the exciting porter ("I *do* hope he's a Christian!" thought the Grandmother), surrounded and almost eclipsed by hand-baggage and Aunty's extra parcels, they settled, crying and exclaiming, like shore birds, and said goodbye to Mr. Jackson. "All Aboard!" cried someone. ("Listen to that! 'All Aboard'!" said Aunty.) The train creaked, groaned, shuddered, and started on its long journey West.

When the three women got onto the train in Montreal station, their visible baggage filled seats, racks, and floor, but was as nothing compared to the baggage not immediately visible which they brought with them. The Grandmother took onto the train her powerful spiritual awareness and lasting gentle domination, and her other-worldliness. Her daughter Rachel took all her anxieties, her fierce sense of duty, her integrity, and a great deal of practical irritable commonsense which, although hampered as yet by inexperience, could readily be applied in nearly all circumstances which affected those who were in her charge at any place or time. Of herself, Rachel never had time to think, and so in her the habit of anxious responsibility to which she was disposed had taken root and was to grow. It became as a beech tree, and, under its fine shade, unessential flowers of ease and frivolity were apt not to flourish, and luxury could not grow where the beech leaves fell.

Topaz got on the train with practically nothing at all. She travelled light. A native toughness enabled her to carry her few strong loyalties without inconvenience to herself, but for the rest, the joy of living was daily renewed in her and was seldom checked by things, people, or events. This joy, which was concerned only with the veriest surface of material and psychic being, allowed her to amuse herself like those "water-gliders" which we see in summer running about on the top of pleasant weed-fringed pools. Unencumbered by boots or boats they run, seldom wetting their feet and, one supposes, unaware of the dreadful deeps below them, in which other beings more heavily weighted are plunged, and swim or sink, caught in the mud or entangled by the débris of circumstance and human relations; and sometimes these heavier beings encounter acute sorrow or acute joy or dull despair of which the water-gliders know nothing. Two or three times in her hundred years Aunty's foot slipped below the surface of her pool, but only for a moment – albeit a long moment – and then she got caught in entangling sorrow and this caused her personal suffering. She at once, on recovery, resumed her running to and fro, and, quite unaware of the realities of the lives of the people whom she met day by day, she went eagerly laughing on. So, equipped as lightly as a water-glider of considerable education, she got on the train.

(It was about half a century later that a great-grandson of the Grandmother's, walking home beside the Rideau Canal in Ottawa, stopped to light a cigarette and looked over the railing at the rather still water of the canal. There came a small invisible wind which ran rapidly along the surface of the water and made its presence known by the sudden pretty dimpling and wrinkling of the stream, and by the deflection of some dry leaves whose time had come to fall. The leaves were carried by the small vagrant wind down the slow-moving canal and sailed for a while until the sluggish current bore them to a cluster of waste twigs and lately fallen leaves at the canal's edge, and no one noticed them any more after that. The wind passed, and the water was again still, and the disturbance was forgotten.

"My Great-Grandmother," thought the great-grandson for some reason or other, looking idly at the water, "needs no memorial. There are forty of us – why, there must be over fifty of us now! – Canadians, up and down the country, who have issued from her or from her issue, and for better or worse we are her memorial. And my Great-Aunt Rachel, whom I just remember, needs no memorial either, because there are still people who knew her and honoured her quite a lot, and anyway, a person like my Great-Aunt Rachel has her own memorial. But Great-Great-Aunt Topaz, who outlived these two, and outlived all her generation, and many of the next generation, and some of the next generation, and who defied these generations in her later days – don't I remember her! – she has gone; there is no mark of her that I know, no more than the dimpling of the water caused by the wind a few minutes ago. She is only a line on granite, 'Sister of the Above.' Yet she lived a hundred years, and is not long dead. Already she is seldom mentioned, and when we meet together as we sometimes do, all so busy, all so occupied, perhaps no one remembers, until afterwards, to mention her name. And the little ones will not even know her name. It is really a shame," thought the great-grandson idly, "that one can live a hundred years with gusto, and be happy, and agitate the stream, and pass at once out of memory. So she has no memorial. . . . I'd better hurry or I'll be late. . . ." The breeze blew and rippled the waters of the canal here and there, and the great-grandson set off briskly and thought of nothing in particular after that until the house was reached. . . . It is pleasant walking home beside the Rideau Canal in Ottawa in the fall, to a good meal and an amusing family and a warm house, especially when there is a nip in the air.)

The forests bordered the railway tracks and ran away up the hills. The forests were more brilliant in colour than any that the travellers had ever imagined. Sunlight was reflected from the gold and flame of each leaf of each tree. The forests seemed to blaze with harmless fire. The travellers' vision was intent on the rose, flame, and yellow that shot towards them, passed them, and fell behind them, remaining stationary and identifiable only on the distant hills; they could not see and did not know that away towards the north (and southwards too) beyond and beyond the northern horizon there was a still world of red, rose, and yellow trees, and they did not think that in a few weeks these forest branches would be thin and bare. And because Time was bounded by yesterday, today, and tomorrow as the train slid and rocked along paralleling Time, they could not know that, decades later, a young grandson of the Grandmother's (not yet imagined, not yet born) would be a bush pilot and would fly in a slow, rather rackety plane above such forests. He would fly above the brilliant woods of the Maritime Provinces, and of Quebec, and of Ontario, and would see below him a flaming earth of boundless maple trees, coloured the tender warm rose and fabulous crimson of a carpet of Ispahan; and he would see small and great rivers shining like steel, widely curving through the bright trees; and he would look down on lonely lakes, great and small, shining like mercury, lying as mirrors to the clouds and the blue sky, and reflecting the rose and flame of the maple woods. The grandson would see all this in a newly discovered dimension as old as Time; yet it would be the same brilliance which they now saw with amazement, and which had transformed autumnal Canadian forests for centuries unknown.

"Oh, look!" and "Oh, look!" they said, as tree after tree flashed shining past in perfection of colour and beauty and was for ever lost. The Grandmother began to tire, and so she took out from her bag her book, Ranke's *History of the Popes*. She fell to reading, reading and looking, reading and looking, until she slept, and the book slid from her sleeping hands and fell upon the floor, and she slept for a long time.

The train jerked, pulled, slowed down, and stopped with a jolt that wakened her, and she found that Topaz had left the drawing-room, and that she and Rachel sat opposite to each other and that Rachel was still looking out of the window. Rain fell fast now and it fell in a straight, vertical curtain that muted the scene which they now looked upon and which they saw as through a fine steel curtain.

The scene upon which the mother and daughter looked had great beauty. They did not recognize it as great beauty because they had always acquiesced in what they saw, not distinguishing beauty unless it presented itself in familiar, obvious, and inescapable form; but there was something strange and old and new in this scene which pleased them. Their coach had come to a standstill opposite a small square field of green which was bounded on its three remaining sides by a shabby once-painted white wooden fence. Beyond the far side of the square, opposite to them – behind the far fence, that is – was a large white wooden church. The church had a belfry and, on the top of the spire, a cross. In spite of the rain and the greyness of the atmosphere they saw plainly, in the belfry, a large bell and a wheel, outlined against the heavy sky. At right and left of the square field, and at right angles to the church, and also behind the fence which enclosed the field, two rows of tall wooden houses faced each other across the intervening grassy space. These houses were painted. One was green, the next was a chartreuse colour, the next was yellow, the next was white, one was blue, and the roofs were red. Never before had Rachel and her mother seen wooden houses painted in random colours. The brightness of the colours was drenched a little and silenced by the driving vertical rain. The green square field across which the coloured houses looked upon each other was a graveyard, and, very strangely, all the tombstones and all the obelisks were of red granite, and all appeared to be new. The red granite shone wetly and the green grass gleamed and satisfied the eye and the scene was complete in its colour and its vertical and horizontal beauty of proportion. Down fell the rain.

"It looks," said Rachel, "as if everyone had died together and everyone had died rich."

"I think it looks very pretty, and very peaceful," said her

mother, whose heart warmed to this place which she understood. "Do you think that the people in these houses are rich or poor, love? I cannot quite make out."

"I don't know. Somehow I think they all speak French though."

"French . . .? Oh . . .? We must get a history at once." The train jerked, groaned, and started, and the unity of the small and homely scene was left behind where it remains to this day in its simplicity.

"That place was Saint Something," said Rachel.

"What a many saints they do have, to be sure!" exclaimed her mother.

"I think most people in these parts are probably Roman Catholics."

"Roman Catholics . . .! I see . . ." said the Grandmother. She pondered this for a while and then said within her heart, "There are many ways to God. We shall all meet there."

Suddenly the door of the drawing-room was flung open and Topaz burst in.

"So there you are, Annie!" she said (as though the Grandmother was likely to be anywhere else). "What *do* you suppose! Oh, I've had *such* an interesting conversation! I have been sitting in the gentlemen's smoking-room . . ."

"*Topaz!* said her sister, and into the eyes of Sister Annie and of Rachel came a rare angry obsidian look.

"Yes," continued Topaz heedless and unwarned, "it has a curtain, you know, and as I passed I heard – oh, only by chance! – one of the gentlemen mention the Palmer House! So, of course, I put my head inside and said, 'What a coincidence! My brother-in-law stayed at the Palmer House when he came to America!' (because James did, you know), and before you could say Jack Robinson I was sitting there, and we had *such* a nice talk!"

"Topaz," said her little elder sister sternly, "I forbid you, do you hear, I *forbid* you ever to do such a thing again! That my sister would invade the privacy of the gentlemen's smoking-room – not that I like their smoking," said Sister Annie sitting erect and almost vibrating, "but it is their prerogative!

You never did such a thing in your life before and pray do not begin now. You are altogether too free!" Topaz had never heard her mild Sister Annie sound so cross.

"Well, what a fuss, I do declare!" said Topaz swaying in the doorway of the swaying coach. "This is a free country, isn't it? We've come to a free country, haven't we? I didn't say I was smoking, did I? Really, Annie, and you too, Rachel – it's no good looking at me like that – now that you've come to Canada, you know, you'll have to be less conventional, you know. You're both very conventional, I don't mind telling you. The gentlemen were very nice indeed and I think they were pleased to see me."

"Not they! Anty," said Rachel, "you don't know anything about men at all! Even if they seemed nice, that was just politeness, and *next* time . . ."

"Topaz," said Sister Annie, "you are right. This is a free country. And gentlemen are free to gather together, if they wish to, without intrusion by you or anyone else. Let this be the last occasion. I do beg of you . . ."

"Well," said Topaz, hurdling her rebukes, "I learned a great deal, I can tell you, more than *you* did, sitting here reading Ranke's *History of the Popes*! They say we shall come in a few days to a part of the country called the Rolling Prairie, all humps and hollows, and Mr. Tomack told me it's caused by thousands and millions of bison, or buffaloes he called them, rolling over and over and causing these humps and hollows – some years ago, of course. We shall not see them actually doing it at the moment, I'm afraid."

"Why ever did they do that?" asked Sister Annie, curious, and forgetting that she was annoyed.

"Come in, Anty, *do*, and sit down for goodness sake," said Rachel. "It must have been fleas, of course, and anyway I don't believe it." The vision of millions of large brown woolly animals rolling over and over seemed improbable. Aunty began to argue.

The train ran on and the countryside ran to meet them and was left behind. The comfortable farms and broad meadows of Ontario which now they saw, pleased the Grandmother.

She understood them and the human toil and planning and thrift which had given them their prosperous dignity. They had a look of home. Here were elms. Here were sheep and cattle. Here was lazy smoke rising from chimneys of white farms. The sheep grazed in an international manner. They did not seem to know or care that they were Canadian sheep and should perhaps behave differently in a characteristic way, like the bison. They might indeed have been sheep of Staffordshire. Neither were the cows different from English beasts in their behaviour, the dear familiar cows. And the horses gossiped silently together as they did in the fields of England, communing secretly head to head through the soft intimate skin of their noses as the train fled past them. "I am rather old," thought the Grandmother, looking at the swiftly passing familiar animals, "to be able to assimilate great change." And the train ran on and on. And the day grew dark. And the windows became black. And they prepared with pleasure for the great adventure called Sleeping on the Train.

The couch of the drawing-room was piled with hand-baggage, of which they had far too much. Rachel and her mother lay in the lower berth, and Aunt Topaz climbed up above with agility and delight, and from the top bunk leaned over in her white calico nightdress, declaiming, "Romeo, Romeo, wherefore art thou Romeo?" and they were all merry. Rachel slept fitfully. She awoke each time the train stopped, and lay looking into the dark until it started again, jolting. How sad and how lonely the train sounded in the night. "O-o-o-oh," it cried on its way in the dark. "Oh oh o-o-oh," mourned the train. Aunty slept and woke lightly too, and climbed up and down at intervals. She enjoyed it.

"What *are* you doing, Anty?" whispered Rachel testily. "That's three times you've been up and down now!"

"Well, I need a goody," said Aunty. "Mr. Tomack gave me some goodies, only he called them candies. Have a goody." And she thrust a rustling paper bag at Rachel, sucking noisily.

"And I *do* wish, Anty, you'd stop flicking your light off and on all night."

"Well, keep your eyes shut then," said Aunty, who was

accustomed to the miracle of gas-light but had never had such a nice little electric light to play with before. "Have another goody. This is all very cosy." And she clambered gustily up again.

If Rachel had kept a diary (but she never could, not being that kind of person, except "May 3rd, Mending shoes 2/6. Stamps 6d."), she should have noted down that something very important happened to her the next morning, and it was simply this. The obligation of disposing of unnecessary possessions in England, of equipping her mother, her aunt, and herself with adequate and quite superfluous wardrobes of a thrifty nature (six pairs of long woollen combies apiece because they were going to Canada; three flannel petticoats apiece for the same reason; a new umbrella In Case, the number one umbrella, and the number two umbrella In Case, and so forth), of making all decisions, of taking nearly all the responsibility for nearly all the details of travel for her co-operative parent and her unpredictable aunt on board ship, the embarkation onto the train – all this had knit Rachel's brows and tensed her spirit. But when she awoke after the first night on the train, dressed, looked out of the window, and saw that they were indeed still speeding westwards (this time through a world entirely different, through millions upon millions of sombre and indistinguishable jackpines), the worry and fret dropped away from her, and she felt a new lightness of heart and a release. She loved even the jackpines which in their rank dark millions are hard to love.

"Anty," she said, turning and smiling at Aunt Topaz who was head downwards uttering muffled cries, trying to get her address-book out of a suitcase which was under the seat, and whose bottom was therefore her only visible part, "I'm so glad I came to this country I can't tell you! Why didn't we come before? It's my kind of country and I never want to go back home again. There's something . . ." Rachel wanted the simple word "free," although no word could express her all-pervading release of spirit – " . . . well, I feel Canadian, just as if I'd been born here. I don't care if we stop – here – now – or if we go on, as long as I can live here all my life." And it was

true. Although Rachel would always be prone to anxiety, she
had for ever, now, a fundamental peace – because she was
where she liked to be. She was in essence as much a Canadian
as those who had trodden Canada's wooded shores two hundred years before, or their descendants. The whole thing was
an accident of time. "I wish I'd come two generations ago."

Aunty scrambled to her feet, scarlet and puffing. "I can't
find it," she said, "and how could you come here two generations ago, what a ridiculous thing to say! I can't find it." But
instead of helping, admonishing, and rebuking her, Rachel sat
smiling at the jackpines which rushed past and vanished in
myriads.

"Poufff!" said Aunty, blowing out her cheeks, and pulling
the address-book and a great many other things out of the third
lowest of a pile of heavy leather cases. "Here it is. McLeod.
Winnie-Peg. Perhaps she has a telephone, they all seem to. A
very lady-like woman. What a name! Winnie-Peg!"

"You'd better be careful what you say about names in a
new country, Anty," laughed Rachel, "or they'll say 'What
about Amen Corner and Petticoat Lane and . . . Cirences-
ter? . . .'"

"And Much Dewchurch!" said her mother.

"And Little Gidding and Sixpenny Handley, to be sure,"
said Aunty. "And, oh, did I tell you what that Mr. Mawdsley
from Newfoundland told me on the boat? In Newfoundland
there's Bare Need, and Seldom-Come-By, and Heart's Ease,
and Heart's Delight, and Heart's Content!"

They smiled at each other and at the lovely names. The
train rocked on through the serried jackpines and they were
all in good humour.

"Heart's Content, Heart's Content," murmured the Grandmother with her shining look. "But, oh, what a many trees! I
didn't know there were so many trees! What do the people do
with them all? But there are not many people!"

And far to the north, and to the south too, unnumbered,
uncountable, stood the crowded jackpines, and among them
lay dark, unreachable, anonymous lakes of blank water. And
soon all this country and north to Hudson's Bay and beyond

would be sealed with iron cold, and with silence broken only by the ultimate shot-like crack of frozen wood or water. And the train ran on and on, and the jackpines showed no sign that they would ever come to an end.

Next day the jackpines had come to an end as though they had never been. During the night as the train had hurried along, mourning as it went, the character of the country had changed, and they awoke to find flat distance – space, space, space. "Why, this must be the prairie!" they exclaimed to each other.

Sometimes they stopped at groups of dwellings so small that they did not conform to the words town or village or hamlet, and so short was the wait at the little station that the porter had continually to prevent Aunt Topaz from getting off the train to "walk upon the prairie," and getting left there. Some of the small wooden houses, which had two eyes, a nose, and a mouth, held a malevolent expression. Some leered out of their windows at the train as it ran past. Some with false pride had false fronts, which concealed and then drew attention to the absence of a second storey. "Well, it may be all very nice, but I'm sure I wouldn't like to live here," said Topaz.

"I would," said Rachel, "I'd love it. Look at all that space! Not *here*, I mean," as the train left behind a melancholy grouping of dolls' houses, "but on a farm – over there," and she pointed to the horizon. "I should like to live on a farm." And she saw herself living on a lonely prairie farm with everything dependent upon her and her industry, and upon her companions and their industry. She would live on this hypothetical farm with a hypothetical brother, not with a husband or a lover. To Rachel all men were indeed brothers, not husbands or lovers. So she saw herself on the farm with her little house and her chickens and her turkeys and a well in the yard and a hypothetical someone, and around her – space.

"Whatever are those? Bones?" said Aunty peering at white piles of bleached something which rushed past them. "Bones I do declare! Well! they must be bison bones!" and, of course, they were.

The train slowed down and stopped. "Regina!" called the

porter. "Twenty minutes to Regina!" and they all got out except the Grandmother.

"I didn't quite hear. May I ask you the name of this place?" Aunty asked politely of a tall sombre young man who felt uneasy with elderly women.

The young man looked at her distastefully. "Formerly Pile of Bones, now Regina. I much prefer Pile of Bones," he said, turning and striding to the other end of the platform.

"Whatever *is* he talking about?" Aunty asked her new friend Mrs. Knox.

"He said it used to be called Pile of Bones and now the name is changed to Regina. When the Indians made pemmican out of buffalo meat they left great piles of bones, and that's how it got its name. I rather like the old name, but some people didn't, and the Governor-General's wife, Princess Louise I think, suggested Regina," Mrs. Knox told her.

"Oh, Regina – Regeena – the Romans, very remarkable, I'm sure," said Aunty vaguely, deferring to royalty. But as they looked abroad on the bare prairie and over the little groups of small angular buildings, she could see nothing to confirm the queerly Latin name in this so very new prairie town. But then Aunty could not look forward and see a vigorous city of brick and stone and wood, of industries, of grain elevators, and a seat of government, with a man-made lake, and hand-planted parks, and a thriving centre of a far-flung community of prosperous wheat farmers. She could not see the courage and vision that absurdly dared to call this place Regina. She could see only the bare sun-drenched prairie, waiting for the wheat and for people.

"Nevertheless I cannot understand," she said to an elderly man, who stood near, "how it is, with all this open space, that the inhabitants of the Old World, crowded as they are, do not flock to this new country, with space and to spare," forgetting as she spoke that only family and circumstances had wrenched her from the cosy crowding of the Old World which she loved so well.

"Jever tend stock'n keep the fires goin' 'n melt the ice for

watter with the thermometer forty below?" asked the elderly
man, whose face was tanned and wrinkled and a little sad.

"Well, no, but . . ." began Aunty.

"Jever spend the winter on a prurrie farm, outer sight of
any human bean?" continued the man.

"No, but . . ."

"Well, I spent twenny-five of them. There's women can't
stand it. Asylums full of farmers' wives can't stand it. Drives
'em crazy. The prurrie don't always look like this," said the
elderly man pointing with his open hand to the far-flung sunny
land. He turned and moved away.

"Oh, now, Miss Edgeworth," said Mrs. Knox to the horrified Topaz, "that's not what you'd call really true. Some
people can't stand it. There were times I found it pretty bad
myself. Tom and I had nearly twenty years of it, but I stood it
all right – it was hard work and it *was* lonely, and now we're
older Tom and I don't feel equal to it so we moved down to
the Coast. But what he said would make you think what isn't
just right . . . oh, here he comes."

The elderly man walked towards them, stopped, and said,
"My wife died in an institution near a year ago," and moved
on.

"There . . . you see . . . oh, the poor man, that's why he said
what he did," said Mrs. Knox. And she and Topaz walked
down the platform together, Topaz rearranging her feelings.
"Oh, Indians!" she exclaimed suddenly.

On the grass, wrapped in blankets, with a plait of hair over
each shoulder, squatted two Indians. Aunty hastened up, and
stopped as one would at a stone wall. The stolid faces of the
two Indians showed no knowledge that she or any other
human being was in the world. How did one address Indians?
"Parlez-vous français?" "How do you do?" all the customary
forms of greeting seemed useless. The two Indians defeated
Aunty. "Well!" she said.

"Come on, Anty, *do*," urged Rachel. "Don't keep looking
at those Indians. They won't like it. They've got a right to sit
there, they were here first."

"Rachel, *did* you hear what that poor man said?"

"Yes, and still I'd like to live on the prairie. It's the most exciting thing I've ever seen in my life."

"*All aboard . . . !* " came the cry, and they turned and ran like chickens.

All day the illimitable prairie spread before them and slipped behind them. Far to the north (and to the south) the prairie spread, defeating imagination, like eternity. They did not know that further north still were great irregular lakes, and rivers, and a great river flowing to the Arctic Ocean, where only a few of the hardiest white men had been. They could not tell, speeding comfortably across the yellow stubble of the prairie, that winter would come and seal, and petrify, and drive away birds, and exact a difficult life and death from fur-bearing animals and their hunters, and maintain in rigidity and without mercy a whole empire in the north. They did not think of these things. "From what I gather, I don't *think* Vancouver will look like this, do you, love?" asked the Grandmother uncertainly. And the train ran on.

At night Rachel was wakeful. She could not see, but she imagined the dark endless prairie lying about them as they ran. "O-o-oh," mourned the train sadly, "oh oh o-o-oh." "Why does the engine blow on the open prairie?" wondered Rachel. "I suppose it's level crossings." "*Oh*," moaned the train, pushing on.

And the next day they still ran along the prairie, but now the land broke into rolling country ("This *must* be the Rolling Prairie!"), and the world became lightly wooded again. Then, beyond increasingly high hills they looked westwards and saw, coldly blue and white against the sky, a tumult of mountains.

In the gullies of the little hills through which they now passed there were aspens and birches whose leaves the early frost had turned from green to gold. The birches with their white maidenly stems and honey-yellow leaves shone against the dark conifers. Far to the north of them, but still east of the Rockies, east of Jasper House, the Athabasca River flowed widely through a land that was all gold. Golden golden golden shone the birch trees in the sunshine in that northern land from north to south, from east to west, spiked here and there by dark conifers. Few travellers along the brave steel way had ever heard of this golden world. But here, as the train hurried towards the mountains, Rachel looked up at the railway cutting and saw, for one moment, poised alone against the blue sky, a single slender white-stemmed aspen tree whose golden leaves trembled and shone and sang in the sunshine. It was there. It was gone. It was hers.

Quickly the mountains were upon them. Each of the travellers had been to Switzerland and the word "Alps" sprang from mouth to mouth, but soon they ceased to speak of the Alps. "This ain't all of it, no, ma'am," said the coloured porter huskily. "It goes 'way 'way up north and down south. This ain't only a little patch of it."

The great peaks advanced upon them and they were as nothing amongst the confusion and welter of the mountains. The train began to pant and toil. What wild extravagance of nature was this. Mist came down, or was it rain or snow, and sometimes blotted the great indifferent torrent-spilling mountains from their sight. "I think, love, that they are rather too big! I could appreciate the mountains better if we had come upon them before we'd seen all the other bignesses. I think," laughing a little, "that my appetite for big things is gone," said the Grandmother.

The mountains ranged themselves on either side of the railway track, peak after peak. The Grandmother looked up murmuring vaguely, "The mountains skip like rams." She would have regarded this statement as hyperbole if the Bible had not said it first. But that is exactly what the mountains did. Silently, silently, they moved one behind the other with surprising speed considering their age and size. They changed their positions as the pushing train sped curving along their bases; so that first one mountain, then another, moved silently, in order, one behind another. The mountains only remained static when the train stood still; but when the train raced along their bases the mountains skipped like rams. "The Lord doeth wonderful things," marvelled the Grandmother gazing up at the moving peaks as they rearranged themselves against the sky, and then gave place to still more mountains which behaved in the same way. This occurred for a whole day, for these were the Rocky and Cascade Mountains. They did not see the gorges of the Thompson River (for night had fallen) nor Hell's Gate.

Morning came in the widening Fraser Valley. The train was running for home now, and the long journey was nearly done. It ran along the shores of Burrard Inlet. As the travellers approached Vancouver they hardly saw the swelling line of the mountains across the Inlet, nor the first waters of the Pacific Ocean, nor the masted schooners and brigs which stood off from Hastings Mill, nor the sea-gulls wheeling and wheeling above the salt water – they sat there ready with their gloves on and their handbags on their knees and their minds forerunning them.

At last the train slowed up and clanked into a modest railway platform. The three women searched the faces and forms of the little crowd.

"Oh, Rachel, I see the Boys!" cried the Grandmother, tremulous. "I see the Boys! I see Andrew!"

"Well, I do declare!" said Aunt Topaz, quite beside herself.

Rachel wrote to her cousin Elise, " . . . it is so lovely, Elise, that I feel I've wasted my life in not living here before. Housekeeping with a Chinaman in the kitchen is odd but I'll soon get used to it. People are so kind. I was rather amused at the church social when a Canadian lady admired my pound cake and said I was so capable you'd never think I was English! It was supposed to be a compliment, I think! Wasn't it funny? Perhaps we're all funny like that because I found myself saying to a Mrs. Barrett the other day that you'd never know she was a Canadian, and I don't believe she was pleased. And Mother couldn't understand it when the bank manager's wife said flatteringly that you'd never think we were Methodists, and then again I heard Aunt Topaz say you'd never dream that Mrs. Shafto was a Roman Catholic! All these preconceived ideas! There seems to be more mixing-up of people here than in Ware, and I like it. And it's so beautiful, you *should* see Stanley Park! . . ."

Aunt Topaz wrote to her friend Miss Peacock – or was it to her other friend Miss Pocock?– " . . . and we have a Chinese cook called Yow with a queue with green silk plaited in to make it longer wound round his head in the house and let down and caught up somehow under his right arm when he walks in the street with Chinese slippers turned up a bit in front and a very good black silk coat and trousers indeed quite expensive with a high neckband. He wears a hat. I can't understand a word he says but he seems very good I'm sure. Our house is called The Hawthorns and we have the only hawthorn trees in Vancouver each side of the door. Fancy that! You will hardly believe it but Stephen drove us carriage and all into a hollow tree where we sat in the carriage and had our pictures taken. I will send you one. Such a size! Oh my dear Lily, you *should* see Stanley Park. . . ."

And the Grandmother wrote to her son George, " . . . we are thankful indeed for Journeying Mercies. I shall never get quite used to being away from you all, love, and the children, and from all the dear associations of England and of home. . . . But this place is beautiful beyond description. The boys have been so thoughtful and we have a deal to be thankful for. The nice house that the boys got for us all is close to the chapel, or church as it is called here. . . . I can, from my bedroom window, see the mountains! The trees here are remarkable. You should see Stanley Park. . . ."

Topaz had at last reached open country. British Columbia stretched before her, exciting her with its mountains, its forests, the Pacific Ocean, the new little frontier town, and all the new people. Here was no time limit, no fortnight's holiday. Here she had come to live; and, drawing long breaths of the opulent air, she began to run about, and dance for joy, exclaiming, all through the open country.

TWELVE

Open Country

IF YOU ARRIVE in Vancouver on a fine day and go up into a high place, to Little Mountain perhaps or even to the top of some high office building, you will come under the immediate spell of the mountains to the north of you, and of dark coniferous forests. You will see high headlands sloping westwards into the Pacific Ocean, and islands beyond. And then you will turn again and look across the blue inlet at the mountains which in their turn look down upon the grace and strength of the Lions' Gate Bridge, upon the powerful flow of the Narrows, upon English Bay, upon the harbour, and upon the large city of Vancouver.

When Topaz came to Vancouver there were no high places built for people to climb into. Modest one- or two-storeyed buildings rose, to everyone's admiration, where the nobler forest had lately been. The forest still was, and winding trails through the woods ended at small hidden shacks, almost within the town itself. Vancouver was only a little town, but prophetically it called itself a city. It was soon to bear the marks of the Klondike Rush. It was the "end of steel," the beginning of the Pacific, and people thought that possibly the place had a future. Who could tell. There was more sail than steam coming into the harbour, but the elegant *Empresses* with their shapely bows came and vanished again into the dim Orient, and the *Islander* crossed the Gulf to Vancouver Island. In the days of tents and shacks by the water edge, and of Gassy

109

Jack Deighton's saloon, the settlement had been called Gastown. Then with a rush of self-consciousness it became Granville. And then came the perfect inevitable name of meaning and destiny – Vancouver. Broad wooden sidewalks bordered the few main streets, but in front of the houses there were just three-plank-wide wooden sidewalks. If you were a little boy or girl you counted your steps to a plank as you walked. You said, "Step across a crack, Break your mother's back," and then you avoided or stepped on the cracks, according to your disposition.

Down came the forests. Chop. Chop. Chop. The blessed forests came down. The men of the chain-gang were driven up in a waggon and with lumbering movements cleared away the fallen trees while their guard stood near, and interested passers-by watched them and speculated on their past and their future. The forests vanished, and up went the city.

Aunt Topaz's nephew Stephen soon began to build a large house halfway between the town and English Bay. This was very pioneering of him, as there was yet no streetcar near there. He built a stable also, and had a fine hitching-post for his horse, and a mounting-block which remains there to this day for children going home from school to play upon. Blackberries rampaged over the adjoining land which itself adjoined the forest. The West End was wooded. Shaughnessy Heights was virgin forest without a name. Stephen's house was painted red. It was with a doll's-house kind of pleasure that Topaz, fresh from bricky England, saw painters painting little wooden houses red, white, green, and even yellow among the standing cedars, fir trees, and maples. The houses all had wooden trimmings and verandahs, and on the verandah steps when day was done the families came out and sat and talked and counted the box pleats on the backs of fashionable girls' skirts as they went by; and visitors came and sat and talked, and idly watched the people too, and watched the mountains grow dark, and the stars come out above the mountains. And then they all went in and made a cup of cocoa. It was very pleasant and there seemed to be no trouble anywhere upon the face of the earth, that you could discern.

Topaz and her sister and her niece all thought that Vancouver was a beautiful name. It was not long before the contours of the mountains became part of their lives. There was the Sleeping Beauty, lying nobly to the sky. There were the Lions rising sculptured, remote, indifferent. Smoke of fires trailed delicately through the trees. Along the topmost generous curve of the westward hills, pine trees cut sharply against the coloured evening skies, and there were always the sounds of the sirens of ships and the cries of the sea-gulls – sounds of ocean.

This, at last, then, was the Canadian city which they came to know. Topaz had hardly observed the towns and cities of Canada, for each one, as is the custom of cities, had presented only its sprawling and unpleasing posterior to the railway travellers, and its face and person could not be seen by them. Now, in Vancouver, whose face and person they soon came to know so well, they also knew for the first time the growth of a young frontier town into a real city.

"Listen, Annie!" cried Topaz, ten years later, "we have a slogan!"

"What is a slogan, Topaz?" asked Sister Annie, looking up from her fine white cotton knitting.

"A slogan is a war-cry for wild Highland clans (or is it Irishmen?), I believe," answered Topaz, perusing the newspaper in a mutter "m-m-m-m-m," as was her custom, "and someone has just discovered the word."

"But we are not Irishmen," said Sister Annie truthfully, "and I am sure we need no war-cry."

"Yes, ah, yes. Here it is," said Topaz, loudly folding and unfolding the paper. "Listen to this:

> 'In nineteen-ten,
> Vancouver then
> Will have one hundred thousand men.
> Move her! Move her!
> Who? – Vancouver.'

There then, fancy that, one hundred thousand men! I wonder if that includes women and children! *There's* a slogan for you, Annie!"

Sister Annie shook her head. "No, Topaz. I like it very well the way it is. I don't want a slogan." And indeed when the Grandmother arrived in Vancouver, and for some years afterwards, it was a very comfortable little place to live in. But no one could stop the changes that came, not even if they had used a slogan to keep people away.

Very soon Aunt Topaz made a great many friends in the little church which was so conveniently near, and her genius for acquaintanceship and activity sparkled and flew about. Societies disclosed themselves, asking to be joined. She joined the Ladies' Aid, the Women's Auxiliary, and the Women's Council, and as time went on, the Y.W.C.A., the Victorian Order of Nurses, and the Anti-Tuberculosis Society and the Ladies' Minerva Club, which had a distinguished book-plate for its small library, but in spite of that could not survive. She went to the Public Library every other day and carried home books. And read late into the night, and before the Public Library became the Carnegie Library she had read every book in it except two on engineering and one on jurisprudence. She had conveyed the entire Library bit by bit, home and back again in a string bag, bursting into the house, loud with exhaustion. She took sketching lessons, and china-painting lessons (bunches of lilac and other suitable flowers, with gilt trimmings, upon cups and saucers), and joined, tentatively, a glee club.

It was not long before Aunt Topaz and Rachel bought bicycles. Rachel bought a light slim bicycle, red, of Canadian manufacture, easy to ride; and on this bicycle she did her errands, riding about the wooden sidewalks among the pedestrians of Vancouver when she had time to do so, saluting with politeness and a smile other cyclists whom she met riding on the wooden sidewalks too; and, for pleasure, she and her various new friends sometimes pedalled in twos and threes around Stanley Park. Their skirts were a little inclined – despite protective inventions – to fly up in front. Their men friends made up for this by wearing natty cycling costumes, trim and manly about the leg. Aunt Topaz bought a noble English bicycle. It was magnificent and too heavy, as if built for Boadicea. It was proud, sexless in spite of its shape, intractable, and would throw you as soon as look at you. It had a large lamp with heavy bevelled glass sides, which was not necessary as Topaz never took the bicycle out at night. It had a bell like a sweet clarion which she delighted to ring; and that was almost all the good she ever got out of it. She became devoted to her bicycle but it never returned her love. It threw her nearly every time she tried to get on it. As she never succeeded in staying comfortably on, even in the most wobbling fashion, she took to leading her bicycle about because it seemed a pity to waste it. It spent more and more time sulking in a dust-sheet. Fifteen years later, when the bicycle appeared rarely, it had acquired under the dust-sheet, over which the years slid by, the look of a grande dame of an early mechanical era, and it attracted attention and comment, which always pleased her.

Aunt Topaz soon became an ardent shopper but was so employed by Rachel only when absolutely necessary, as Aunty was not economical and was usually late in returning home. Together with the other shopping ladies she would go to Cordova Street, meeting and greeting, and arriving at last at Mr. Fader's fish shop.

"Oh, Mr. Fader, how do you do! What a beautiful salmon! It reminds me exactly of a Scottish salmon I once met in, or I should say on, the Tay. . . ." This Scottish salmon was to Aunty the criterion of all fish, and it did not occur to her, as it does to ordinary people, that one fish wears much the same expression as another. The similarity of her salmon to other salmon always surprised her.

Life was further enlivened by the discovery of the Hudson's Bay Lunch Room. There had been no lunch Room in Ware, only the Leopard pub, to which Aunty could not or did not go, though she would have loved it and would have met her match there. To the Hudson's Bay Lunch Room she repaired eagerly, any morning that she had nothing better to do, sometimes accompanied by her bicycle, sometimes alone; and she ate elevenses, a kind of superfluous mid-morning snack, in the cosy publicity of the Lunch Room. She made many friends of many kinds there and would return and tell Sister Annie and Rachel all about them.

"Rachel, I met *such* an interesting American woman! I said to her, 'I see you are an American, you cut up your meat and then lay your knife down and eat it with your fork.' She *was* surprised."

"Well, I should think she was very much annoyed with you! That is no business of yours, you know, Anty, going round telling people about their knives and forks."

"Oh, she was intensely interested, and told me all about her sister. I joined her and I asked her to come to Annie's next At Home day. I said, 'My sister Mrs. Hastings would be delighted to see you. She is At Home on the first and third Tuesdays, and she is very fond of Americans.'"

"*Anty!*" Rachel would exclaim, helpless and aggravated.

For by this time the Grandmother and her family were established with At Home days, like all the other people who knew what was what. Aunty derived a great deal of pleasure from dressing herself with unusual care (she was indifferent about clothes, yet "dressy"), and paying and returning calls, but most of all she loved the first and third Tuesdays. There was a fearful pleasure in considering whether no one would call, and they would have to sit alone with the best tea-things all afternoon, or whether the room would be proudly over-flowing. It was found best to have something or somebody in the kitty, and most ladies took the precaution of asking a trusted friend or two to come in as a nucleus and to save face if necessary on their At Home days. True, Aunty loved what was beginning to be called Society, but she found people who were not designated as In Society equally delightful.

One day, when about five years had passed, Rachel and Topaz looked up to see the Grandmother walk into the sitting-room with tears running down her face. She held a letter in her hand.

"Mother, what is it?" asked Rachel.

"Robert has died," said her mother speaking through tears. Her face was convulsed with grief.

"Rose must come to us at once," said Rachel decisively.

"Robert *dead*!" exclaimed Topaz in distress.

Here was a young death, not one of those old deaths with which Topaz was now familiar. When the tall dark handsome Robert had walked straight into the family affections and had married Laura, who was the Grandmother's eldest daughter and a second mother to all the Grandmother's sons, he had become one of the family. It had been forgiven him for his charm and sincerity that he had taken Laura to a benighted Africa where in her second childbirth she had died. And now Robert, who had returned to England with his baby daughter Rose, had died, too, and the small eight-year-old Rose was left alone. Wholehearted plans were at once made by the family of six adult people to bring the child to Canada, and Rose, after spending some months with compassionate relatives in England, arrived, a small surprised child, dressed in black. "Take off that black," said the uncles, "and let the child wear colours!"

"We can't waste her *best* black," said Rachel, "but she shall have colours for every day." And now Rachel added to her duties the great care of a child.

It was about the time that Rose arrived in Vancouver that Aunt Topaz, in whom the success of belonging to so many societies had mounted to the head, ran herself into trouble. Since it was obvious that she was a great deal better educated – in her own peculiar way – than most women, and since she had great affability and was particularly get-on-able-with, and since she had unlimited leisure, executive committees in several societies decided separately but simultaneously that Miss Topaz Edgeworth must not be wasted out of office. Aunty therefore accepted, with almost delirious enthusiasm, nominations to office in three or four societies at the same time. The experience was novel and exhilarating, until she gradually became entangled in the horrible web of the responsibility which goes with office. Then began the period of the Great Moan. As decisions had to be made, succinct letters had to be written, reports had to be made out and read, and exact information ascertained, Aunty's pleasant life dimmed and became uniquely horrible. A blackness crept upon the bright and lighted chamber of her mind. She awoke in the morning, and while her nephews were still in the house, she moaned softly. The Hudson's Bay Lunch Room saw her no longer, and the bicycle stayed in the shed and its bright bell remained unrung. Aunty went to her bedroom after lunch, closed the door, lay upon her bed, and then went to work moaning in good earnest. She moaned and moaned and moaned whenever her nephews were out of the house, and the sound of her moaning was heard everywhere by all except the Grandmother, who was becoming very deaf.

One day Rachel found Rose standing outside Aunt Topaz's closed bedroom door, listening to the uninhibited bellowing that went on inside.

"Aunty Rachel, why does Aunt Topaz moo?" asked the child.

"Aunt Topaz isn't moo-ing, Rose," said Rachel genially, "she is moaning because she is the head of a committee to select the new carpets for the new church." And Rachel went about her work. She found Aunty's low spirits rather a relief. It seemed to equate things somewhat. To Rachel, always reserved, always controlled, except for surface irritation, Aunty's indifference to her listeners was funny and very astonishing.

Rose, entranced, remained listening. Words were mingled with the moans.

"Oh. Oh. Oh," roared Aunty like a suffering bull. "Those carpets. Oh. Oh. Oh." And she buried her face in the pillow and continued to roar, which gave her moans a fog-horn note.

Rose did not analyse her feelings about her Great-Aunt's moaning, but nevertheless her feelings were mixed. She was a child who was already schooled to change. She had discovered that grown-up people were not all the same. In Father there had been all that was more gay than grave, more kind than severe, and in him a dearness and a oneness that was simply "Father." She could say her silliest word to him and it was not too silly. But since the world which was Father had gone, she had lived in a world of many different grown-up people who all regarded her with the compassionate kindness and love which they felt for Laura and Robert's little girl and which an orphaned child inspires. But she had already begun to lose the habit of blurting everything out, and had begun to consider. And as she stood outside Aunt Topaz's door with her hands behind her back and her head rather on one side, she considered.

"O-o-o-oh," moaned Aunty.

"Imagine a grown-up making a noise like that," considered Rose. "I don't think it hurts her. I think she likes it. I don't feel sorry like if it was a cat. I couldn't bear it if it was a cat. Aunt Rachel wouldn't do that, nor Grannie, nor Uncle Frank, nor Uncle Stephen, nor Uncle Andrew, and Father never would and they wouldn't let me if I wanted to." At that moment Aunt Topaz, moving as usual with precipitation, blew her nose loudly, let out one more moan, got up, and burst out of her room to go to the bathroom and Rose only just had time to skip.

As soon as the church carpets were bought, and each Annual Meeting came round in turn, Aunty resigned from her offices. She took her delightful unresponsible place again as an ordinary member of society and societies, and resumed running about the open country in a way which she now more than ever appreciated. The Hudson's Bay Lunch Room welcomed her again, and the superb and indifferent bicycle was wheeled abroad. Rarely, in the years that followed, did she allow herself to become entangled in responsibility.

One only office she cherished. During the visit of the Duke and Duchess of York to Vancouver, Aunty had assisted in the pleasant task of presenting the Duchess with a Book of Views. She had talked as volubly to the Duchess as her allotted space of time would allow, and had recalled to the Royal memory the name of her friend Miss Peacock (or was it Miss Pocock?) who helped the Duchess in her own private charities. And so it was that Aunty was asked to establish a branch of a Needlework Guild in Vancouver with Royal encouragement. It was, to begin with, a one-woman affair, and Aunty joyously collected knitted garments from her knitting acquaintances, and forwarded them to the Duchess. And as years went on,

Aunty was joyously sending knitted garments to the Queen of England, for which she received charming and grateful letters through the Queen's Lady-in-Waiting. Aunty gave these letters with all speed to the newspapers, and then rejoiced to read in the news:

Miss T. E. P. Edgeworth of Vancouver has received the following letter from the Lady-in-Waiting to Her Majesty the Queen:

Buckingham Palace

Dear Miss Edgeworth,
    The Queen commands me to thank you for . . .

And friends and strangers would accost Aunty and say, "Oh, Miss Edgeworth, I see you've had another letter from the Queen!" and Aunty would be gratified.

And friends and strangers would accost Aunt Rachel and say, "Oh, Miss Hastings, I see that your Aunt has had another letter from the Queen!"

And Rachel would go home and say crossly, "Anty, I do wish you'd stop putting the Queen's letters in the paper. They are really personal letters, and I don't think the Queen would like it at all. It's very self-important of you."

And Aunty would retort, "Everyone but you likes to see them! The trouble with you is, you have no loyalty! No loyalty whatever!" "Me! 'No *loyalty*!'" Rachel would splutter, and an argument would begin.

And late, very late in Aunty's life, when Rachel and Annie were dead and gone, and Aunty was more alive than ever, and had entered into her apotheosis, she was commanded to go to see the Queen. And the Queen, dressed in blue, with glorious sapphires, received her kindly in Buckingham Palace, and Aunty lived happy ever after. She could not have dreamed that her future might hold such bliss.

THIRTEEN

"I have a Father in the Promised Land"

YES, LOVE, I understand," said the Grandmother at the head of the table, soothing one of her sons who made strong objections to going to the revival meeting, "indeed I do understand that you prefer another way of worshipping God. But since Mr. Pratt is our new minister and he has called his congregation together for this service, it ill behooves us to stay away. Nay, and if the Lord should speak to us and bless us, we shall be well repaid. Come, let us all go." Grandmother spoke in her little careful ornate way that was her natural form of expression, and looked with such sweet sincerity upon her household, that, of course, they all went to the revival meeting, willy-nilly.

They walked into the pew, pushing a little, but decorously. There were the Grandmother, the Great-Aunt Topaz, Aunt Rachel, Uncle Frank, Uncle Stephen, and Uncle Andrew. There was also the lovely Miranda, fiancée to Uncle Frank. There was Rose, aged eight, small, curly-haired, still wearing the good black in which she had been warmly and suitably dressed following her adored father's death the year before. They all sat down, then they dropped upon their knees. The uncles remained there for a brief and manly instant. The Grandmother became charged with emotion immediately on closing her eyes. The Aunts communed silently and respectfully for a moment, and Rose stayed down as long as they. On rising they settled themselves on the long pew which curved at the side of the church. The lovely Miranda, knowing herself the object of interest to her young friends as she sat among her dignified relatives-to-be, gazed pleasantly round, acknowledging charmingly and almost imperceptibly the bright glances that shot to her across the church. Radiant she sat there among her dignified relatives-to-be. The Grandmother gazed at nothing, rapt and suffused by her own inner vision, unaware of the congregation. Rose looked this way and that with youthful interest. She noted the bonneted old ladies as they stole to their pews, their plain and bearded husbands, the pretty Miss Moores, the fathers, the mothers, the families that streamed in. Most of them dropped to their knees. Fleetingly she wondered what they all really did there. But some, oh horrors, sat smack down and looked round frankly and with interest upon their neighbours. No stained glass shed its warm and romantic radiance upon the congregation. The amenities of coloured windows, pulpits, surplices and the like were not there. No, they were suspect a little of the delightful worldliness of the Church of England.

A door opened. On to the platform, garnished with chairs and a reading-desk, strode the Pastor. When this man of God was sent from Ontario to minister to the West, doubtless the Fathers in Israel shaded their eyes and gazed towards Vancouver. They looked west across the Great Lakes. They looked across the prairies, all wheat, cattle, cowboys, and Indians. They looked again across the foothills, the forests, the Rocky Mountains, the mining camps, the saloons, the gambling hells, to the wild shores of the Pacific Ocean where a young and turbulent city was growing. They looked towards the Klondike Rush. They looked, and then they said to each other, "Let us send the Rev. Elmer Pratt, he's just the man for the West." So now here was the Rev. Elmer Pratt, full of zeal, swarthy, black-visaged, and violent of feature. Beneath his black hair shone his bright black eyes. Beneath his bright black eyes jutted his large nose. Beneath his large nose sprang and flourished his magnificent black moustaches. Beneath his vigorous chin rose up his high and stiff white collar, with a splendid white four-in-hand tie. The face, coarse and vigorous, was perpetually at war with the sanctity of the starched white collar and tie beneath. He used strange words. Rose, accustomed to the suave tones of her native England, was constantly amazed at the flat and grating voice of the Rev. Elmer Pratt. Whereas the ministers of the Gospel to whom she had listened Sunday by Sunday since infancy spoke gently of the love of God, the Rev. Elmer Pratt thundered about brothels. She supposed that brothels were places where broth was made and decided that the broth must be very bad or the Rev. Elmer Pratt would not be so angry. He also spoke frequently about "foaming out your shame upon your city streets" (see Hosea), in a way that made her feel personally responsible, and she could only conclude that he had reference to the nasty habit of spitting that she had noticed and disliked among men in the streets of this little western town. There seemed to be no other explanation. Many strange things were uttered by the Rev. Elmer Pratt, and little of it did Rose understand. But once his sermons of wrath and denunciation were over, he became a human and kindly being.

This evening as he mounted the platform he was almost in tender vein. He prayed long and enjoyably. Chiefly he desired God's blessing upon the week of revival services on which the congregation was entering. Much stress was laid upon the Last Chance. For example, it might be that Tuesday night next had been selected for some dear brother (or sister) to be saved, and if they stayed away on Tuesday night the chance might pass by for ever. This became very important. Rose had never before been to a revival service, in fact there had been some discussion at home as to whether she was too young to come. But, the Grandmother having been saved at the age of five, here she was.

By the time they were again vertical in their seats, the church was filled with a lively emotion. The congregation Rose and sang, their thoughts uplifted, "There is a fountain filled with Blood," a terrifying hymn to Rose, because she had seen fountains. Then they sat down, their gaze upon Mr. Pratt. Even the lovely Miranda, her thoughts forcibly removed from her trousseau, gazed upon Mr. Pratt. He became as one a little transfigured by darkness. His grating and powerful voice was subdued, vibrant, and touching. His black glances played over the congregation, loving them, frightening them, yearning over them. He held up to them their lives of sin and shame. He showed them the dreadful, the almost inescapable doom. Strident his voice rose to the horrors of the hereafter. Softened and vibrating with tenderness he described to them as if he had been there the Kingdom of the Blessed where they fain would be. Did they not, urged the Rev. Elmer Pratt, as a strong inducement, wish to see their Dear Ones who were undoubtedly waiting for them in the Heavenly Home? "Is there no one waiting for you?" thrilled Mr. Pratt. "My brothers, my sisters, have you no one waiting in Heaven for you? Come now," said he encouragingly, "who has a Father in the Promised Land? Who has a dear dear Father waiting in the Promised Land? Come now, stand! Stand up now, any person who has a dear dear Father waiting in the Promised Land; do not be afraid; stand up, ah, bless you, my brother; bless you, my sister!" Thus exhorted people began to stand up, one here, one there, looking downwards. Rose's heart was ready to burst. Her Father, her dear dear Father, whom she loved better than anyone on earth, Father with the dear voice and the kind laughing eyes, was waiting, waiting. She slipped to the floor and stood up. "Bless you, my child," said the Rev. Elmer Pratt kindly.

Rose burst into tears.

"Let us sing," said the Rev. Elmer Pratt, "let us sing together." And he sang in his grating voice:

> "I have a Father in the Promised Land,
> I have a Father in the Promised Land,
> My Father calls me, I must go
> To meet him in the Promised Land."

"Come now," said Mr. Pratt, "all those standing, sing – 'I have . . .'" and everybody sang.

Rose sang sobbingly, sniffingly, to the mute distress of Great-Aunt Topaz, Aunt Rachel, Uncle Frank, Uncle Stephen, Uncle Andrew, and the lovely Miranda. The Grandmother, touched and pleased, wept gently beside her.

The song finished. Relieved, the bereaved ones sat down. Rose wiped her eyes.

"Now then," said the Rev. Elmer Pratt, rubbing his hands in a pleased way, "who has a Mother, a dear dear Mother, waiting for them, waiting to welcome? Stand up, those who have a dear Mother in the Promised Land."

This startled Rose. She had thought the affair was over, and had settled down comfortably in the pew to her grief. But others, the more knowing among the congregation, had suspected this. Sadly Rose stood up again. Her mother had died when she was eighteen months old, at the birth of a little son. In fact, as far as Rose was concerned, she had never had a mother and felt no grief at her loss. However, there she stood, still weeping for her father. One by one the people stood. More handkerchiefs came out. The Rev. Elmer Pratt witn innocent ghoulish pleasure welcomed and encouraged them as they stood. "Bless you, my brother; bless you, my sister. Bless you, bless you, my child." Thus blessed, they stood, looking downwards. "Let us sing," said Mr. Pratt, "let us sing, my dear folks, those who have lost a Mother.

> "I have a Mother in the Promised Land,
> I have a Mother in the Promised Land,
> My Mother calls me, I must go
> To meet her in the Promised Land."

They sang. "Sit down, sit down," said the Rev. Elmer Pratt. The bereaved ones sat. Well, that was over.

"Has anyone," said the Rev. Elmer Pratt enquiringly, "lost a dear brother?" Now this came as a surprise to everybody, and hastily the congregation tried to remember if they had lost a brother. A bit of mental fumbling here. Rose recollected that Father had once told her that her baby brother, christened Edward, had died when he was three days old, and lay buried beside her mother in South Africa. Once only her father had spoken of his grief. "Did I ever see little Edward, Father?" she had asked. "No, dear," had said her father. And now, here was little Edward! Did she have to stand up for Edward? He must have been so very small, hardly worth standing for. Time

was pressing. Poor little Edward, no one to stand up for him!
But, strictly speaking, would little Edward be able to welcome
her in the Promised Land, being so very small? This was
puzzling, but there was no time for advice. Little Edward won.
Rose stood up again. The family looked up in surprise. They
had forgotten about little Edward. "Sing, friends," com-
mended the Rev. Elmer Pratt, "sing together,

> "I have a Brother in the Promised Land,
> I have a Brother in the Promised Land,
> My Brother calls me, I must go
> To meet him in the Promised Land."

They sang. The tune, now familiar, rang out cheerfully.
The bereaved ones sang sturdily and without sobs. Apparently, inured as they now were to loss, they could more easily
support the presence of a brother in the Promised Land.

"Sit down, folks," said Mr. Pratt with real satisfaction.
They sat down. "Well," thought Rose, "I'm down now safely,
for I never had a sister." But poor Miranda! Her turn was
coming. Rose looked along the pew at the lovely Miranda.
Miranda was turning her engagement ring this way and that.
She tilted her charming head with its pretty pointed chin. She
looked at her ring. Rubies and diamonds, rubies and diamonds. Look up, look up, Miranda, it's your turn next!
Miranda looked at the ring and smiled sweetly, dreamily.
Only yesterday, as Rose had sat admiring her while she
brushed her beautiful hair, they had talked about Miranda's
family. "And was that all of you, Aunt Miranda?" Rose had
said. "Yes, dear," said the lovely Miranda, her mouth full of
hairpins, "except a tiny tiny baby sister, but she died, stillborn," murmured the truthful young Miranda through the
hairpins. Rose had enquired further, "Did you say 'stillborn'?
What does 'stillborn' mean?" Miranda had not answered. Her
mouth was full of hairpins. All this Rose now remembered.
She looked along the pew. The tiny tiny sister, stillborn, how
sweet! She yearned over Miranda, so soon to be haled to her
feet by the inexorable Pratt. Even now he was speaking
tenderly, tenderly. "Any person here lost a sister?" he said, "a

dear dear sister, stand, stand up!" Heavily, without alacrity, people stood. Rose looked at Miranda. Miranda looked fondly upon her ring. Rubies and diamonds, rubies and diamonds. Oh, the little stillborn sister – forgotten – Miranda, how could you? You couldn't have heard Mr. Pratt! But indeed now the people were singing glibly, pleasantly,

> "I have a Sister in the Promised Land,
> I have a Sister in the Promised Land,
> My Sister calls me, I must go
> To meet her in the Promised Land."

Rose looked along the pew. Her whole mind besought Miranda. The little stillborn sister! But the lovely Miranda tilted her charming head with the pretty pointed chin the other way and gazed upon her ring.

Rubies and diamonds, rubies and diamonds.

After the service was over they all walked home.

Aunt Topaz, standing in front of her mirror and drawing the hatpins out of her boat-shaped hat, was frozen in her attitude by a thought. It had not occurred to her during the revival meeting that perhaps she, Topaz Edgeworth, was also a bona fide orphan, and should have done something about Mr. Pratt's appeal.

"I do declare!" she exclaimed aloud. "Father's in the Promised Land, and so's Mother and Mother Jane, and so's Mary and Joe and what a many uncles and aunts – they've been there for years, some of them – and I never thought to stand up! *Wouldn't* Father be annoyed, oh dear! Well, what a bobbing up and down that would have been, to be sure!" She laughed merrily, but she felt that she had missed an opportunity.

FOURTEEN

Down at English Bay

ONCE UPON a time there was a negro who lived in Vancouver and his name was Joe Fortes. He lived in a small house by the beach at English Bay and there is now a little bronze plaque to his honour and memory near-by, and he taught hundreds of little boys and girls how to swim. First of all he taught them for the love of it and after that he was paid a small salary by the City Council or the Parks Board, but he taught for love just the same. And so it is that now there are Judges, and Aldermen, and Cabinet Ministers, and lawyers, and doctors, and magnates, and ordinary business men, and grandmothers, and prostitutes, and burglars, and Sunday School superintendents, and dry-cleaners, and so on whom Joe Fortes taught to swim, and they will be the first to admit it. And Joe Fortes saved several people from drowning; some of them were worth saving and some were not worth saving in the slightest – take the man who was hanged in Kingston jail; but Joe Fortes could not be expected to know this, so he saved everyone regardless. He was greatly beloved and he was respected.

Joe Fortes was always surrounded by little boys and girls in queer bathing suits in the summer-time. The little boys' bathing suits had arms and legs not to speak of bodies and almost skirts on them; and the little girls were covered from neck to calf in blue serge or alpaca with white braid – rows of it – round the sailor collar and the full skirt, and a good pair of black wool stockings. This all helped to weigh them down when they tried to learn to swim, and to drown the little girls, in particular, when possible.

Joe had a nice round brown face and a beautiful brown body and arms and legs as he waded majestically in the waves of English Bay amongst all the little white lawyers and doctors and trained nurses and seamstresses who jumped up and down and splashed round him. "Joe," they called, and "Look at me, Joe! Is this the way?" and they splashed and swallowed and Joe supported them under their chins and by their behinds and said in his rich slow fruity voice, "Kick out, naow! Thassaway. Kick right out!" And sometimes he supported them, swimming like frogs, to the raft, and when they had clambered onto the raft they were afraid to jump off and Joe Fortes became impatient and terrible and said in a very large voice, "Jump now! I'll catch you! You jump off of that raff or I'll leave you here all night!" And that was how they learned to swim.

Rose was one of the children who learned to swim with Joe Fortes, and she was one of the cowardly ones who shivered on the raft while Joe roared, "You jump off of that raff this minute, or I'll leave you there all night!" So she jumped because the prospect was so terrible and so real, and how threatening the wet sea by night, and who knows what creatures will come to this dark raft alone. So she jumped.

Aunt Rachel did not let Rose go swimming in her good blue serge bathing costume with white braid and black wool stockings unless some grown-up was there. Aunts and guardians feel much more responsible for children than parents do, and so they are over-anxious and they age faster. Aunt Topaz was not very much good as a guardian because she did not bathe, could not swim, was irresponsible, and usually met friends on the beach with whom she entered into conversation and then forgot about Rose.

One day, however, Rose persuaded her Aunt Rachel to let her go to the beach with Aunt Topaz who was quite ready for an outing, and in any case wanted to take her bicycle for a walk. So Rose and her Great-Aunt started off down Barclay Street in very good spirits on a sunny July afternoon. Tra-la-la, how happy they were! They talked separately and together. Aunt Topaz wheeled her bicycle, which gave her a very sporting appearance, and she wore her hat which looked like a row-boat. She carried some biscuits in the string bag which was attached to the shining handle-bars of her noble English bicycle. Rose carried a huge parcel in a towel and swung it by a strap. She further complicated her walk by taking her hoop and stick. So Great-Aunt and Great-Niece proceeded down Barclay Street towards English Bay, Rose bowling her hoop whenever she felt like it.

When they arrived at English Bay Rose rushed into the bath-house with five cents, and Aunt Topaz got into conversation with a young man called Eustace Flowerdew, with whose mother she was acquainted. Eustace Flowerdew wore a stiff straw hat attached to him somewhere by a black cord, so that if in his progress along the sands the hat should blow off, it would still remain attached to the person of Eustace. He wore pince-nez which made him look very refined. His collar was so high and stiff that it hurt him, and his tie was a chaste and severe four-in-hand. He collected tie-pins which were called stick-pins. Today he wore a stick-pin with the head of a horse.

"Oh, good afternoon, Eustace," said Aunt Topaz, "how nice you do look to be sure. How is your mother what a nice horse!"

After taking off his hat and putting it on again, Eustace hitched up each of his trouser legs and sat down beside Aunt Topaz, and looked over the top of his collar. In so doing he jiggled the bicycle which was unusually heavy and was inexpertly propped against the log on which he and Aunt Topaz were sitting. The bicycle intentionally fell on them both and knocked them down. This bicycle was very ill-tempered and ingenious, and was given to doing this kind of thing when possible on purpose. Aunt Topaz lay prone, and Eustace Flowerdew crawled out and lifted the bicycle off her and led it away to a tree where it could not touch them any more. Aunt

Topaz exclaimed a great deal, got up, dusted the sand off herself, and Rose was as forgotten as though she had never existed.

"What are you doing on the beach at this time of the afternoon, Eustace?" asked Aunt Topaz.

Eustace did not want to tell Aunt Topaz the truth, which was that he hoped to meet a girl called Mary Evans in whom he had become interested, so he told her a lie.

"I have come here to forget, Miss Edgeworth," he said, looking at the ocean over his collar.

"And what do you want to forget? . . . Oh, I suppose I shouldn't ask you if you want to forget it! How very interesting!"

The young man took his hat off and passed his hand over his forehead wearily. "He is good-looking, but he looks rather silly," thought Topaz.

"The fact is that I am writing a play," he said at last.

Topaz was frightfully excited. She had never before sat on a log with someone who was writing a play. Memories of Sir Henry Irving, Ellen Terry and the Lyceum Theatre in general romped through her mind and she did not know where to begin. She bubbled a little but the young man did not seem to hear. He was still looking out to sea. How beautiful it was, beyond the cries and splashings of children who crowded round Joe Fortes. There is a serenity and a symmetry about English Bay. It is framed by two harmonious landfalls. Out stretches Point Grey sloping to the south-west. Undulations of mountain, mainland, and island come to a poetic termination on the north-west. Straight ahead to the westward sparkles the ocean as far as the dim white peaks of Vancouver Island. Sea-gulls flash and fly and cry in the wide summer air. Sitters on the beach regarded this beauty idly.

"What are you calling your play, Eustace?" asked Aunty when she had recovered.

"*Break, Break, Break*," said the young man. "Who is this uncommonly plain little girl standing in front of us? How very wet she is!"

"That?" said Aunt Topaz, suddenly seeing Rose. "Oh, there you are. How do you do, Rose? That is my great-niece. Yes, she is plain, isn't she? When wet. When dry she looks better, because her hair curls. Now run away and enjoy yourself and make sure you don't drown. Well what is it?"

"May I get a biscuit?" asked Rose, who had come up full of rapture and talk now quenched.

"Yes, yes. Get a biscuit but be careful of the bicycle. It's against the tree."

Rose looked hatingly at Eustace Flowerdew and went over to the bicycle, dripping as she went. No sooner did she touch the heavy bicycle than it rushed violently away from her down the beach and hurled itself into the sand where it lay with its pedals quivering. Rose looked, but the two had not seen this. So she went and pulled up the bicycle and led it over to the tree again. She propped it up against the tree as best she could, dusted some of the sand off the biscuits, ate them grit and all, and ran off again to the heavenly waves and children surrounding Joe Fortes.

"What does your mother say about your writing a play? I should think she would feel very nervous. Are you introducing the sex element at all . . . illicit love, so to speak . . . or are you, if I may say so, keeping it thoroughly wholesome?" asked Topaz.

"My dear Miss Edgeworth," answered the young man pityingly, "I trust that you do not still regard Art as being in any way connected with morality!" He saw in the distance a figure that looked like Mary Evans, and his muscles were already flexing to rise. A shadow fell across Aunty and Eustace.

"Well, I do declare!" exclaimed Aunty joyously. "If this isn't Mrs. Hamilton Coffin! Mrs. Coffin, let me present to you a rising young . . ." but the rising young playwright was no longer there. He was striding away down the beach.

"Do sit down, Mrs. Coffin!" said Topaz. "This *is* nice! How very athletic you do look!" She was filled with admiration. Mrs. Coffin was tall and the black serge bathing suit which she wore did not become her. On this fine summer day

Mrs. Coffin, warmly dressed for swimming, displayed no part of her body except her face and ears and her arms as far up as her elbows. "How delightful!" exclaimed Topaz sincerely.

"I have lately, Miss Edgeworth," said Mrs. Coffin, who was a serious woman, "come under the influence of Ralston's Health Foods, and so has my husband. We are making a careful study of physical health and exercise and right thinking. We eat Ralston's Health Foods and a new food called Grape Nuts" (" 'Grape Nuts!' that sounds delicious!" said Topaz) "twice a day. Already complexion is brighter, our whole mental attitude is improved, and I *may* say," she lowered her voice, "that faulty elimination is corrected."

"Faulty elimination! Well, well! Fancy that!" echoed Aunt Topaz, and wondered "What on earth is she talking about?"

"I have also made an appointment with Mr. Fortes for a swimming lesson and I hope very soon to have mastered the art. This is my third lesson."

"Never too old to learn! Never too old to learn!" said Topaz merrily but without tact. She had no intention of taking swimming lessons herself. "I will come down to the water's edge and cheer you on." "I wonder if it's her costume or her name that makes me think of the tomb," she thought cheerfully.

Mrs. Coffin and Aunt Topaz went down to the water's edge. Joe Fortes disentangled himself from the swimming, bobbing, prancing, screaming children, and came out of the ocean to speak to Mrs. Coffin. He looked very fine, beautiful brown seal that he was, with the clear sparkling water streaming off him.

Mrs. Coffin advanced into the sea, and unhesitatingly dipped herself. "How brave! How brave! Bravo!" cried Topaz form the brink, clapping. Joe Fortes discussed the motions of swimming with Mrs. Coffin, doing *so* with his arms, and then *so* with his big legs like flexible pillars, and Mrs. Coffin took the first position. Joe Fortes respectfully supported her chin with the tips of his strong brown fingers. He dexterously and modestly raised her rear, and held it raised by a bit of bathing suit. "How politely he does it!" thought Topaz, admiring Joe

Fortes and Mrs. Coffin as they proceeded up and down the ocean. When Mrs. Coffin had proceeded up and down supported and exhorted by Joe Fortes for twenty minutes or so, with Topaz addressing them from the brink, she tried swimming alone. She went under several times dragged down by her bathing suit but emerged full of hope. She dressed, and came and sat with Aunt Topaz.

"I understand, Miss Edgeworth," said Mrs. Coffin, "that you are the President of the Minerva Club!"

"I! President! Oh dear no!" said Topaz laughing merrily. "Never again will I be President of anything as long as I live! I was for a year President of our Ladies' Aid, and the worry nearly killed me! I'd as soon be hanged as be President of anything – much sooner, I assure you! No, Mrs. Coffin, I am the Secretary of the Minerva Club – Honorary you understand – and Mrs. Aked, the President, promises that I can toss it up! toss it up! at any moment that I wish!"

Mrs. Coffin seemed to be about to say something further when a miserable-looking object appeared in front of them. It was Rose, blue and dripping.

"J-J-oe F-F-Fortes s-s-says that I'm b-b-b-blue and I must g-g-go home," stuttered Rose shivering. "I d-d-d-don't want to. D-D-Do I have to?"

"Oh dear me, what a sight!" said Aunt Topaz who had forgotten Rose again. "Certainly, certainly! Rush into your clothes and we'll walk home briskly and have some tea! What a delightful afternoon!"

On the way home the two pushed their impedimenta. Rose took the superfluous hoop, and Aunt Topaz wheeled her bicycle. The bicycle kicked her with its large protruding pedals as often as possible, and became entangled in her long skirt from time to time, so she often had to stop. When she was disentangled they went on. The bicycle bided its time, and then it kicked her again. Their minds were full of their own affairs, of which they talked regardless.

"A very silly young man, I'm afraid, but he may grow out of it. It is possible, however, that he has talent. . . ."

"I swam six strokes alone. I swam six strokes alone . . ."

"I'm sure Mrs. Hamilton Coffin deserves a great deal of credit at her age. . . ."

"Joe Fortes says that if I can just master the . . ."

"But what she meant by 'faulty elimination' I cannot imagine. It may have something to do with the Mosaic Law. . . ."

"Joe Fortes can swim across English Bay easy-weasy. A big boy said that Joe Fortes could swim across the English Channel easy-weasy . . ."

"I do wish you'd stop saying 'easy-weasy' . . . oh . . ." The bicycle, behaving coarsely, swerved, turned, and tried to run Aunt Topaz down.

"And Geraldine has been swimming longer than me and she can't swim as good as me. . . ."

"As well as I. 'Grape Nuts' sound delicious! A combination of grapes and nuts no doubt. . . ."

This kind of conversation went on all the way home, and after they reached home too, until Rose went to bed. It was plain to Rachel and her mother that Aunty and Rose had enjoyed going down to English Bay, and Rachel was greatly relieved that Rose had not been drowned.

On the next afternoon Aunt Topaz prepared to go to the meeting of the Minerva Club. She dressed very prettily, and wore a feather boa. Her success in dress was a matter of luck rather than taste, but today she looked uncommonly well. "How nice you look, Anty!" said Rachel admiringly. Aunty was very happy. She pranced up Barclay Street, carrying her Minutes of he previous meeting – which were brief – in her hand.

There were nine ladies gathered at Mrs. Aked's house for the meeting of the Minerva Club. Tap, tap went Mrs. Aked on a little table. "We will now call the meeting to order, and our Honorary Secretary will read the Minutes of the previous meeting – Miss Edgeworth."

Everybody admired the experience and aplomb of Mrs. Aked.

Topaz arose and smiled at the ladies. Nine of them. When it came to reading aloud, even Minutes, she enjoyed herself thoroughly. But if she had to utter a single impromptu word in public, on her feet, she suffered more than tongue could tell. Therefore she was careful never to place herself in a position where she might have to make a speech. Considering that she had spent her whole life in speaking, this was strange. But human beings are very strange, and there you are.

Topaz reported, smiling over her Minutes, that at the previous meeting the Minerva Club had listened to a paper on Robert Browning and that selections from that great man's less obscure poems had been read aloud. It had been decided that today's meeting should include a brief comprehensive paper on "Poets of the Elizabethan Era" by Mrs. Howard Henchcliffe who certainly had her work cut out, and that selections from the verses of Elizabethan poets would be read by Mrs. Isaacs, Mrs. Simpson, and – modestly – Miss Edgeworth. Then Aunt Topaz sat down. How she enjoyed this!

"Any business, ladies?" enquired Mrs. Aked. "Ah, yes, one vacancy in the Club. The name of Mrs. Hamilton Coffin is up for election. Any discussion before we vote Mrs. Hamilton Coffin into the Club? I think not."

But a rather pudding-faced lady raised a tentative hand. She cleared her throat. "Pardon *me*," she said. "I hope we are all friends here, and that discussion may be without prejudice?"

Mrs. Aked nodded, and the ladies murmured and rustled and adjusted their boas.

"Before voting on the name of Mrs. Hamilton Coffin," said the pudding-faced lady, "may I remind ladies present that the reputation of our members has always been beyond reproach?"

"I'm sure Mrs. Hamilton Coffin . . ." began a small lady with sparkling eyes, in outraged tones. "Whatever can this be?" wondered Topaz.

The pudding-faced lady again held up her hand.

"Pardon *me*," she said, "I have nothing at all to say against the personal reputation of Mrs. Hamilton Coffin. But *do* the Ladies of the Minerva Club know that Mrs. Hamilton Coffin has been seen more than once in a public place, bathing in the arms of a black man?"

A rustle of indignation ran through the room, whether at the pudding-faced lady or at Mrs. Hamilton Coffin it was impossible to say.

Suddenly in that inward part of her that Topaz had not known to exist, arose a fury. She who did not know of the existence of private life because she had no private life of her own, she who feared so greatly to speak in public, she who was never roused to anger, rose to her feet, trembling and angry. She was angry for Joe Fortes; and for Mrs. Hamilton Coffin; and for herself, a spectator on that innocent blue day. She was aware of something evil and stupid in the room.

"Ladies," she said, shaking, "I shall now count ten because I think I shall then be better able to say what I want to say and because I am very frightened. Excuse me just a minute." And Topaz was silent, and they could see her counting ten. All the ladies waited; emotions were held in check. Then the plain and interesting face of Topaz lighted with its usual friendly smile.

"Ladies," she said, "I was present yesterday when that admirable woman Mrs. Hamilton Coffin had her swimming lesson from our respected fellow-citizen Joe Fortes. I know that the lady who has just spoken," and Aunty smiled winningly upon the pudding-faced lady, "will be quite properly relieved to hear that so far from swimming in the arms of Mr. Fortes, which any of us who were drowning would be grateful to do, Mrs. Hamilton Coffin was swimming in his finger-tips. I feel that we should be honoured to have as a fellow-member so active, progressive, and irreproachable a lady as Mrs. Hamilton Coffin. I therefore beg to propose the name of Mrs. Hamilton Coffin as the tenth member of the Minerva Club." And she sat down scarlet-cheeked, shaking violently.

"Hear-hear, hear-hear," said all the ladies – including the pudding-faced lady – with one accord and very loud, clapping. "Order, order," cried the President, enjoying herself immensely. "I hereby declare Mrs. Hamilton Coffin a member of the Minerva Club, and I instruct our Honorary Secretary to write a letter of invitation. I will now call upon Miss Topaz Edgeworth to read the introductory selection from one of the poets of the Elizabethan Era."

The ladies slipped back their boas and emitted releasing breaths of warm air (the room had become close), adjusted their positions, and adopted postures suitable to those about to listen to the poets.

Aunt Topaz stood and read. This was her great day. How beautifully she read! Her chattering tones were modulated and musical. The training of the classical Mrs. Porter had made Aunty a reader in the classical style. She was correct, deliberate, flowing, unemotional, natural. She was very happy, reading aloud slowly to the Minerva Club. She read clearly –

> "Even such is Time, that takes in trust
> Our youth, our joys, our all we have,
> And pays us but with earth and dust;
> Who, in the dark and silent grave,
> When we have wandered all our ways,
> Shuts up the story of our days.
> But from this earth, this grave, this dust,
> My God shall raise me up, I trust."

Everybody clapped.

Aunty went home disturbed and happy; and that evening she told her sister and Rachel about the meeting, and her indignation rose and fell and was satisfied. She told it several times.

The Grandmother said, "I am glad you spoke as you did, my dear sister. You were right."

Rachel put down her work. She thought, "How often I am angry with Aunty! How often I scold her! She *is* aggravating, but just see this!" Rachel looked across at Aunt Topaz with eyes at once sombre and bright that were Rachel's only beauty. "Yes, Anty," she said, "that's true. I have never heard you say an unkind thing about anyone. I have never heard you cast an aspersion on anyone. I really believe that you are one of the few people who think no evil."

Aunty *was* amazed! Rachel, who seldom praised, had praised her. She – Topaz – who was never humble and embarrassed became humble and embarrassed. What could she say. "I think," she said, "that I will go to bed. I will take the newspaper." And she stumbled upstairs in her hasty way.

Above, in her bedroom, they heard her singing in that funny little flute voice of hers.

FIFTEEN

Christmas Eve

WHEN FRANK and Stephen were married and living in their own homes near by with their wives ("Yes, charming charming girls, Canadians, born in this country!" which seemed to establish the whole family as finally and indisputably Canadian), the Grandmother, Topaz, Rachel, Andrew, and Rose moved to a smaller and peculiar house. Andrew was now the man of the house; but as he went before long to live in Montreal where he established connections for the firm, Rachel herself became and remained the man of the house. At the time of his marriage, Andrew returned again to Vancouver, and the family branched out again. Thereafter it continued to branch, and the history of families like the Hastings family is to some extent the history of the city of Vancouver, but it will not be written for a long time.

The house in which the Grandmother now lived had a bastard architectural excrescence at its corner which resembled both a Norman turret and a pepper-pot but was neither. Houses with assertive pepper-pots may still be seen in the older sections of Canadian cities, and date from aspirations held in the eighteen-nineties. Although from the outside the pepper-pot was a nasty bit of work, from the inside it provided many windows and much light, and a pleasant more than semicircular window-seat in the Grandmother's bedroom. This window-seat was the perfect place for a household of women to gather in, and read their letters to each other, drink tea, sew, mend, and turn sheets sides-to-middles. And below the Grandmother's bedroom was a similar curve and a similar window, which changed an uninteresting small square drawing-room to a room of considerable charm, in which, on the first and third Tuesdays, the Grandmother's At Home days were prinked out.

This was now a household of women in which the usual filaments of pull and push, understanding and failing to understand, love and forbearance grew, and grew stronger than hawsers, binding the four together and pushing them apart. But their faces often turned outwards too, and the ties which bound them to their old home held steady. The Grandmother wrote industriously in her delicate hand to her sons in England – Lancelot, Samuel, and George – and to their wives, and their children, and to Rose's paternal relatives to whom she felt responsibility. Rose's letter-writing was negligible. Topaz wrote furiously and continuously. She and her surviving correspondents were the kind who upon receipt of a letter sit down in short order and write a voluminous answer, and thus drive dilatory correspondents mad. They belonged to the dwindling generation of letterwriters. So in the curved upper window of the pepper-pot, Aunty triumphantly read aloud letters from Mme Roux in Grenoble, old Signora Castellani in Rome, Mr. Heaton (a widower) in Ware, Miss Pocock, and also Miss Peacock, the never-yet-seen but ageing and indistinguishable twins Tilly-and-Sassy in India (the babies of Mary), Brother Blakey in Australia, Brothers George and John in England and their wives, and several assorted ladies throughout Canada.

When Brother John and Topaz had both lived in Ware, John had tried to sneap Topaz whenever he thought it good for her, which was often. But now that six thousand miles separated them, John's letters flew with a lover's frequency, and Aunty in the pepper-pot happily read to the others of John's encounters with Members of the House of Commons and the House of Lords, with the Lord-Lieutenant of the County, and other Great Ones, his roarings against the present policy of the Government, pious memories of Mr. Gladstone, news of his cold and of his wife's cold, and of their visitors of whom they had a great many.

Rachel disliked writing letters and so she wrote none. At Christmas-time, duty made her send a few non-committal cards. In any case she was far too busy.

Those were days of agreeable simplicity in Vancouver. Since then we have learned to wrap our Christmas parcels in coloured and decorated papers, have tied them with prodigal tinsels, have adorned them with stickers, stars, and bells, and have outwitted ourselves in the enfolding of lingerie, decanters, and face powders. But we remember a time when we wore not lingerie but underclothes, when reputable noses went bare, when we offered not decanters but bedroom slippers, as again we do. Then people wrapped their parcels neatly in brown paper, and tied them with good string.

Rose returned home with a rush, after delivering most of the tidy and identifiable parcels at the homes of Uncle Frank and Uncle Stephen. At each house there was a baby or two, and at each house there were gay greetings and rushings about and the delicious mounting excitement of Christmas Eve. But the treat of the day lay ahead. Every Christmas Eve Aunt Rachel and Rose had their own special and peculiar celebration. After the hall and downstairs rooms had been decorated with greenery, and the last carefully observed preparations for the large family Christmas Day gathering had been made; after the Grandmother had been escorted to her rest, behind drawn window blinds; after the Grandmother had been awakened and helped to dress for the evening; after the completion of a multitude of details of which Rachel alone knew the meaning and necessity, she – Rachel – was ready.

Evening had come, and with it a light pretty snowfall. When Rachel stepped out into the dark exciting air with Rose, and closed the house door, she shut the door on a small, warm, and well-conducted world which she had created and which she maintained. Grannie, the admired and titular head of the house, was now really the child of her daughter Rachel. It was Rachel who, with a selfless filial piety, and sometimes with sharp admonishings, was still her mother's proud servant. It was Rachel who was the only subduer of the effervescent Aunt Topaz. It was Rachel who had cared for her younger unmarried brother Andrew. It was Rachel who looked after her orphaned niece Rose, and made her hair shine, and disciplined her, and loved her. It was Rachel who controlled the wily and violent Chinese cook, Yow. And it was Rachel who was regarded by the family as the responsible person in her wonted place. And for what reward did Rachel spend her days? For no reward other than the fulfilment of her own fierce integrity and sense of order, and the confidence and placid affection of her family.

Rachel and the young Rose walked arm in arm down the snowy sidewalk, and waited at the street corner for the tram. They would have walked to town, but that their planned and joyous occupation when they reached town was to be the peculiar one of twice walking slowly the length of Hastings Street, from Granville Street to below Cambie Street and back. Rachel was already tired, and so they took the tram.

When they jumped off the tram at the corner of Granville and Hastings Streets, and began walking, there was the stirring feeling of something shared and gay in the air. Snow sparkled on the roofs of the small shops. The streets and the shops were bright, and the people walking slowly on Hastings Street in twos and threes with no regard for right or left, laughed, talked, and gave themselves up to the pleasure of Christmas Eve in a random strolling fashion. On this respectable street there was no noisy behaviour and no drunkenness. Families and friends walked happily, just as Rachel and Rose also walked. It is true that on near-by Cordova Street, when Rose accompanied her aunt on Saturday morning shoppings, she sometimes saw glorious ladies dressed in fashionable black, who sauntered, often in pairs. These ladies were beautiful. They did not shop. They sauntered lazily with a swaying of opulent hips and bosom, looking softly yet alertly from lustrous eyes set in masks of rose and white. "Aunt Rachel, Aunt Rachel, *look* at those pretty ladies, who are they, just look!" Rose had sometimes whispered. But Aunt Rachel did not look. She behaved as if she were blind and deaf. It appeared that she did not know the pretty ladies at all. The town was small, and Aunt Rachel knew everybody, at least by sight, so this struck Rose as queer. But tonight, on Christmas Eve, these ladies were not to be seen. Only the families strolled and talked and laughed and gazed at the shops along Hastings Street. Well, that is all that Rachel and Rose did too. And then they got on the tram and went home again. Even the tram was full of Christmas.

Aunt Topaz was impatient for them. She had just helped the Grandmother to bed, and was in the kitchen munching. "Well, who did you see?" she enquired eagerly.

"Anty, what *are* you eating?" asked Rachel as she set about making some cocoa for them all.

"Oh, just a bitta cheese and some mustard pickle," said Aunty airily.

"It's a marvel to me that you don't have nightmares," said Rachel, measuring the cocoa.

"Well, I don't have nightmares, and that's a fact," said Aunty. "A little gas sometimes perhaps, but no nightmares," laughing and patting her diaphragm elegantly with her spread fingers and continuing to eat pickles and cheese. Aunty had the gift of belching delicately, when and where and as often as she chose. She enjoyed this. It amused her. Rachel was not amused when Aunty belched, because the example was bad for Rose, who thought it funny.

Over and through the small things of home flowed the excitement that was Christmas Eve. In a gust of secrecy and love Rose kissed her aunts good-night. She took Grannie her cocoa, and sat carefully on the edge of Grannie's feather bed. As she talked to the Grandmother, Christmas hung and glittered in the air, just as if the slow walk along Hastings Street had been a festival, just as if the parcels lay wrapped in silver. Tomorrow is Christmas Christmas Christmas! She went to bed.

When Rachel came upstairs, long after the lively Aunt Topaz had proceeded with ejaculations up the stairs to her room, the Grandmother called sleepily, "Is that you, Rachel?

Tuck me feet up, love," and Rachel reached in her capable and accustomed hands under the bedclothes and wrapped a shawl around the Matriarch's tiny feet. "Now go to bed, love, do." "Good-night, Mother."

Rachel lay tiredly awake for a time, and then turned her face into the pillow and slept. She was the daughter, the maiden. Never having known the lights and music of marriage, never having known the joy and care of being a mother, she was yet the wife and mother of her household. She was to this home as the good bread upon the table, as the steadfast light upon the stair.

SIXTEEN

Family Prayer

ONE DAY Rachel walked up to her mother who was sitting in the pepper-pot window of her bedroom mending some lace, and said in a tone of grave announcement, "Yow is going to China."

Her mother looked up dismayed and said, "Yow going to *China*? Why?"

"Because," Rachel said, "he is going to have a baby. In three months."

"But, my dear Rachel, that is impossible. Yow cannot possibly . . ."

"I know, I know," said Rachel irritably because she had just had a scene with Yow. "Just the same he is going to China for the purpose of having a baby. He will live with his wife for three months, and at the end of that time he assures me that he – or I suppose she – will . . . will . . ."

"Of course. I understand," said her mother who did not think it was nice of Yow to have discussed with her daughter the probabilities and mechanics of his having a baby. "But if Yow has a baby, I think we should invite him to bring it here, and then it would be a little Christian."

"What's this, what's this?" exclaimed Aunt Topaz coming hastily into the bedroom. "Yow having a baby! Well, what next! What a surprise, to be sure!"

"Hush," said Rachel, "here's Rose coming!" But Rose was already there, and the sealed faces of her three elders added another mystery to her expanding but muddled mind.

Down in the kitchen Yow and a thin Chinese friend sat on

144

two chairs opposite each other at the kitchen table and kept up a rapid Chinese conversation in the Cantonese dialect. The door opened with a rush and Topaz bounced in.

"Well, Yow, what's this I hear! How do you do, how do you do!" to the second Chinaman who showed that he knew how to behave in a white house by standing up and taking off his round hat. He was neatly dressed but much smaller and thinner than Yow. His queue was not bound around his head for working purposes as Yow's was, but hung down in a neat plait which was augmented and lengthened by a twist of green cotton, so as to reach up and be hooked invisibly under his right arm. Yow did not stand up, because he enjoyed being ill-mannered.

"And is this a friend of yours, Yow?" enquired Aunt Topaz gracefully.

"No. He not my friend. He my kah-san," said Yow rather sullenly.

"But how can he be your cousin and not be your friend? I should think . . . At least in *our* family, cousins are closer even than friends!" This was true.

Yow proceeded to be rude. "Canadian people no savee nothing. China people more different. Last February China New Year my family have large party seven hundred people. All my kah-san. All my generation. You no care. You not ask all your famuly. I not hear you go telephone seven hundred people, all your generation. You not know all your generation. You not care. I care. I know all my generation. I all same Queen Victoria."

For a moment Aunt Topaz could not answer, because she was trying to discover any likeness between Yow and Queen Victoria.

"Queen Victoria he know he generation eight hundred year," continued Yow, while the other Chinaman remained impassive, standing. "Queen Victoria generation King in England eight hundred year. My generation King in China eight hundred year." "I think he means 'relations,' not 'generations,'" explained Rose who had joined her Great-Aunt in the kitchen doorway.

An idea had blossomed in the mind of Topaz. She forgot all about her intended enquiries about Yow's absence, his baby, and his successor, and turned. She hastily climbed the stairs and entered the room with the pepper-pot, taking a good deal of breeze in with her.

"Yow says he is like Queen Victoria," she announced.

"Now *that* is *quite* impossible," said the Grandmother, smiling at all these careless statements flying about. Rachel stopped her dusting, and listened.

"No. It is credible," said Aunt Topaz. "And he has given me a very good idea, with which I hope, Rachel, that you will agree and co-operate." Rachel looked at her Aunt, but was already set to disagree with any idea born under these auspices.

"He says," continued Aunty, "that his ancestors were kings in China at the same time that Queen Victoria's ancestors were kings in England. He seems to set a great deal of store by family, and I'm sure I for one don't blame him. He says that last Chinese New Year his family – or clan, I suppose – anyway all his cousins had a party of seven hundred people in Chinatown. He seems to think very badly of us because we don't do the same kind of thing."

"Well, he can think badly of us for all I care. I'm not going to ask seven hundred people to this house in order to keep Yow's good opinion, I'm sure," said Rachel, "and I'm telling you now."

"Wait, wait," implored Aunty. "Can't you wait! In this new country it is very important that we should not lose track of family history. Tradition tends to die." Rachel went on dusting.

"My suggestion is this. I have reason to believe that my ancestors came over with William the Conqueror" ("What about mine, then, I'm your niece," said Rachel.) "and I'm sure, Annie, that the same must be true of the Hastings family. It stands to reason! Look at the name! I shall write to *The Times*. I shall ask all those who can trace their descent from the Norman Knights who came over with William the Conqueror" ("How can they tell? They might have been kitchen boys," said Rachel.) "to have a meeting. We could call it a rally. We could meet on the beach at Hastings, or in Normandy, or even here! I shall certainly write to *The Times*!"

"And I shall certainly leave home if you do!" said Rachel vehemently. Her dark eyes flashed. This was too much in one morning.

"I think I'd wait a little, love," said the Grandmother gently. "Why not try to substantiate your own claim first? That would be very interesting, I'm sure. You could write to the Staffordshire Archives and you might get some splendid information about the family."

"Yes, and she might get some information she wouldn't like," said Rachel, shutting a drawer with a bang.

While this conversation continued upstairs in the room with the pepper-pot, the Chinese conversation went on in the kitchen. Yow was smoking a very stinking small cigar. He only did this to show off, as he was not supposed to smoke in the kitchen. Translated into simple pidgin, the Chinese conversation went something like this.

"All right. I give you this job for three month. You give me ten procent wages," said Yow.

The small thin Chinaman, whose name was Fooey, blinked his mild eyes behind his steel-rimmed spectacles.

"I give you five procent."

"You give me ten procent."

"Lady Fowkes down by Stanley Parks like me go cook for her. She give me forty-five dollars a month. No procent."

"You lie. I know Lady Fowkes. I know her cook. He heap smart. Lady Fowkes pay fifty-five dollars a month. Six children. Three housemaid nurse. Three breakfast. Three lunch. Afternoon tea with sandwich and hot biscuit and small cake. Three dinner. You no can do. You very small. You very thin. You not strong. You all time cough. I think pretty soon you die."

Fooey sat respectful and silent. All this was true.

"You come here," said Yow wheedling a little. "This very easy job. Not much cooking. Bossee lady" (this was Rachel) "heap stingy. All the time milk pudding. Very easy. Dinner very oily" (early). "Dinner Lady Fowkes half-past seven. All time wash dish Lady Fowkes' house."

"What time dinner here?" asked Fooey.

"They say dinner half-past six. I say dinner six. I make dinner six. They no like. I no care. You get out oily. Every night I go Chinatown play fan-tan. Sunday I go two o'clock go Lung Duck play fan-tan all day all night."

"Lung Duck tell my kah-san you lose plenty money."

"He lie. Sometime I lose twenty-five cent. Sometime I win one two dollar. He crazy."

Fooey thought for a minute. "All right," he said, "I take this job three month while you go China get baby."

"Ten procent?"

"Ten procent."

Something else occurred to Yow.

"Listen," he said, "you care for old Mrs. Hastings. She good. She all same God. You care for her like she your sister." Yow was too proud to say that he loved the Grandmother. Just the same he loved her beyond anyone; far more than he loved his wife or his mother. "Two times every day you go Famuly Prayer."

"I not know what you call Famuly Prayer," objected Fooey.

"Old Mrs. Hastings heap like talk to Jesus Christ," said Yow, only Yow said "Jee Kly." "After breakfast she talkem Jee Kly. After dinner she likee talk Jee Kly."

"Why she all the time talk Jee Kly? What she say?" asked Fooey.

"I not know what she say," said Yow crossly, putting out his stinking cigar. "I no care. You no ask. After breakfast she tell you come. You come."

"What I do?" enquired Fooey.

"You look see. Very easy. After dinner you go Famuly Prayer too."

"How long time Famuly Prayer?" asked Fooey dubiously.

"Maybe five minute. Maybe seven minute. Not long."

"All right. I go Famuly Prayer," said Fooey. He slipped

fifty cents to Yow for letting him have the job, and the bargain was sealed. Yow was well pleased. Fooey was not strong and could not aspire to a difficult or expert job, and he was so poor a cook that Rachel would not want to keep him when Yow returned. Everything, then, was right; Yow would go to China for three months and do his best to have a baby, and would return to Mrs. Hastings to this comfortable billet which was only a side-line to his game of fan-tan.

The family had now descended to the sitting-room. Yow went in, followed by the mild thin Fooey, hat in hand. Yow led Fooey up to the Grandmother.

"Missee Hasting. This Fooey. He my kah-san. He very good cook. He likee work for you. I tell him be good boy. I show him everything. He care for you. He likee Famuly Prayer. He not usem much cream. He heap stinge."

Thus introduced and qualified, Fooey bowed, and the Grandmother looked up at him confidingly, sensitively, kindly, and he knew and trusted her.

"I hope you will be happy here, Fooey," she said. "Yow is *so* good, *so* kind." (The Grandmother really believed this, and perhaps he was.) "We shall miss him very much, but I know you will look after us."

Fooey was very much surprised to learn that anyone thought that Yow was good and kind; but as the two races had always to understand or believe in each other across a great area of fog-like confusion and misconception, he was prepared to try to believe anything at all.

"Well, he looks very thin, I'm sure," said Aunt Topaz.

"He welly strong. He more strong than me," said Yow and swaggered out of the room with Fooey following submissively.

Only a day or two after Yow left, the imitative Fooey was performing all Yow's duties in such a way that hardly any change could be observed in the conduct of the house. This was what Rachel, who was conservative, desired; and this was what Yow, who was conservatism itself, would have desired too. There was the added advantage to Yow that although the atmosphere of the house in general was more peaceful,

Fooey's cooking was tasteless, and his cough was incessant; otherwise Rachel would have preferred to keep Fooey.

Time passed peacefully enough, with friends and family coming and going, and the At Home day on the first and third Tuesdays; but always there is something ahead, isn't there. And now the family looked forward to the visit to Vancouver of the eminent Dr. Carboy.

Dr. Carboy was the President of the Methodist Conference, and he came from Toronto. Both these attributes elevated him in the estimation of the Grandmother, and her estimation of him spread downwards through the family, until at last Dr. Carboy's psychic presence preceded him and hovered all over the house. His name was constantly on the tongue of Aunt Topaz. Dr. Carboy was asked to dinner. Dr. Carboy, by letter, accepted. He accepted gladly, because of the goodness and fame of the Grandmother, who was indeed a Mother in Israel, and because the Grandmother had given a home to a young nephew of his during the previous winter and Dr. Carboy was grateful.

"I shall be very glad indeed to accept your gracious hospitality, dear Mrs. Hastings," wrote Dr. Carboy. "Dr. Fensom, the Executive Secretary, thanks you for your inclusion of him in your kind invitation to dinner, but will, on that occasion, visit his mother-in-law, who is very aged and resides in Vancouver. He deeply regrets . . ."

"Well, well. 'Gracious hospitality!' Very nice, I'm sure," said Aunt Topaz, and proceeded to talk of Dr. Carboy every day until her niece Rachel nearly went out of her mind.

The Grandmother's hospitality forever outran her means. Her table – simple enough to excite the scorn of Yow – was always ready to receive the guest without a real home; and in this small seaport town, where transient travellers came and went, many visitors having a tenuous connection with the Grandmother's long life in England were made welcome. And on Sunday afternoons came the Boys and their own young families. Poor Fooey! Yow could manage all this small hospitality with ease and disdain; but poor coughing Fooey could hardly keep up, and so it was that Rachel and her mother decided that Dr. Carboy should come alone, and there should be no dinner-party. Just Dr. Carboy.

How nice Dr. Carboy was! A small pleasant stubby old man who made you feel at home at once. They had been warned that Dr. Carboy, coming from Toronto which had a peculiar and unfair fame, might show a little cultural and spiritual "side". But no, there was none.

As long as the volatile Topaz would permit it, the Grandmother and Dr. Carboy talked the same spiritual language, though in a different dialect. The Grandmother's was the dialect of the soul; the minister's was the dialect of the executive officer of the Church, dry and succinct; but they comprehended one another, and would have communed long together if Topaz had not been on hand to show Dr. Carboy her photograph album, where relatives appeared serious or with dehydrated smiles, and her birthday-book, which by this time was of unusual interest because it contained the autographs of several suicides.

During dinner the supersensitive Rachel was aware, and so was the young Rose, that, although Aunt Topaz was very amusing, and kept Dr. Carboy in a dry crackle of laughter, she overstepped a good deal. But they could do nothing about it. And so, when the time came for Family Prayer, Rachel welcomed the imposed silence.

The Grandmother, so small that her granddaughter had begun to overtop her, moved with her accustomed gentle stateliness to her accustomed place. Dr. Carboy was ushered to the large easy-chair on which Great-Aunt Topaz usually knelt at prayer-time. ("*Why* do you have to be different, Anty?" Rachel used to say. "*Why* do you have to kneel on an easy-chair when everybody else kneels on the floor?" "I have a perfect right to kneel upon a chair. Do you suppose that your posture is the only one acceptable to the Lord? Mohammedans put their heads on the floor and Quakers stand up, and if the Lord doesn't mind, why should you? Anyway, it's because of mice." "*Mice!!* What a . . ." "Now, now, love. What does it matter where Aunty kneels, as long as she prays from a full heart?") So tonight Topaz was dislodged from her big chair and had to sit and kneel like other people.

What is it, Oh God of Love and Battles, that you have given to the saints of the earth and that you have withheld from the earth-bound of the earth? Dr. Carboy read from the Word. The Grandmother leaned forward. Her soft eyes were upon him. She listened with her ears and with her soft eyes and with her luminous countenance and with the other-worldliness and selflessness and consecration that made her a saint, as if she had never heard the familiar holy words before. Her earth-bound granddaughter Rose, who was young but alert, would have been quick to detect the least scent of hypocrisy or of self-awareness in her Grandmother. There was none. Rose marvelled. She could not enter, but she marvelled. (She thought, "It must be a gift like music. It must be a special gift of religion that other people haven't got. Aunt Rachel has it a lot, but not like Grannie. Aunt Topaz hasn't got it at all. And I? No, I haven't got it.") When Dr. Carboy ceased reading and closed the Book, they all got up, turned round, knelt down, folded their hands, closed their eyes, and Dr. Carboy began to pray.

"We thank Thee, oh Lord," he prayed. "We thank thee for . . ." and Dr. Carboy thanked the Lord for twenty-five different things. He then prayed for Country, King, Church, Heathen, Family – both the Grandmother's and his own – using a perfected formula for each petition.

("It's very hard for him," thought Rose as she knelt, watching him with bright eyes, "to find anything fresh to say, isn't it. But he seems to mean it. I wonder how they made the pattern in the back of this little cane chair." She poked. "The cane goes in here and out here and the other piece goes out there and in here. I like this little chair. I wonder if it's ebony. No, there's some paint off here. Do they paint ebony? Gild the lily and refine the what. Oh, look at Dr. Carboy's beard going up and down. He's praying for *us* now. I must pay attention." And she shut her eyes very tight.)

("Oh God," prayed Rachel, "enable me to keep my temper

with Anty. Enable me to bring Rose up properly, and give me a gift of true goodness and make me worthy. That joint was far too big. We'll have it cold tomorrow, and Italian Delight – or Cecil – on Friday if it keeps this weather. If Yow had only been here we could have had Frank and Miranda and the Johnsons and little Percy Beardmore in to eat it up. I think Fooey has consumption. If he has, what had I better do? What am I thinking of? Oh, my God, I am no better than a heathen with wandering thoughts." And she pressed her hands over her eyes and listened to Dr. Carboy. Italian Delight – made with minced ends of meat, and tomatoes, and the macaroni that was supposed to delight Italians, and a baked meatloaf with the surprising name of Cecil, were the final states of any joint entering the Hastings home. Rachel often had to banish the cares of housekeeping from her prayers. It was one of her "besetting sins"; so – "Save me," she prayed, "from my besetting sins.")

("Carboy, Carboy," thought Topaz. "I forgot to ask him if he could be any relative of that old Mr. Carboy that Father did business with. He used to wear a square hat. A most unusual name. Irish?" She looked at Dr. Carboy. "He doesn't look Irish. No brogue. I would call that an Ontario accent myself, but it's all the same in the sight – or sound I should say – of God, no doubt. It's very difficult, I must say, to keep one's mind intent during a long prayer. I feel quite sure that God – who made us and not we ourselves when all's said and done – will quite understand. Ah, the *Rubaiyat*! Beautiful and so true!

> 'Oh Thou who didst with pitfall and with gin
> Beset the path I was to wander in,
> Thou wouldst not with whatever is it
> Enmesh me and impute my Fall to Sin.'

I quite agree. Oh, look, grapes! I didn't see that fine bunch of grapes! Rachel must have hidden it. I *would* like a grape!")

("Our Dear Heavenly Father," breathed the Grandmother, "Thou hearest this good man Thy servant. Pour down Thy Blessing upon Thy children gathered here and upon all Thy poor children gathered everywhere. Give us all a sense of the close reality of Thy Presence. Draw us near to Thee. Purify us. Yes, indeed we thank Thee, dear Father, in the Name of Thy Beloved Son." And the Grandmother listened to the prayer of Dr. Carboy, and her communion spread like a natural radiance straight to God, either in that room or wherever He might be. Posture of body did not change her heart. When she stood up or walked she was as close to God as when she sat or kneeled or lay down.)

The Chinaman Fooey knelt with his head bowed, eyes squeezed tight shut, and his thin hands knitted together, thinking in Chinese of God knows what.

When Dr. Carboy's voice fell, and ceased, all those kneeling except Fooey collected themselves and joined reverently in the sublime words of the Lord's Prayer. A short pause, and they rose. Fooey departed. Rose took away the Bible. Dr. Carboy stood still. He seemed to be thinking. The Grandmother, still looking through a mist, sat down.

"Ah! A grape!" exclaimed Topaz, darting. She went through the half-closed sliding doors into the dining-room, and returned with the best Spode comport laden with green and purple grapes, peaches, and pears. Rachel looked desperately at her – this fruit was destined for later in the evening – and then she fetched plates and fruit-knives and forks.

"Let me show you how to eat a grape, Dr. Carboy," said Topaz merrily. "You impale it – so! – on the fork. You lift the skin a little, and – you see – off it comes! Then you cut the grape in half – out pop the seeds! – and you eat it. Delicious! Delicious!"

"Thank you, Miss Edgeworth," said Dr. Carboy in his deliberate dry and rather grating voice, "I can handle this prahposition myself." And he swallowed down the grapes one at a time, stems, skins, seeds and all. Rose laughed so hard that she had to be sent out of the room.

About a month later Yow returned and said he had had a good time.

"And what about the baby?" enquired Great-Aunt Topaz with gay interest.

Yow shot her a dark look and went into the kitchen and made banging noises. Rachel began to talk. "Anty, you are outrageous!" she said.

Every few weeks whenever the thought happened to enter her mind, Aunty nevertheless enquired of Yow if there was any word of the approaching baby. After some months Yow announced that his wife had given birth to twin boys. Topaz congratulated him warmly and gave him two dollars each to send to the babies. Rachel and Rose, however, believed that Yow had made it up. There did not seem to be the right ring about his announcement. They felt quite sorry for him, because he had done the best he could.

The family settled down into its place once more. They settled down to one At Home day a month instead of two. They were busy people now. Yow jockeyed them into early dinner again, but always came in to Family Prayer. Family Prayer continued as a loving reality to the Grandmother, and as a "very good thing" and an accustomed order to Topaz and Rachel. Rose was inclined to dodge Family Prayer. She did not care for it, except for her Grandmother's sake, and yet in after life she affectionately treasured the memory and the sincerity of the communion. It all seemed to centre in and radiate from her Grandmother.

SEVENTEEN

The Innumerable Laughter

"WHAT A LOVELY morning! Oh, look, there's a bird!" said Aunt Topaz as she hastened down the steps from the verandah of the small summer cabin which her nephews had caused to be built upon the high rocky shores of Benbow Island. "And the sea, oh, look!" she said to no one in particular, for there was no one there. "'The many-twinkling smile of ocean!' 'The innumerable laughter of the sea!' Just like the Greeks I do declare! I wouldn't be at all surprised! Who would think that this is the Pacific Ocean! Much the same rocky . . . What is that? Voices? Voices? Who *can* it be?" and she quickened her steps towards the rock which overlooked the lonely bay.

Aunt Topaz, hurrying forwards, reached the rock and looked down. "Well!" she said.

On the smooth expanse of the little bay below her floated two small yachts, and in the bay, swimming about with lusty and happy shouts, were several young men with nothing on.

"Well I never!" exclaimed Aunt Topaz, bending down so as to see better. "Nothing on! Very pleasant, I'm sure! Oh, can that be Mr. Morland? Good-morning, Mr. Morland, good-morning! And *can* that be that nice young man in the Bank? I do believe it is!" said Aunty, delighted to recognize two young men of her acquaintance so far from home, even though they had nothing on.

At the sight of Aunty who smiled and called and waved the handkerchief which she had rummaged from the front of her blouse, Mr. Morland and the nice young man in the Bank uttered warning cries. All the swimmers immediately turned face downwards and swam about, vainly trying to escape from the orbit of Aunty's vision. Aunty now saw nothing but posteriors swimming vainly away.

"Oh," said Aunty, vexed, "if only they'd turn right side up, I'd be able to see if it really *is* Mr. Morland! I *must* tell Rachel!"

Aunt Topaz, who was a great imparter of news, turned and went back at top speed to the cottage, where she saw her niece Rachel standing in the doorway.

"Rachel, Rachel, what *do* you suppose," she cried, "there are nine young men swimming about the bay with nothing on, and I do believe that one is Andrew's friend Mr. Morland, and I *do* believe that one of them is that nice young man in the Bank! If they would only turn right side up I might be able to see! I called and called but they did not reply!"

"What does it matter if it *is* Mr. Morland?" said Rachel wrathfully. "A great pity if young men can't have a bit of a swim without people staring at them. I sometimes think, Anty, that you have no modesty."

"*Me!* No modesty!" exclaimed Aunty with indignation. "Well, really! Here I am clothed from head to foot, and they haven't got a stitch on! Who's immodest, I'd like to know! Oh, Annie, so *there* you are! What do you think, there are nine . . ."

Just as the Grandmother appeared at the door, Yow, domineering as usual, came round the corner with a large breakfast tray.

"I puttem breakfast verandah. Plenty sun," he announced, without asking them whether they wanted to have breakfast on the verandah or not.

"Ah, bacon, bacon! How nice!" said Aunty. "Delicious! Annie, did you know that there are nine young men . . . Oh dear me, there's a serpent!"

"Why, there's a snake!" said Rachel, looking over the verandah railing at a snake which lay curled on the warm grass.

"A serpent?" said the Grandmother in surprise.

The garter snake slid, coiled, stopped. It slid, coiled, stopped, and slid shining away through the grasses.

"Well!" said the ladies, who had seldom seen snakes before, except in a zoo.

"Can it be poisonous?" asked Rachel.

"Is it venomous, do you think?" asked the Grandmother. They all left their bacon and peered over the verandah railing after the vanished snake.

"Mr. Oxted says that snakes in this part of the world are never poisonous," said Aunt Topaz. "Mr. Oxted has lived in British Columbia for years and years and years. Mr. Oxted says that Mrs. Oxted. . . ."

"*Anty*," said Rachel in extreme exasperation, "if I hear you mention Mr. Oxted once more . . . if I hear you quote Mr. Oxted once more . . . I've heard nothing but Mr. Oxted ever since we started coming up here, for two whole months. You'd think that no one but Mr. Oxted had ever gone camping before!"

"Mr. Oxted is a very nice man and a very *fine* man," said Aunt Topaz. And then she proceeded to give a good example of the way she could shift an argument to suit herself. Since no one could prove whether the snake was poisonous except by being bitten by it, and being sent down as a corpse to Vancouver, Aunty adroitly shifted her stand.

"His wife is a very handsome woman, and she sings in St. Andrew's choir. A fine contralto. Some people say that St. Andrew's choir is the best choir in Vancouver."

This was not kind of Aunty. Rachel had been for five years a faithful choir member and a leading soprano in Wesley Church. But Aunty achieved her end, which was to irritate Rachel just a little. Rachel had rebuked her in the matter of the young men, and Aunty was still mildly annoyed. She succeeded in irritating Rachel.

"How can you say such a thing!" cried Rachel. "Everyone who is anyone and knows anything about music knows quite well that Wesley Church choir is the leading choir in Vancouver, and if St. Andrew's . . ."

The Grandmother held up her hand. "Let us have no rivalry," she said gently. "Although we do not belong to the Presbyterian Church, there is no doubt but that, in their own way, the Presbyterians praise God with equal . . ."

"Oh, do look at Yow!" exclaimed Aunt Topaz.

Yow stood nonchalantly in the doorway. He looked at the ladies with his peculiar facial cynicism. This was not difficult, as his right eyelid drooped by nature with a sinister effect, and gave to his face a cynical and even diabolical appearance without any effort on Yow's part. Between his fingers he held the tail of a snake. The snake, hanging head downwards, looked uncomfortable, and squirmed in an angular and unnatural manner, quite unlike its usual fluid performance.

"I catchem snake. I puttem stew," said Yow, looking with indifference upon the breakfast party. Cries arose, but Yow did not stay to listen. He departed, taking the snake with him.

"I do believe he will!" they breathed one to another.

It was the habit in this family of three ladies that even the slightest move on anyone's part should be prefaced by a brief and candid explanation. If Rachel should at any time arise, and go out of the room without some such announcement as "I am going to get my sewing cotton," the Grandmother and Aunt Topaz would say mutually in amazement, "Where *can* Rachel have gone?" as if she might have gone to China or to Peru or to bed.

Aunt Topaz therefore did not surprise anyone when she said, "I have a call," and got up and walked in her hasty pounding fashion in the direction of the rear of the cottage.

She returned by way of the lean-to kitchen where Yow was making loud noises in the dish-pan.

"Yow," said Aunt Topaz, "you wouldn't *really* put that serpent into the stew, would you?"

"Sure," said Yow rudely, and went into the house.

As Aunty returned dismayed to the verandah, Rachel arose and said, "I am going to get some more hot water." She then repaired to the lean-to kitchen. Yow looked at her malevolently.

"Yow," said Rachel, using her mixture of pidgin-English

which she admired but could not achieve, and the King's own English, "I absolutely forbiddem you puttem snake in stew. If you puttem snake in stew, I shall tell Mr. Andrew when he comes next Saturday. If you puttem snake in stew, Mr. Andrew will be extremely angry."

"I no care," said Yow, and went on being noisy.

When Rachel got back to the breakfast table, the Grandmother stood up in all her small dignity and said, "I am going to speak to Yow about that serpent," and sailed like a little black schooner into the house.

"Yow," she said, lifting her limpid brown gaze to the Chinaman, "*please* don't put that little serpent into the stew! I shall not relish my stew at all if you do. Please, Yow!"

Yow looked upon his darling. "I no puttem snake stew, Missy Hasting," he said. "You no likee, I no puttem. I makem little fun. I foolem. They heap clazy. They no savvy nothing. I no puttem stew."

"Oh, I do thank you, Yow," said the Grandmother gratefully. She returned, saying to her sister and daughter, "Yow declares that he does not intend to put the serpent into the stew. He says . . ." but her sister and her daughter did not hear her.

"I have every intention of doing so!" declared Aunt Topaz. "Mr. Oxted says that Mrs. Oxted says that she finds it most beneficial. She says that he says, I mean he says that she says . . ."

"Oh, for goodness *sake*, Anty!" said Rachel.

"What can this be?" asked the Grandmother, diverted from the serpent.

"I am going to sleep on this verandah tonight," said Aunt Topaz. "It will be most delightful. Mrs. Oxted sleeps on their summer cottage verandah all summer. She sleeps like a top. I shall sleep like a top too. I shall sleep on this little couch. It will be quite comfortable and it will be very invigorating."

"Yes, and you will be going around with one of your sniffly colds for the rest of the summer. *I* know," said Rachel, "and breakfasts in bed and the wash full of those pocket-handkerchiefs of yours."

"Now, love," said the Grandmother mildly, "let Aunty do what she likes. Let her try it for one night. I'm sure if I were young I should enjoy it."

"Young!" said Rachel, and she looked at the shining spacious sea, and the sky, and at the fringe of the dark bright forest. *If I had been here when I was young. If I had come here before I was an elderly woman looking after two older women, and my brother, and my sister's child . . . all this beauty. If I had married Tom Shaw, or Mr. Calverley when he asked me, I might have been a married woman and important like my sisters-in-law . . . but I could never have married Tom Shaw or anyone else. Only this life that I lead is tolerable to me. I could not endure to be other than I am. Oh, what a beautiful beautiful morning!*

There was within Rachel a virgin well into which beauty silently seeped. She could receive the beauty of the morning without speaking. She did not have to transmute this beauty into conversation. So, now, she did not need to say to her mother, "Look, the smooth bark of the arbutus tree is like copper in the sunshine, isn't it? See how the draped branches of the cedars wave seriously! Listen to 'the innumerable laughter of the sea'!" But she turned to her mother, content, and then cried in her anxious way, "Mother, what *are* you doing! Come, Anty, let us move Mother's chair out of the sun!"

When the evening came, Aunty's plans for the night caused so much confusion that no one could sit upon the verandah couch without being asked, several times, to get up. Even the mild Grandmother felt that the experiment demanded too much fuss.

"I shall take my walking-stick," declared Aunty, pounding in and out with her busy tread.

"Whatever for?" asked Rachel.

"Well, I might want to walk down the steps in the night. And I shall take my umbrella and my parasol that belonged to Elijah's wife."

"Both of them, love?" asked the Grandmother.

"Yes, both of them. In Case. Because it might rain in on me, or in the morning the sun might prevent me sleeping. And, you see, I shall take a glass of milk."

"That will attract slugs," said Rachel.

The slugs of Benbow Island are large and gross. They appear to be inert, but are really very mobile; they cover long distances at night and may be found in the morning glued to the edges of containers of food. They are very intelligent, although they do not look it.

"Slugs! Oh. Then I shall take some biscuits and a little bit of chocolate instead," Aunty announced.

Rachel did not say "That will attract mice," although she felt that it should be said.

"I shall take my quilt and Grandfather's shawl," continued Aunty, plumping up her pillow. "And I shall take a hat."

"A hat! Whatever for?" enquired Rachel.

"Because I should like to have my hat with me. In Case. I might wish to sit up during the night, and then it would be nice to have my hat on," said Aunt Topaz.

"Anything else?" asked Rachel.

Night drew on, and the coal-oil lamp was lighted. Yow, the protector, had gone to bed in his outside room. Night finally declared itself, dark and moonless. The lamp shone reflected in the jet-black windows. This was the time when the three women felt within themselves a turning towards sleep. The Grandmother was settled by Rachel; Rachel settled herself; and Aunt Topaz at last closed the door on the warm small room, instinct with habitation, and went out into the uncharted dark. She was excited.

After some stumbling, and some rearrangement on the floor of her equipment, she turned back her neatly made bed, got in, and pulled the bedclothes up to her chin. She looked up into the dark. "This is most delightful," she announced to herself.

She lay for some time looking into the darkness which did not become less opaque. Objects did not emerge from this darkness. Sometimes she turned and regarded a patch of starred sky which the slope of the verandah roof disclosed. All was very still, except for the small continuous sound of ocean upon the rocks. There had been a wind earlier in the day. The wind had died, but a slight wash of the salt sea remained, and with the wash against the shore only a small continuing sound, which grew more faint. The usual commotion and breeze caused by Aunt Topaz in the business of living had ceased abruptly with getting into bed and pulling up the bedclothes. She would have liked to cough, for something to do, but the austere solitude of the night forbade her. Her own stillness and the dark cosmic and planetary silence outside the cabin really disturbed and deprived Aunty a good deal, but she determined to enjoy herself.

"This is indeed *most* delightful," she thought again, but she was restive, feeling a need of someone to express herself to. There was no one. Even the young men in the bay had long since sailed away. She lay awake. She was not afraid, but, with her genius for communication, she felt deeply the need of a listener, to whom she could explain how delightful everything all was. This became more needful as she continued to lie awake. But there were no human ears at hand to oblige her; so she conversed with herself, within, or fell silent, pinioned in the bedclothes.

There are on Benbow Island many deer of small and medium size. These beautiful bucks and does – with their elegant heads, their poetic and nonsensical eyes, their delicate feet and their fine russet or beige rumps – together with their pretty dappled children inhabit the forest where they stray safely, because there are no predatory beasts indigenous to Benbow Island. The only predatory beast is man, occasional man, and the deer are reasonably safe from man except for a few months in the year. Knowing and suspecting man, the deer stray in the forest in the day-time, but when night comes they emerge from the woods, and enjoy cropping tender shoots in the grass that often surrounds the small houses where men seem to keep themselves at night; and, if possible, the deer enter men's enclosed vegetable gardens and eat up their green peas, and sometimes get shot out of season for doing this.

Around Aunt Topaz's nephews' cottage which was in solitude, there were no green peas, but there was some good lush grass. The deer knew this, and because they were as conversant with the dark as with the day, they came out by night one by one, to the number of three or four, and cropped this good grass undisturbed, but Aunt Topaz did not know this. She soon heard an alien sound.

For there were now, near her, sounds as of small footsteps, a little movement, a little rustling. Aunty raised herself cautiously on her elbow and peered. She could see nothing, nothing. These small sounds came from in front of the cottage, and from either end of the verandah. They were closing in. Crop, crop, crop. Rustle, chump, and a nipping of grasses. "Dear me," thought Aunty, "it sounds like a very little cow! But there are no cows. Or a sheep! Certainly it sounds like a grass-eating animal. Could it be a deer? Or an elk? Or a moose? Or *could* it be a bison? Is it dangerous if surprised? However, since it seems to be a vegetarian it is unlikely to attack me." She began, nevertheless, to feel nervous. The sounds ceased. They began again. Aunty strained her eyes this way and that into the unrevealing night.

In the woods, so near the cottage, owls began to cry. Hoo-oo-oo, came the sweet quavering cry. Hoo-oo-oo, came the answer out of the forest. "Owls," thought Aunt Topaz, "I do believe! I hope indeed that they will not think of pecking out my eyes! . . . And if owls, then mice, and what else – rats, perhaps, and weasels. This is, when all is said and done, a very wild country, and only newly inhabited. Truly the New World. Oh, there's the owl again!" She began to wish that she had never met Mr. Oxted, and as the unexplained, unexplainable rustlings continued near the verandah, she wanted to gather up her bedclothes and go in from the unknown and elemental to the comfortable familiarity of the cabin. She was wide awake, and her usually impercipient senses were alert. But she was too proud to get up and go inside.

A great shooting star tore red across the patch of silent sky and went out. Aunty felt elated, and then subdued. "And to think that Rachel is sleeping, and Annie too!" she reflected, bitterly.

"If I thought about Father, perhaps I could go to sleep," she decided, and reverted easily to her life's habit of youngest daughter. She saw at once his noble bearded head. "What a fine beard! You never see a beard like that now. How queer those nine young men would have looked today swimming about with beards on! Very odd. Very much in the way. There must be some reason for it, I suppose." She now indulged her favourite habit of enumeration. "Let me see, beards, beginning with Father. And then Uncle Montague. And Uncle Edward. And Sam Rathbone – all long and well-combed except Uncle Edward's, a very unpleasant beard. And *not* Matthew Arnold – side-whiskers when we knew him, very peculiar. And all my brothers, little pointed ones – the decline of the beard, I suppose. Mrs. Porter's husband hadn't got a beard, but then he was a very unprincipled man. And, oh, William Sandbach – the most *beautiful* beard!" She tried to evoke tenderness at the thought of Mr. Sandbach and his beard, his benign, deceiving, heartless, hypocritical beard. But no, her love for him was long dead. She who had wept so much could not now evoke even a spurious sigh. "How could he have made me so unhappy?" she asked herself with surprise. A dreadful cry grated and rent the night. Aunt Topaz stiffened and her eyes started. She did not know that a blue heron was protesting as it awoke, and was now beating its great wings slowly against the adjacent air. She had never heard of a blue heron. The harsh and frightful cry was repeated near at hand. "That is not human!" thought Aunty trembling, and, of course, it was not. What Aunty meant was that it was hellish, which it was. All her bearded company had flitted, like the lot of silly shadows that they were. They had never been. The only reality was the dark and preposterous night. "If I turn over," thought Topaz unhappily, seeking refuge in a phrase, "I shall sleep like a top."

The owls had ceased their whistling, the deer had moved

slowly on, and with the passing of time even the slight sound of the sea against the rocks was stilled. Aunt Topaz turned over, and it was when she began to pull the flannelette sheet about her ears that she heard the voice.

A voice? Voices? Sweet, high, clear, and very faint. A dropping cadence of semitones. A foreign tongue? A sound never heard before, followed by a light sigh, a groan. Aunty listened with her whole being. Again the sweet, descending, unmeaning cry, followed by a sigh, a groan. It came from the shore. No, it came from the ravine. No, it was nearer than that. It was farther away. In the dark was no proportion, no guide. Whence did it come? From the ravine? Again! Is it a voice, is it a cry, or is it music? Is it a flute? Yes, it is a flute. "Oh, my God!" thought Aunty, and cowered in the dark, remembering.

(Yes, said Mrs. Porter when she had finished reading to her young pupils sitting safely about her beside the fire, now, girls, you understand where the word Panic comes from. The Greeks, you see, believed that whoever should hear the fluting of the pagan god Pan was in danger of a revelation which would turn him mad, and whoever should see Pan – who was not even a human type of god, if I may say so, but resembled also a goat – might die from the experience. How much more fortunate are we than the Greeks – we who have the benefits of the Christian religion, that we do not suffer from these and other unsatisfactory superstitions!

But, Mrs. Porter, asked Eliza Pinder and Topaz Edgeworth, both speaking together, and only half convinced, wasn't there really a god Pan in those days? The Greeks were quite sure of it!

No, certainly not, replied Mrs. Porter turning her fine eyes upon them, except . . . well . . . it may be possible . . . that before they had the benefit of the Christian religion, when their world of rocks and trees was so new . . . and in its natural state . . . who can say . . . no, we cannot say . . . why, even Homer . . . Benbow Island is as new as Greece ever was, and newer, newer, much newer). Again the descending notes of the flute, and a groan, dropping into the night.

Inside the white satin body of Topaz – satin white until the day of her death – there opened a dark unknown flower of fear. Slowly it opened, and through the orifice of this flower fear poured into the darkness. Her whole body dissolved listening into fear which flowed into the terrible enclosing night. She, all alone, became only a frightened part of the listening elements.

The high sweet sound continued again into a groan. She could not tell whether the fluting came now at regular intervals. It came. It came. It was light but clear, and stronger than the silence into which it fell. "Oh God Our Help. Oh God Our Help," said a residuum of Topaz blindly. She could not remember anything more to say. But the sweet sound came again, undefeated and unperturbed by the Holy Name. *Then I must go or I am lost this is Panic I have heard it now at any moment I shall see him close in the darkness I shall feel his breath!* And she sprang up, not knowing what she did, and seized soft quilt and Grandfather's shawl, and stumbling, trailing, upsetting, she found the door. She wrenched the door open and rushed in. She shut the door and locked it. How dark was the room!

"What on earth *are* you doing?" said Rachel crossly from the bedroom.

Topaz stood against the wall, breathing heavily, her quilt fallen about her. Directly she stood within this frail unlit shelter of walls, doors, windows, and humanity, even before she heard the comfortable crossness of Rachel's voice, Pan, so very near at hand, became impotent and withdrew into his own place. Her living family and all her bearded memories rushed about her in confusion.

Rachel lit a candle and, blinking from sleep, saw Topaz standing there, white and staring. "Were you frightened, Anty? What frightened you?" she asked curiously.

"I have a cold, I think," said Topaz, chattering. "I think I have a chill." She laboured across the floor dragging her quilt and cast herself upon her naked and deserted bed. She pulled the quilt over her.

Rachel got up and stood with the candle in her hand. "Would you like a bit of a rub?" she asked.

"Yes," said Topaz, with her eyes closed, and still shivering, "I would like a bit of a rub." She longed to feel the hard comfort of Rachel's capable hand upon her.

"What is it, love?" murmured the Grandmother, stirring distantly in sleep.

"Nothing, Mother, turn over, turn over."

Rachel bent down and rubbed and rubbed. She wondered amazedly "She isn't talking! She isn't saying a word! Why is she so quiet?" Her knowing capable hands swept up and down the flaccid white back and shoulders of her lively, voluble, silent aunt. Aunt Topaz felt their solace, mournfully.

"There then," said Rachel, and stood up. She looked down on Topaz who still lay without speaking. "She looks as though she were suffering," she thought.

"Anty," Rachel said at last, "why did you lock the door?"

But Topaz did not answer.

The wind having so long dropped, the ocean became at last still, and there was no movement at all in the waters of the bay. Long before dawn broke and there came the sounds of birds and of day, the faint regular musical rub of the boom log against the little wharf, wood against wood, wood against wood with the slow sway of the water, ceased its clear petulant cry, its chime, its rhythmical sighing.

EIGHTEEN

Rather Close in the Sitting-room

THEY ALWAYS had dinner earlier than they wanted to because Yow, whose domination had increased over all these years, wished to get out. When he got out he walked with his swaggering gait straight to Vancouver Chinatown and shed his cloak of West End respectability. He belonged to a very fast set. He became deeply and darkly a Chinese gambler. This occurred every night of the week, but his nicest and most gambling day was Sunday when he got out very early. Yow looked like a dangerous criminal, and later in life he had, unfortunately, to go to prison. No one knew what his early life had been. He was in some ways a very bad and unscrupulous man, but during the day-time he guarded the interests of his blameless household of ladies in a bullying and efficient way. Such is the power of goodness, that Yow (who was quite the wickedest person that the Grandmother had ever seen, only she did not know this) revered the Grandmother deeply. Each morning and evening this scoundrel continued to "come in" to Family Prayer, and as the little Grandmother knelt and raised her earnest and tremulous petitions to the Lord, he also knelt without either compulsion or contempt. When they all arose from their knees, Yow swaggered out of the room in a more bullying manner than usual, probably in order to reestablish himself in his own esteem, and also in order to reimpose himself on his ladies.

Between Aunt Rachel, since she was the housekeeper, and Yow, there was for ever war. Sometimes one of them lost

ground, sometimes the other. When Yow lost in the great
kindling dispute (he liked to cut it too long for the grates),
Aunt Rachel lost in the thick-toast-for-afternoon-tea battle.
Each was daily comforted by some small victory. When Aunt
Rachel showed her superiority by ordering fifteen cents'
worth of soup-meat from the butcher instead of the twenty-
five cents' worth demanded by Yow, then it was music in her
ears to hear the defeated Yow muttering as he went about his
work, "Stinge, stinge, stinge, no can make good soup fifteen
cents soup meat, all a time velly stingy." When she heard this,
she affected not to hear, but she enjoyed it as Yow's admission
of defeat. And Yow, when he succeeded in announcing dinner
at six, at twenty minutes to six, at twenty-five minutes to six,
at half-past five instead of at half-past six, regarded Aunt
Rachel's annoyance and bafflement with sneering satisfaction.

Between Yow and Great-Aunt Topaz nothing existed. She
was the freelance of the family. She gave no orders, and
received none, and although she set forth daily on her own
immaterial and engrossing affairs, often leading with her the
obstinate bicycle, she returned more or less in time for meals.
She talked continuously when the presence of any other
person, Christian or heathen, made this profitable. And in the
solitude of her bedroom, for lack of any immediate listener,
she talked to herself. During Aunty's flings at public office,
when she used to retire to her room and bolt the door and moan
there, Yow would stand and listen and then confide to Rose,
"He clazy," and depart swaggering to the kitchen. Yow regarded her incuriously when she addressed him, answered her
briefly, and was often heard to say as he departed, "He clazy."
But Great-Aunt Topaz never heard him say this, as, of course,
she was still talking. Neither did the Grandmother hear him,
as a great deal of her time was spent in listening deafly,
charmingly, and attentively to her sister. Aunt Rachel and
Rose, who were not deaf, charming, or attentive, felt as time
went on that Yow should not be allowed to say this, even in
the hall, and that something should be done about it. But, on
the other hand, they each felt that they were getting a bit of

their own back, as Great-Aunt Topaz's rather continuous monologue used to drive them silly, but unlike Yow they were unable to say "He" (or she) "clazy," and get up and go into the kitchen and make unnecessary and deafening noises there. A little thing like this shows plainly the disadvantages of a good upbringing. Or put it another way – what is civilization?

Between Rose, now nearly grown up and a very innocent young lady who had only lately begun to pry into life, and Yow, there was a kind of camaraderie. They sometimes disliked each other, but they were united by a common tug against Aunt Rachel who was a little prone to command. That, however, was her rôle. Yow was fairly polite to Rose, except when she was ironing. It was understood that Rose should iron her own silk blouses. When Rose prepared to iron her blouses, she clamped the handle on each iron in turn, as the irons lay heating on the top of the kitchen stove. She raised each iron in turn to her cheek to test the heat, but she could not tell. So she spat on the iron, a delicate spit, sizzle, sizzle, that told her exactly how hot the iron was. This always enraged Yow. He would not allow Rose to spit upon his irons. When Rose spat upon his irons Yow roared, "No spitty Iron!" in such a menacing way that Rose was quite frightened. She used to try guile. She would go through the form of putting the irons to her cheek, while Yow watched her closely, and then, apparently making her selection, she would go into the little laundry with the chosen iron. There she would cautiously spit upon it to see if it were really right. A very little spit indeed, sizzle, sizzle. But Yow never trusted her. Like a cat he would follow her into the laundry, just in time to catch her spitting. Then he would roar with ferocity, "No Spitty My Iron!" and the simple girl was caught again. Sometimes Rose would brazen it out. She simply could not iron her blouses if the irons were not just right. Defiantly she would spit upon the iron. But Yow had two dreadful punishments for her. One was that he would pull his loose eyelids away from his eyes, above and below, exposing large unpleasant red areas. Then he would roll his bloodshot eyes in all directions apparently independent of each other. As in any case he was violent of face, this was formidable, but somehow Rose could not help gazing upon him. She had to look. Yow did another thing. With a quick flick of his fingers he turned both eyelids inside out, and advanced into the little laundry with what looked like two great gobs of raw meat hanging where his eyes should be. The effect of this as he advanced upon Rose so terrified her that she always cried submission at once, and untruthfully promised never to spit upon the irons again. Sometimes in consequence she scorched her silk blouses past repair, but Yow did not mind. He just unflicked his eyelids and returned to his business. This was queer of Yow, because it is well known that his compatriots in the laundry business are not so finicky.

This, then, was the tyrant who induced the four ladies to sit down unwillingly to dinner at five-thirty instead of at half-past six, and to whom the game was this night conceded. Yow was thus ensured a good long evening with his fellow-rowdies, but for Rose this particular evening was unendurably lengthened thereby. From this early meal both Aunt Rachel and Rose therefore got up in middling humour. Their ill-humour had been increased by the garrulous Great-Aunt, who, finding little response from her niece and great-niece, had been driven to repeat some of her observations an irrelevant number of times. This mood did not always prevail at the table. There were times when the irrepressible Great-Aunt was very funny; when, indeed, they were all funny together, wittier and wittier. Then they laughed and laughed until the tears ran down their faces, and until the little Grandmother, who mistrusted too much laughter, looked around with some concern and said kindly, "There, there, that will do. We have laughed," and they stopped being so divinely silly.

But on this evening Rose got up from Family Prayer in the sitting-room after dinner in a haughty and irritable frame of mind. She was aware that the veil of her irritability hung between herself and her Maker, but she clung to her veil and wrapped it round her in defence against her Grandmother's piety, the Great-Aunt's impervious loquacity, and the domination of Aunt Rachel. As Rose put away her Grandmother's Bible she looked enviously at the retreating Yow. He was on his way to a gambling hell. He was lucky. Tomorrow he would approach her, black with temper and lack of sleep, and would borrow twenty-five cents from her. Lucky unlucky gambler Yow. What, oh, what should she do? She wandered over to the piano. "Oh, for goodness' sake," exclaimed Aunt Rachel, "let us have a little peace! What with Anty talking, talking all dinner-time, I want to read my book in peace." The Great-Aunt was offended. She became superior.

"It is well known," she said, "that the difference between civilized and uncivilized man is that civilized man converses with his meals, and uncivilized man eats his in silence. Except, I suppose, for grunting. I at least prefer intelligent conversation."

"To sit and listen to you telling us about Miss Jackson's brother's bedroom slippers several times isn't conversation," said Aunt Rachel. "I like to eat my meals in peace, they digest better. And, anyway, that's not conversation, that's mono-logue."

"Well, if you can't take your part in an intelligent conver-sation, I can't do anything for you," said Aunty, still nettled. "Where's the newspaper? Nobody speak a word, if you please." Decidedly everyone was in a bad humour.

"Rachel doesn't mean it, Topaz," said the peace-making Grandmother ("I do," said Aunt Rachel.), "but perhaps it would be nice to have a little quiet." (" 'Quiet'! Heavens above!" murmured Rose, dramatizing.) "Rose, love, what is that book you have, is it a novel?"

"Yes, Grannie," said Rose. "It is a novel."

"What is it called?" asked Grannie.

"*Poppy*, darling," said Rose.

"Is it a good book, dear?"

"Well, it's all about Africa, you know, darling," said Rose. And so it was. Dark, sensual, amorous Africa, night on the veldt, Poppy in Africa, plagued by dangerous Love.

"That's nice, dear," said Grannie, thinking, Rose knew, of

missionaries. "Where are me reading glasses, and where's the Missionary Magazine? *Now* we're all settled. Poke the fire, love."

"Well, well, *well*," exclaimed Great-Aunt Topaz in agitation, "the Duke of York!" They all looked up.

"Well what?" asked Aunt Rachel. "Oh, a cold," said Aunty indifferently, rattling the newspaper. She was sucking a plum stone.

"I *do* wish, Anty," said Aunt Rachel desperately, "that you'd put that plum stone out!"

"I'll do no such thing," said Aunty, "a plum stone gets sweeter and sweeter and – dear me! 'Arm broken in three places'!"

Everyone tried to fix their looks downwards. Grannie went on reading a report from the Congo with living interest. Aunt Rachel turned a page of *Adam Bede*, and Rose read to herself, "I am not beautiful," said Poppy, "but I have good bones." "Good bones. Have I got good bones?" thought Rose. She looked at her wrists, and saw that she had not got good bones.

"Well!" said Aunt Topaz. She sucked loudly, and they could hardly hear her words on account of the plum stone. "Did you see this?" The newspaper always excited her dreadfully. "This must be *our* Mrs. Bromley! It says –" They all looked up. Mrs. Bromley was one of their more exciting friends. "Oh no," said Aunt Topaz, "it can't be our Mrs. Bromley because this one lives in Kansas and it says 'a widow aged 64.'" Aunt Rachel glared at Aunty, but Aunty did not see. She was engrossed in the newspaper. She sucked and rattled her plum stone.

"Eh," said Grannie wistfully, "if some of you would take a little more interest in these articles from Dr. Mawdsley. They're good, so good – I can't think why you –"

"Her own mother!" exclaimed Aunty with indignation. "Listen to this!"

She rustled the paper furiously, folding it this way and that.

"Is it in Kansas, Aunty?" said Rose in a tired way, "because if it's in Kansas –"

"Yes, listen," said Aunty, "it says 'Adeline Leavenworth,

formerly of Liverpool, but now residing in New York, when asked whether – ' "

"Oh, Anty, *will* you be quiet, we've all read the paper!" said Aunt Rachel.

"A pretty funny way you read the paper," said Aunty looking at Aunt Rachel. "None of these things that are so interesting have you read a word of, it seems to me. You must read the paper very badly, it seems to me. You miss a great deal."

"Well, I miss what I want to miss and I read what I want to read," said Aunt Rachel.

"I miss nothing," said Aunty loftily. "I read everything. You never know what . . . Well!!"

For a few minutes there was silence broken only by the plum stone. Everyone read.

"Here's a letter," said Aunty, "a very good letter 'From One Who Knew Gladstone.' I wonder *who* that could be! I'm sure I could write about Gladstone. I shook hands with him when he came to Ware. Father was on the Committee. He –"

"I think I'll go to bed," said Rose getting up with "Poppy" who was being rather sensual in Africa. Rose could not concentrate. She went over to her Grandmother, stooped and kissed her.

Grannie looked up from her reading. "Going, dear? So early? Not tired, are you?" "Not exactly," said Rose. She turned to her Aunt Rachel.

"Would it be all right if I went to stay with Marcella Martin over Easter?"

"Oh . . . Easter . . ." said Aunt Rachel slowly. "I hoped you and I might go away for the week-end together. Perhaps to Chilliwack."

Rose was silent. "Well . . ." she said. She wanted to stay with Marcella.

"When you say 'week-end,'" said Grannie gently, "it grieves me a little to think that we can speak of the Lord's Day as being the week-*end*. It is the *beginning* of the week, the beginning of a new week of endeavour and of service to our Loving Heavenly Father."

"Well, Mother, the week-beginning then," said Aunt Rachel, still looking up at Rose. Her eyes were bright and a little anxious.

"This week-end habit," said Aunty coming out from behind the newspaper, "is pernicious. It's growing. Everyone says it's growing. What my father would have said! A fortnight, I always had. A fortnight once a year with Mrs. Grimwade to go to the Academy, and then a week sometimes . . . Why, off to Bermuda!"

"Who?" asked Aunt Rachel, diverted for the moment. But Aunty had moved on. "Who? Who what?" she said, "oh . . . Bermuda! Some people from Nanaimo, I believe. Walker it said."

"Anty, you are aggravating!" said Aunt Rachel passionately, but Aunty did not hear her.

"M-m-m-m-m-m," she read secretly, "well I never! Well I *never*. Oh, nothing, nothing." And she sucked her plum stone. She would take it to bed with her.

Rose went slowly upstairs with "Poppy" to Africa. She didn't want to hurt Aunt Rachel but she did want to spend the week-end with the laughing and popular Marcella.

"Did you see *this*?" said Aunty violently. "Well, of all the outrageous statements! A man in Australia . . ." and she went on reading to herself.

"Is there something wrong with Rose?" asked Grannie.

"She seems to want a change," said Rachel. "But she gets plenty of change, I'm sure, more than ever I used to get. Last Sunday Stephen and Margaret and the children came to tea and next Sunday Frank and Miranda and their children are coming to tea. And she was out with Marcella Martin on Tuesday. And last week young Mr. Anthony called."

"*I* think she's in love with him," said Aunty, looking up from her paper and sucking hard.

"She *says*," said Rachel, "that she can't bear the sight of him. She *says* she hopes he never comes to the house again, and she *says* that if he does, *she's* going to bed."

"Well, I'm sure, I tried to make it a pleasant evening, I'm sure," said Aunty. "Rose sat as mum as a mouse, and I had to talk to him all evening. He stayed and stayed. I found him a very intelligent young man though. I asked him all about his aunt at Dunstable. I know Dunstable well. Father and I were there in '84. There are some very fine gardens in Dunstable. I'm sure we were all very polite. Why, even Annie waited up to see him. What more could Rose want?"

"She says he wants to take her for a drive," said Rachel.

"A *drive*!" said the startled Grannie. "Do you mean a drive alone with a horse?" Rachel nodded.

"I call such an idea ridiculous, and very *common*," said Aunty, suddenly censorious for the fun of the thing. She resumed sucking operations and furled and unfurled her paper at arm's length. "Well, what does this say? Ostrich feathers! The Duke of Sutherland! Laughing gas! Ah, here we are. But I do call that very ridiculous."

"I don't want Rose to begin that kind of thing," said Grannie. "I hope that young man is not going to be troublesome. Oh dear, I do find it a responsibility, Rachel. . . . Well, shall we have a little game of dominoes? That would have been nicer for Rose. We are too quiet, I think sometimes, for young people . . . Three's not so good quite, but would you mind having a little game, Topaz, and Rachel?"

"Dominoes? Dominoes?" said Aunty folding the paper noisily. "Good, a little game before we go to bed. But what's this?" with rising excitement. "It says Puccini's new opera, oh no, that's in London! Well, where are the dominoes?"

And as they rattled the dominoes Rachel thought, "I believe she doesn't want to go with me. Oh no, no, it can't be that. She's all the youth I have. I've always done everything for her. She couldn't not want to go with me! How thankless, how selfish they can be!"

"*There* then," said the Grandmother, "now, who has double six?"

"I have," said Aunty with a flourish.

Upstairs Rose read, "The stars glowed like lamps in the scented African night. Poppy could almost hear . . ." Without taking her eyes off the romantic page Rose reached vaguely for another sweet. The hasty trampling steps of Aunt Topaz were heard upon the stairs. Quickly the damsel turned out the light.

NINETEEN

Saturday Morning

NOTHING exciting ever happened on Saturday afternoon, nor, come to that, on Saturday evening. Nevertheless there was a delicious air of preparation about Saturday morning. They walked quickly along the narrow dark passage that led to the bathroom (there was a lot of traffic to and from the bathroom on Saturday morning, and some impatience and knocking . . . "Anty, are you taking all the hot water?"), and as they met each other going and returning they enquired, "What are you going to do this morning?" and the news was relayed.

Grannie, having finished her breakfast, sat up in bed reading her devotional books. She looked up at her daughter Rachel. Grannie was such a pretty old lady. Later, when she got up, she wore a morning-cap of white net in Mary Stuart design. It had no streamers. From tea-time on she wore a white net cap of similar design that had two long white net streamers. But for morning wear in bed she had white lace over her head. For sleeping, she put on a tiny frilled white spotted muslin nightcap that tied under her chin. Never had she been seen bareheaded. As she sat up in her bed she wore shawls. One shawl in summer, mounting to four or even five in winter. Her Bible, her Prayer Book, her Hymn Book, a little pile of devotional books and some small religious magazines lay beside her. All these books looked alike to her granddaughter Rose. They were just "Grannie's books." But to the Grandmother they were strikingly and thrillingly various. She read these manuals to a soft cooing accompaniment of praise and sorrow. "Oh Lord." "How great indeed is Thy Mercy to us, Oh Lord." "Oh, indeed we *do*, Lord." Her soft brown eyes were dewed with tears. Her spiritual life was all-pervading. Communion with God, a great and infinitely loving Father, was the great fact of Grannie's life. Morning and evening, indeed throughout her conscious life, Grannie communed.

From this gently solemn occupation she looked up at her daughter Rachel, and wiped her misty eyes. "And what are you going to do, dear?" she asked.

"I am going to make a Milk Jelly," said Aunt Rachel rather importantly. She did well to sound important. Around this simple delicacy had grown up a legend. Rachel's Milk Jelly could have been made by anybody else, certainly by the capable Yow, who could make anything, but it was only made by Rachel. If the visiting minister came to dinner on Sunday, a Milk Jelly was considered suitable. Or perhaps on Saturday evening some young friend of Rose's might (on invitation) come to dinner, or some of the family. Then the Milk Jelly was felt to be just the thing. Grannie's sons and their exhilarating wives and children were the delight of this family. Their visits brought infinite pleasure and variety to this sedate household of three ageing ladies and one young girl.

This is the way that Aunt Rachel's Milk Jelly was made:

> 1 oz. gelatine (nearly)
> ½ lb. white sugar
> 1 breakfast cup of milk
> 2 lemons
> 2 eggs

Put the gelatine into a breakfast cup of hot water until dissolved. Add the beaten eggs and the juice and the grated rind of the lemons to the sugar. Stir all together, adding the milk last. Pour into a mould and set.

It will be seen that the Milk Jelly was not a complicated dessert. The theory that Yow could not make it was untenable. In its scrupulous simplicity it typified this innocent household. It was fresh, clean, sweet, tart, economical, clear and sparkly in places, in other places opaque, of a pale-primrose distinction, and the recipe was English. Also it had been poured into a mould and had set. Also it was controlled by Aunt Rachel.

"Oh, *here* you are, Annie. Did you now that Rachel is going to make a Milk Jelly?" enquired the lively Topaz, bouncing into the Grandmother's bedroom after a hasty pounding progress along the passage. "Oh, *there* you are, Rachel! Who is coming?"

"Well," said Rachel, "it's just In Case. And what are *you* going to do this morning, Anty?"

Aunt Topaz went to the window. "It's such a lovely day, I think I shall go for a ride," she said. "Oh, look, there's a bird! Whee-whoo! Whee-whoo! There, he answered me. Such a pretty bird! And there's Mrs. Andrews, I *do* declare! She's got a string bag! She must be going to the town! I think I shall go to the town! Yes, I shall ride to the town!"

"*Do* be careful, Topaz," begged Grannie. Only last week a young man pedalling merrily down the Long Hill in Stanley Park had lost control of his machine and with pedals whizzing madly had pitched over at the bottom of the hill and had broken both his legs. But Grannie need not have cautioned Aunt Topaz. It was unlikely that she would break a leg, as it was rarely now that she tried to mount her bicycle. She usually led it all the way to town and pushed it all the way back again. Before being taken for a walk, Aunty's good English bicycle, whose organs were laced into a kind of flat corset, and whose beautiful lamp shone, was dusted off with care. Aunty led it through the garden gate. She then gave one or two abortive hops as of one about to mount a bicycle. This was done for the benefit of anyone who might be looking out of windows. Then as if dismissing for the moment the idea of mounting, she set off, wheeling her bicycle. Thus, throughout her ride, Aunty presented to the passer-by the appearance of a lady who, owing to the heat of the day perhaps, is for the moment wheeling her bicycle which she may at any instant decide to remount. Aunty rather enjoyed "going for a ride." Many opportunities occurred to stop and chat with friends, and it would have been a great pity always to leave such a good bicycle at home. Aunt Rachel and Rose had been inclined to tease Aunty about taking her bicycle for an airing, but they realized that they would spoil things for her, so they had stopped long ago.

A door was heard to slam. There were young steps coming down the hall and Rose came quickly into the bedroom. She looked young and fresh and eager as she joined her elders. "Oh, hello, Aunt Rachel, I thought you were in the kitchen. Yow told me you were going to make a Milk Jelly. Who's coming?"

"Well, it's just In Case," said Aunt Rachel.

"Come here, love," said Grannie. She reached up to smooth Rose's billowing fair pompadour from her brow. Rose and her young friends were rather stylish and wore their hair in an extravagant fashion with a swoop up and a dip down over the brow. The brow was mostly concealed, as though it were an immodest thing, a sort of second bosom.

"Couldn't you take your hair straight back from your face, dearie? I should like it so much better."

"Oh, Grannie, it would look perfectly *awful*."

"I wish, love, that you would try not to use those slang words. 'Perfectly awful!' I know it is fashionable, but it is not pretty nor suitable," said Grannie gently. "I even heard Mrs. Bromley say the other day that she felt 'awfully well.' How could one feel awful and well at the same time?"

"*Awfully well* indeed," said Great-Aunt Topaz, "what a contradiction! But there is no need to copy Mrs. Bromley. She even shakes hands high up – like this" (and Aunty minced about the room in a burlesque of the fashionable Mrs. Bromley shaking hands), "in a most affected way. How d'you do! How d'you do!" mimicked Aunt Topaz holding up her right hand in an affected manner. "But what are *you* going to do this morning, Rose?"

Rose was readjusting her prized pompadour at Grannie's mirror and laughing at Aunty's performance. "Marcella Martin is calling for me and we are going to town."

"To the *town*, dear?" asked Grannie, "what takes you to the *town*?"

"Marcella is going to buy a new hat, and she asked me to help her." Rose tried to make this pleasant expedition sound virtuous, but the fact was that she and the beautiful Marcella were young and vain, and the nicest thing that they could possibly think of on this fine morning was to tie on their new blue veils over their fresh unpowdered complexions and their tilted sailor hats and go to town and try on something dashing.

"Poor Marcella has, of course, no mother and no aunts to help her to choose her hats, so I'm glad you are able to help her, dear." Rose knew that this speech meant "No going off with Marcella to choose *your* hats. That is Aunt Rachel's prerogative."

The door-bell rang. It was the ravishing and elegant young Marcella. Rose patted her pompadour and the front of her blouse, settled her waistline, smoothed down her hips, kissed her Grandmother, and flew for her hat, veil, and gloves. Aunty watched from the window.

"Well, they look very nice to be sure, those two tall girls, but a little inclined to attract attention. They should know by this time that no lady puts her gloves on in the street. I don't know that I quite like them walking about the town together like that, I *must* say, do you, Rachel? It may perhaps be all right in Vancouver, but in Ware I know it would never do. However. Well, I must be off," she said busily, the gay idler.

Before Aunty led her bicycle down the path and out onto the sidewalk, she tested the sweet-voiced bell which she so enjoyed ringing, and attached the little string bag to the handle-bars. It was convenient for carrying things home. You never knew what Aunt Topaz would find to buy. All sorts of things took her eye. "Anty, what *have* you bought now!" the thrifty Rachel would exclaim. And Aunty would protest.

As Great-Aunt Topaz wheeled her good bicycle up Barclay Street this bright June morning, two little boys across the road were trying out their new words. "Skidoo," they said to each other, "skidoo skidoo, twenny-three for you, twenny-three for you, skidoo skidoo skidoo." They liked saying it. The words wafted after Aunty as she pushed her bicycle up the street. "Skidoo for you, skidoo, skidoo," and fainter and fainter, "twenny-three skidoo."

Aunty smiled. "What funny little boys! Why, there's Miss Butterworth ahead, I do declare! I believe I can catch her if I try. What a *beautiful* morning!"

TWENTY

The Voice

SUDDENLY Rose surprised her grandmother and aunts by growing up and getting married. No sooner had they begun to recover from their surprise than the German armies marched unwarranted into Belgium. This event made apparent the continuous fusing of Time and Place and Effect everywhere, and people (startled and rallying from shock) in all places found that their lives were not their own and were no longer assured, because the Germans (who had not consulted them) had decided to march into Belgium. Rose's husband left, and went overseas. She, in common with other innocent dwellers on the Pacific coast and elsewhere, had long since relegated war to the old pages of history. And here was war, violent and not to be denied, taking away her husband and jouncing her out of her delightful new existence, back into the too cosy seclusion of the house with the pepper-pot, hurt and anxious. Life in the pepper-pot house thereupon seemed to close down again and settle into its old simple yet involved forms. "Something," thought Rose, "is unreal about this . . . I have had nightmares. . . ."

From August the fourth, nineteen hundred and fourteen, until November nineteen hundred and eighteen, were days of severe trial and sorrow. Each evening – in that war – the newspapers published a casualty list of the last recorded day, in round numbers. The lists would read thus – killed 385, wounded 979, missing 211.

Rachel and Rose, who had too much imagination, read

daily with unwilling eyes these dreadful lists, and felt in their bodies the loss and anguish of wives and parents. Aunt Topaz, who had almost no imagination at all, read the lists also, and to her the numbers were not people but numbers. She was not susceptible to the depression which afflicted Rachel and Rose as they unwillingly read these numbers which to them were people, and she often chided them.

"Dear me, we'll never win this war if people give way to their feelings like that! Take the long view, like me! These lists will only serve to stiffen the determination of our men!" And, noisily folding and unfolding the newspaper, "Well, what's this? 'Lady Haig visits hospital for Canadian soldiers.' Good. Good." Rachel and Rose looked at her and thought her incomprehensible. It is true that if Aunty had been allowed to march into battle with "our men" she would have marched joyously. But she could not do that. So she knitted linear miles of scarves, bought raffle tickets lavishly, and won two raffles; when she did that, you would have thought that "our men" had carried two major victories. Aunty did what she could, and as she often remarked, there is no virtue in feeling low.

One morning late on in the war Rachel went to her mother's bedside to awaken her, and her mother did not answer.

When it was made clear to them that the Grandmother would continue to lie there, unknowing, unseeing, unspeaking, for an indefinite time, Rachel and Rose divided the care of her between them. Aunt Rachel slept in the Grandmother's room and cared for her during the night. Rose did the active nursing during the day. There were times in the afternoons when both Rachel and Rose were away, and then, provided that everything had been done for her sister, Aunt Topaz took her books and her knitting and sat beside the bed. Now, when young men were lying on beds of pain, the once-beautiful Grandmother, with her long and good life behind her, lay without suffering, with eyes closed, unspeaking, cared for by the loving devotion of three women. Rose's tenderness overflowed to her Grandmother, yet she saw with envy the young men and a few young women going away to where the war was, and her mind was continually divided.

One afternoon Rose sat beside her Grandmother's bed, knitting and not knitting, wondering when the war would be over, wondering about her own engrossing problems, wondering if Aunty would come in time to let her go and play tennis, wondering where her Grandmother really was, wondering if there would be another mail today. The vagrant, unsatisfactory, familiar wonderings came and went. She was bored. She got up abruptly and went and looked out of the window of the pepper-pot.

"It's not fair," she thought rebelliously. (Rose often seemed to think "it's not fair.") "It's not fair. Look at this war. Going on and on and on. And us separated. And me *doing* nothing. It's been nearly Four years now." (Four years seemed to be all her life, then.) "Every day people getting killed and crippled. Every day people made miserable. When's it going to stop? When are they coming home? Look at Grannie. She's no more than a bit of broken china in that bed. She's never done one unkind thing in her life or said one unkind word" ("Not like me!" she thought with a gust of shame), "and she gave Aunt Topaz a home at once when she needed one and look at Aunt Topaz! Oh, she *can* be aggravating! And she gave me a home when I needed one and all the love there is, and she'd give anyone a home. And she's never bought one extra thing for herself, she gives every bit away." ("The tithe belongs to the Lord, love," Grannie had said simply. "We don't begin to give until we have given our tithe and until we do without things.") "And she hasn't any spiritual pride like she might have. She's not a bit a prig. She's just like crystal. She's got the gift of religion like Paderewski has music. I haven't got it but I can see it. And look at her!" (The girl turned again and looked at the small figure in the bed.) "Where is she? Where is she now, this minute? It's not fair. I wish the war would stop. I *do* wish . . . If Aunty doesn't come I won't get any tennis. Oh, blast." And she knelt on the window-seat of the pepper-pot and drummed on the window-ledge. She was furiously bored. Life was a mystery; so was death. She wished Aunty would come. She wanted to play tennis.

The door opened and Aunt Topaz tiptoed noisily in. "Oh, so *there* you are, Rose!" she said. "Am I late? Is everything all right? Did you feed her? I've got my books. You can go, you know."

"All right, Aunty," said Rose, gathering up her knitting. She bent over her grandmother, lifted the little mask-like head, softened the pillow, and set the inanimate head with its closed eyes gently on the pillow again. "She's all right. I gave her her milk, and Aunt Rachel or I will be back. But do keep the fire in, won't you." So often, now, Rose, the young one, felt immeasurably older than Topaz, the old one.

Rose left, and Aunty took her place beside the bed with her pile of books. She chose a book and began to read. Sometimes she looked at her sister. The Grandmother lay unmoving, as always now. Aunty went on reading until the light faded; but like an owl, if an owl could read, Aunty could read in the dusk. She did not put on the light. She read on and on.

She laid down the volume of Frazer's *Golden Bough* and took up her book of Sherlock Holmes stories. "Let me see, now," she thought, flicking the pages, "*The Speckled Band*. Yes, *The Speckled Band*." And she continued to read.

A young voice in the room called urgently, "*Rachel!*"

Topaz slowly lowered her book and looked over the top of it through the dusk at her sister. The room was still except for a dropping of ashes in the grate. The Grandmother lay as ever, eyes closed, unmoving. Her face, which was not any more the serene face of sister Annie, had gradually become a shadowed anonymous mask of extreme age and approaching death – infinitely tragic in its mystery and anonymity. Over the top of the book Topaz gazed upon the ivory shadowed mask of her dear sister.

The Grandmother's lips moved, and the voice, which was clear and young, said urgently, "*Rachel! I want you.*" The eyes remained closed. It was very strange.

"Oh, dear," said Aunty within herself, "whatever shall I do? Annie wants Rachel! If I try to tell her that Rachel isn't here and that she's coming I shall muddle things and spoil it . . . she might never speak again. . . . But *is* it Annie speaking? Oh dear, why isn't Rachel here! Whatever shall I do?"

The mysterious voice called again, "*Rachel!*"

Topaz made her decision.

"Yes . . . yes . . . Mother . . ." she faltered.

"*Did you marry him, Rachel?*" asked the voice.

"No . . . Mother . . ." said Topaz leaning forwards, her hands flat out on her open book.

"*Then are you happy?*" asked the voice.

"Yes . . . Mother . . . I am very *very* happy . . ." said Topaz, breaking into a sob. "Oh," she thought, "what is it? Oh, Annie."

"*I am very thankful, love. God bless you always, Rachel,*" said the clear mysterious voice, and ceased.

The book slid to the floor. Topaz fell on her knees beside the bed. "Annie," she said. Then "Annie, Annie!" she cried in distress. "Annie, speak to me too! It's me! It's Topaz! It's your little sister!" Aunty put her hands almost roughly on the little form and, "Annie," she cried, "won't you *please* speak to me too? Just one word to me! I'm Topaz, Topaz, calling you! Oh, Annie! I'm Topaz, the youngest one!"

"How many hours," the thought flooded through her, "Annie and I have sat and talked together, and now can't I have just one word? This is our last chance," she thought desperately.

But whatever had come had also gone away again, and the Grandmother made no sign. It was as though she had never spoken.

Topaz stood up and looked wildly round the darkened room. "What shall I say to Rachel when she comes?" Shock had given way to compassion. Pity for Rachel crowded out pity for herself and for her dear sister lying so still. Rachel was good; she was constant and devoted, and after all these years of service she had not received her mother's message and her blessing. This pity for Rachel, which was in itself an unfamiliar emotion to Topaz, wiped out her natural curiosity and quickened an unusual sensibility in her, disclosing to her a sure knowledge that something in human relations of which she was unaware, or which she was incapable of feeling, existed between Rachel and her mother. Aunty knew blindly that she had stumbled into some private ground that belonged to the reserved Rachel, and with this sensibility that was rare in her she felt that she must not disclose the whole of the strange scene, or Rachel would feel her life (which was all that she had) invaded and deprived by Aunty.

She sat down. She rehearsed herself. I shall say, "Your mother called your name, Rachel, and then she said, 'God bless you always.' . . . She called your name, and then she said, 'God bless you always.'"

Aunty did not see that the fire had gone out. She had been close to a mystery, and her mind was confused. She wiped her face with her handkerchief, pulled her skirt over her knees and tried to compose herself.

Before long the bedroom door opened and Rachel came in briskly. "What are you in the dark for? Oh, Anty, you've let the fire go out! Is everything all right?" and she turned on the light and went over to the fireplace.

Aunty sat blinking. She said rather stupidly, "Rachel, your mother spoke."

Rachel stood still. "Spoke?" she said, "Mother spoke? You're imagining, Anty!"

"Your mother spoke . . . loudly," said Aunty, nodding her head, hardly believing her own words.

"What did she say?" asked Rachel.

Aunty said her part. "She called *you*. She said your name twice and called you 'love', and then she said, 'God bless you, Rachel, always.'" Then Aunty said with a rush, "I was so surprised, I couldn't . . . but she didn't say any more after that. I *asked* her and *asked* her!" She gazed up at Rachel.

Rachel looked down for a minute at the little ivory and shadowed face which lay upon the pillow, and which was her mother who was so saintly, and was her care and so dear to her, and was soon going to leave. Then she turned and went out of the room, and down the passage, and into the little room that used to be Andrew's bedroom before he was married. She looked through the dark window at nothing but darkness, and her heart felt hot and sad and proud within her. "Oh," she thought, "It's me she asked for . . . after all these years it was me she wanted. . . ." She stood there a long time and then she went back and made up the fire.

It was weeks later that the Grandmother died. The mysterious voice was not heard again.

Rose knew that this death was not really sad, although it made every one of the family sad because they had all always loved the Grandmother ever since they could remember, and she was their mother. She knew that the right time had come; but she and Topaz and Rachel were very unreasonably sorrowful.

With the death of the Grandmother, the house with the pepper-pot tower was "broken up." Rose and her husband, now returned from the war, went to live in a house on the hill opposite a green open park. Rachel and Topaz after much discussion left on a visit to England, which cheered and excited Topaz very much. Yow became cook to a newly married couple and stole all the bride's trousseau bit by bit to give to a white lady-friend of his. He would never never have done anything like this if he had still been with the Grandmother. Yow had to go to prison in spite of everything and the white lady-friend formed other connections.

TWENTY-ONE

Apotheosis

DURING THE year after the Grandmother died, when Rachel and Topaz went to England, certain events induced a sort of catharsis in Rachel, and her small complaints and impatiences were shed away. Rachel became very gentle but Aunty did not notice this. New relations had gradually established themselves between aunt and niece, and Aunty became the leader and decider, although of course it was always upon Rachel that the brunt of arrangements fell.

The following year Rachel and Topaz left England and travelled to Italy. They went with Elise, still the unrivalled beauty of the family among young or old, and now a widow, living sometimes in Florence. Aunt Topaz often took much pleasure in recalling that forty years ago she (as chaperon) and Rachel, and the haughty beautiful young Elise had gone to Paris with Elise's father, Aunt Topaz's brother George. Topaz and the two young girls had stuffed their bustles (which were not Frenchily large enough for Paris) with newspapers, and had crackled wherever they went, until some young Frenchmen had poked them in the bustle, and Elise had flashed round and enchanted the young Frenchmen with her fury and it was worse than ever (but wherever Elise went there was this kind of trouble), and they had had to go back to the hotel with bits of newspaper sticking out of their behinds, and take it all out. What adventures for three young women from Ware in the eighteen-seventies!

This time it was Elise, still, at her age, in brilliant scornful beauty, who led, followed by Rachel (her occupation gone) and by the hastily pounding Aunt Topaz whose gait had become more vigorous in motion than ever. There were many tilts and flashes between Aunty and Elise, but there was much laughter too, as Elise had by nature and experience a disturbing sense of humour. They all laughed a good deal but, afterwards, Aunty forgot the laughing, and remembered the picture galleries, and the encounters with people, in the trains, and in the pension dining-rooms, and on excursions. They went as far as Rome.

It was about two months after their return to England that the dreadful event – too tragical to contemplate – occurred which took the life of Rachel with great suffering, and spared Aunt Topaz. The impossible had happened. Rachel had left her and was dead.

Aunty lay in her last phoenix fire of sorrow. She did not know that it was a phoenix fire which consumed her, and that, in her own remarkable way, she would arise from this fire and become more resilient, more strong, impervious to grief and even to love, and that now, at the age of seventy-five, she was entering into her own little apotheosis, and nothing mortal, not even death itself, would be able to move her or hurt her any more. And so it was that one day, as she uttered her constant and touching cry, "However can I live without her? Oh, if only Rachel were here to scold me! Why wasn't I taken too? I wish I was dead. Oh, Rachel, Rachel, I am a poor old woman and I shouldn't be here," she suddenly thought with surprise, "That isn't true! I'm only pretending now! I am not a poor old woman at all! I'm not afraid of anything!" It was as when, after a dire illness which might have reduced her to the lowest in human weakness and dependence, and which might have continued through weeks of disheartening and uncertain convalescence, a day had come in spring and she had looked at the poignant world of buds and birds and sky (which appeared somehow different) and felt, with life in her body and in her face, "I am better! Oh, I am well again!" So it was with Great-Aunt Topaz after her weeks in the valley of the shadow of Rachel's sudden and violent death. She looked around her with interest, and was immune for evermore from chance and mischance. And it was at this moment that a large square envelope arrived, with a crown on the back of it, and Aunty was commanded to go to Buckingham Palace to see the Queen. Topaz instinctively turned at once to Rachel, but Rachel was not there.

Uncle John hurried up to London. Here he was, a Justice of the Peace, and County Councillor, a sitter on Boards of Directors, an industrious and valuable public servant, dropping at once his multiple activities and coming to the help of his inexperienced sister Topaz in London. "I will manage the whole affair. I shall take charge." Aunty moved from the nursing home where she had been taken after Rachel's death, to a repulsively respectable hotel in Bloomsbury which you would really think that Uncle John owned, by the way he treated it. You could use the old-fashioned phrase "he patronized that hotel," because Uncle John patronized the hotel and everyone in it, and began by patronizing Aunt Topaz. He found that although he had patronized her, off and on, for seventy-five years, Aunty was no longer patronizable, and this disconcerted him.

Uncle John at the age of seventy-eight was still a handsome man whose trouble was that he had always looked like an earl, much more like an earl than earls do, and was thus usually taken for one when in places frequented by earls, and that he had been called Giovanni ever since he was twenty. He had a habit of fluttering his eyelids, which looked sublime and put one a little in one's place. At concerts, before taking his seat, he would stand and turn round (sometimes in an opera cape) and, gazing about him with pure delight and looking very distinguished, would, across invisible nobodies, discover a friend and would exclaim, "Ah, do I see my dear old friend Forsyth?" These attributes caused affectionate admiration, pleasure, and amusement among acquaintances, and among coarse people something like fury. He had an undeniably kind heart as many in need could testify, and he came up to London well equipped in every possible way to help his poor sister – who had recently suffered so frightful a bereavement and had, herself, barely escaped the grave – through the overwhelming emergency of going to Buckingham Palace.

After four or five days of coping with Aunty, Uncle felt that something had become unmanageable; but his mind was not supple enough to understand that his sister could no longer be coped with, and so he went on trying.

"I will order a good carriage, Topaz," said Uncle John, "and *I* will take you to Buckingham Palace myself. It would not be suitable for you to go without an escort, and I had better go in with you to see the Queen. I could tell you what to do." Aunty opened her mouth and shut it again. She had no intention of giving John the glory. Uncle John knew the idiosyncrasies of a man's wardrobe and was always well dressed and well groomed, but he did not know about the details of women's dress and prayed that Topaz would look "right" for this grand occasion, for she often looked "wrong."

On the great morning, Aunt Topaz emerged jangling from her bedroom, looking right and also looking wrong. Rachel would have curbed her here and there, especially in the matter of necklaces and bracelets to which Aunty was addicted. However, Aunty looked nice in her own particular unfashionable yet individual way, and she was very happy indeed. She stopped each chambermaid whom she met, and announced (because she couldn't help it and because such an announcement was bound to give them pleasure), "And where do you suppose I am going? You'd never guess! I'm going to Buckingham Palace! There! I knew you'd be surprised!" And the chambermaids regarded this happy old lady prancing along the hall with a warming of heart or with disbelief.

"Ah, John, so *there* you are!" exclaimed Aunty, radiant, "what a beautiful carriage! Oh dear, I haven't got me other little bag with me other hanky! Well, this will do! How do you do, how do you do," to the doorman, "where d'you suppose I'm going? I'm going to Buckingham Palace!" And to the cabby, "Ah, what a beautiful day! I'm sure it isn't every day you drive someone to Buckingham Palace, is it!" And bent down and laboured happily into the cab.

All this effervescence disturbed and annoyed Uncle John;

in fact the past few days had made him very nervous, as Aunty had caused him, in his passion for correct behaviour, to suffer. He recalled their Italian journey together. Association with Topaz would be a trial, he felt, in public, to any man of position. No longer could he thunder, "Topaz, be silent! May I not be permitted to speak at my own table?" for several tries of this sort of thing had been easily squashed by his sister.

"I do wish, Topaz," he said in a pained way as he settled himself beside her on the carriage seat, putting his stick between his knees and leaning upon it in an elegant manner, "that you would try to control yourself, and – er, *conform* a little. You really sound very Colonial sometimes."

Aunty flew to battle. Her words leapt like little jangling jaguars onto Brother John.

"'Colonial!'" she said sarcastically, "'Colonial!' You do indeed make me laugh, John. You're too conventional to breathe. 'Colonial!' You don't know what the word means! You say the word as if it were something to be ashamed of! Well, it isn't. I'm Colonial and I'm proud of it."

"I only –" began Uncle John.

"Yes you did," continued Aunt Topaz. "You have no sense of history, that's what's the matter with *you*! When colonists left Greece and colonized every corner of the Mediterranean" (Aunty flung out her arms and batted Uncle John on the prince-nez with a bag flying from her wrist) "you don't suppose those colonists were ashamed of the word 'colonial'? No, indeed, it was their pride . . ."

"I only –" said Uncle John.

"And," Aunty went on, giving her necklaces a toss (the carriage rolled pleasantly along) "those who left this country as colonists, and established colonies in the New World have a deal more to be proud of than you who stayed at home and were comfortable . . . a deal too comfortable, I don't mind telling you! It's a word that anyone should cherish and be proud of if they've any sense of history at all, whether they stayed here in comfort or are descendants of those colonists who so nobly landed on those rugged shores." Aunty blew a gust of breath. She had become an orator. She trumpeted at her brother who sat with immaculately gloved hands on the silver head of his walking-stick, his handsome face with its pince-nez and its Van Dyck beard looking straight ahead like that of a well-bred martyr. "If they haven't any sense of history," Topaz continued, "I'm sorry for them and I'm sorry for *you*, but I can't do anything about it." You would have thought that Aunty had hewn down the forest and raised the home and killed the wolves and planted the garden herself.

"My dear Topaz . . ." said Uncle John in a tone of defence, "I only –"

"That will do, John," said Aunty grandly and kindly. After all, who was going to Buckingham Palace, she or John? "Well, look at all the people, I do declare. *Wouldn't* they all be surprised if they knew that we were going to Buckingham Palace!" Aunty had indeed won, because they were back exactly where they had started the argument, and not a word from Brother John.

When the tiff had subsided, Great-Uncle John and Great-Aunt Topaz, seeming to any observer to be an old gentleman and an old lady (although, of course, they were actually only little John Edgeworth and his sister Topaz, grown old), rolled along in the nice carriage, looking out at the London crowds and buildings, all familiar to John but always fresh to Topaz. Topaz rolled along in the heaven of happiness reserved for one specially commanded to Buckingham Palace, but Uncle John was only in the second-class heaven reserved for the relations.

"It must have been very funny," laughed Aunt Topaz to Miranda when she was back in Vancouver a few months later. "I didn't notice it at the time because I was very excited – oh yes, very excited indeed – but when John said to the nice young man in a lordly way, '*I* will escort my sister to see Her Majesty!' I don't remember what happened but the nice young man was very polite and the next thing I knew John was left sitting in a beautiful room, waiting, you know, and I was walking with the nice young man along wide corridors with fine carpets on, oh very fine carpets, and large paintings on the walls. John *was* sneaped, I can tell you," said Aunty retrospectively and very much pleased. "John had always been so important and a J.P. and a County Councillor and exactly like a lord to look at, and *he* had to wait! And me, *I*, his little sister that many's the time he'd sneaped, walking with this handsome young man all along those corridors – we *did* have a nice talk – and going to see the Queen."

Aunty stopped for a moment and savoured her memories. Miranda looked at Aunty whom she had known so long – although she was only a niece-in-law – and pictured, smiling to herself, the figure of Aunty pounding busily down the palace halls, all her necklaces dancing, the pearls, the amethysts, the jet, and perhaps the amber underneath for luck, and catching up with and passing and falling behind the escorting young man, telling him meanwhile about herself, about Vancouver, and that she remembered seeing the great exhibition of Winterhalters in 1873 – " . . . that *is* a Winterhalter, I think!" as she pointed here and there at a Royal portrait with her best walking-stick.

"And when we got to the door of the large drawing-room – oh, tremendous – me knees trembled and I thought they wouldn't support me, and there was the Queen standing, oh such a long way off it seemed to me, all in blue and she had on those blue stones – sapphires they were" (Aunty had telescopic vision) "she looked *beautiful* and I thought, oh dear me, how shall I ever get there, and I went forward, and would you believe it, the Queen came forward to meet me! And she took my hand and led me to a chair and sat down in front of me and said (and I thought to meself, this is *The Queen* speaking to me, Queen of Great Britain and Ireland and of the Dominions Overseas), yes, she said, 'Now, Miss Edgeworth, we have just half an hour and then the American Ambassador is coming. Tell me all about Vancouver. I remember how beautiful it was. I suppose the city has grown out of recognition.' And she put me at me ease and I told her all about you, Miranda, ("Oh my goodness!" thought Miranda) "and about Rose, and Rose marrying Charles, and Charles coming back from the war, and about the Boys and all about the children, and about everybody, and Annie and Rachel, of course. Oh, Her Majesty *was* interested!"

"I'm sure she was!" said Miranda politely.

"And then," said Aunty, "it seemed like two minutes and I had a deal more to say" (now that Topaz was old, she used old colloquialisms and Staffordshireisms, "jannock" she would say for "kind and pleasant"), "and Her Majesty was very jannock with me, and then she told me that the half-hour was gone and she must receive the Ambassador, and she got up and, of course, I got to me feet too, and I suddenly remembered again where I was at the end of that long room, and how would I get to that door, backing all the way as John had told me, and I would bump into the furniture and me knees turned to water and I thought oh dear. But the Queen didn't let me do it. She walked all the way down the room with me to the door and made it oh so easy and then she stopped and picked up this photograph – she'd written her name on it – and said, 'I should like you to have this, Miss Edgeworth,' – and here it is! Look!" said Aunty in effulgence of pride.

Miranda took up the picture of the Queen, who stood superbly dressed for an occasion of State, wearing a small diamond crown, and jewels, and orders. Her eyes looked steadily out of the photograph, the eyes of a woman who could bear pomps, and cares, and dignities, and the anxieties of a wife and of a mother; and could be an example to her people; and could keep her own counsel; and could summon to her an old woman who, six thousand miles away, had served, a little, the Queen's poor people of London, over a long period of years; and she could crown this old lady's life, and walk with her to a door, and send her away with undying happiness. This was the photograph of Queen Mary that Miranda now held in her hand and looked at, thinking of these things.

"And John," laughed Aunty, "poor John! I think he enjoyed himself after he got over feeling sneaped. When we drove away in the carriage – because we kept the carriage waiting, John said spare no expense – and after I had told him all about the interview as we were driving back to the hotel,

John said, 'I will admit to you, Topaz, that I felt a certain pang of envy. But that is gone, and I can assure you of my deep satisfaction for you.' John was really very good," Aunty said kindly, "I can see him now," and she sat back and closed her eyes in a lofty manner and regarded inwardly that memorable day.

Now, for the first time in her life, Aunty had her own home. She reigned for the first time alone, and in her own apartment. And yet not alone, for there was a constant struggle for mastery with her companion Mme Brizard. Life was always exciting. Aunty enjoyed her duels with Mme Brizard, because she always felt that she (Aunty) won, and because she was fond of Mme Brizard as a worthy friend and adversary, and because Mme Brizard was related to a Cabinet Minister.

Mme Brizard she would introduce thus. "This is Mme Brizard . . . my Companion . . . ma dame de compagnie," airily, "English. Of very good family. Well connected. Sometimes speaks French." And Aunty would flip an explanatory hand as if Mme Brizard were a waxwork, and then would hiss whisperingly in parenthesis, "Her husband was French, you see, poor man!" Why Aunty was sorry for M. Brizard was because he was dead, not because he was French. She had a high opinion of the French, and felt that the inclusion of even an imitation Frenchwoman in her household conferred on her – Topaz – a good deal of chic. "Mme Brizard is the sister-in-law of a Cabinet Minister," Aunty (vague as to whose Cabinet) continues ineffably, "and comes from West Africa."

"Argentine, Argentine, Miss Edgeworth," protests Mme Brizard.

"Very well then, the Argentine, if you insist," says Aunty in a fatigued manner, closing her eyes, and putting Mme Brizard almost in the wrong. This she could do quite unfairly whenever she chose, simply by closing her eyes, although she had noisier methods. Mme Brizard seemed to admire Aunty's adroitness, as one would say "Ts – ts! Well, well! Behold!" In fact, each admired the other – a sound basis. . . . Mme Brizard, alternating between exasperation and devotion, managed Aunty very well.

Topaz spoke often of Rachel. Then, as time went on – you know how it is – her memory reverted and reverted until she spoke very seldom of Rachel, and more of the friends of the moment or of the friends of her youth.

TWENTY-TWO

Aunty spends the Day

GREAT-AUNT Topaz now ruled from her eyrie in the tall apartment house over her whole world, which was small; yet she did not know that it was small, for it extended as far as her interested vision could reach. She not only ruled her own world, but she took it, and tossed it off like a drink, and it intoxicated her, and, renewed daily, it intoxicated her again. Around and beyond her spun the barren and often silly 'twenties. She knew little enough about them; but that she could amble with the times was evident as, laughing, she passed cigarettes to her younger great-nieces Carlotta, Helen, Peggy, Isabel, and Anne. Ten years before, she would as soon have passed them strychnine. She ran about her world in her relatives' cars or in taxis. The proud and obstinate bicycle had long since been sold at a loss after many years of monastic retirement in a shed, and Aunty's age and unsure bounce prohibited the use of street-cars. Each week rose to two peaks of happy personal excitement (what more can one wish for at eighty? At eighty-five? At ninety? – her Sunday visit to one of her nephews and their spreading families, and the regular Friday afternoon visit to Rose. This Friday visit, originally scheduled for early afternoon, soon began at mid-morning. Mme Brizard, fighting a losing battle and urged on by Aunty since daybreak ("Now then, this is the day I go to Mrs. Forrest's, you know!"), compromised on ten-thirty, and so did Rose. All the preparations, dispute, and commotion involved, added the pinch of conflict required by Aunty to season her day and make it perfect. She arrived alone each Friday morning in the captious good humour of a ruffled and recent victor.

Rose hears her Great-Aunt mounting the front steps and runs to receive her multiple burden. Great-Aunt Topaz, small, resolute and aged, thunders up the steps on large and important feet. This grand and ancient woman carries a parasol ("it belonged to Elijah's wife"), a walking-stick, a large chintz bag, a small leather bag, and a tiny black silk bag. She carries a muff of grey fur. Protruding from the largest bag, which contains books, papers, shawls, slippers, and sweets, is a garden hat trimmed with a mauve ostrich feather. In Case. She talks as she pounds resolutely up the steps. A taxi-man dodges anxiously behind her with a rug and an umbrella.

Rose begins, "Oh, Aunty, I'm so sorry, I didn't hear the taxi . . ." but Aunt Topaz is speaking and does not listen. She seldom listens. She enjoys speaking. She enters the front door. She fills the house. She casts everything down.

"Well," says Aunt Topaz in a powerful and carrying voice, "so here we are. Friday again. I've had some very interesting letters this week . . . catch . . ." (the letters fall like snow) "a very good letter from Tilly-and-Sassy, and one from Miss Peacock and one from Miss Pocock, and one from Elise who seems to be very much annoyed, and, oh, such a good one from Sam Skadding, very fond of me is Sam Skadding. He's an orphan, you know, he's had that school in Surrey for over forty years."

"He can't be a very young orphan," suggests Rose, helping Aunty off with her coat and hat.

"Young? Of course he's young. He's my second cousin. He can't be more than fifty . . . sixty . . . well, seventy years old." At what age does one cease to be an orphan? wonders Rose, who, although an orphan at the age of eight, hasn't felt like one for years and years. This orphan is also a widower, it appears, and has a long life-history. So have all his relations. Up wag the dogs. "Oh, doggie, *there* you are! Come and be scratched. You see, they like to be scratched. What? Lunch? Out of the way, doggie, out of the way. I want to wash me hands."

The bathroom door closes on Aunt Topaz. Peace descends upon the house. Then the door opens. Aunt Topaz comes out. She rubs her hands vigorously, refreshed. Bracelets jangle. Necklaces of jet become entangled in necklaces of gold, of amber, of pearls. She wears five necklaces. She is small, she is shrinking in size, but she fills the house from the front door to the back.

"There then," continues Aunt Topaz, "give me me stick. Well," sinking heavily into a dining-room chair and dropping some bags, "it's nice to be here again, I'm sure. You haven't told me what you've been doing since last Friday. Oh, been in bed with a cold. You should be like me. I'm never ill. Well, I think I had a headache once, but I'm not sure, and here I am over eighty and I can read and sew without glasses! Oh, what's this? Soup! Mushroom soup! Good! Good!" says Aunt Topaz, stirring her soup with relish. "Do you know Bishop Empey? A fine old man Bishop Empey. My age. Walks with a stick. Well, he came to see me yesterday, and he came in and said, 'Ah, Miss Edgeworth!' and I held out me hand and Bishop Empey took it and he shut his eyes and raised his other hand and began giving me a sort of introduction to God, and he went on praying over me hand . . . you know the sort of thing . . . and I looked at Mme Brizard and I began to laugh, and I covered me face with me other hand," and Great-Aunt Topaz spreads her gemmed and crooked fingers over her face and looks wickedly through her fingers, gulping with laughter (she has not tasted her soup yet) "and the good man thought I was weeping and he went on praying all the more. And I wrenched me hand free and I *ran* along the hall," picture to yourself Aunt Topaz's frail but heavy flight, "and rushed into me bedroom and flung meself upon me bed and laughed into me pillow. And when I'd got over it and wiped me eyes I went back. And Bishop Empey thought I'd been overcome with emotion and weeping in me bedroom. Oh, he *was* pleased!"

She stirs her soup. "What do you say? Cold? I like it cold. How you *do* gobble your food, to be sure! No wonder you're not strong. What do you say?" stirring harder than ever, "I can't hear what you say. I never could endure to sit silent at a meal. It's uncivilized to sit mum as a mouse. Don't hurry me. I can't bear to be hurried at me meals."

Rose continues to sit with a hostess expression above her long-emptied soup-plate while Aunty continues to pour out the racier news of the week. Then, piteously, "I can't eat all this soup. I'll just have a bitta cheese. Oh, but oysters! . . . good! . . . Did you know that oysters are an aphrodisiac? Oh yes, indeed. It's well known. What big oysters! Charles Dickens said he'd as soon eat a baby as one of these large oysters!" She prods her oysters.

Aunty talks of Charles Dickens and the joy of reading the instalments of his stories as they came out in *Household Words* and *All the Year Round*. She continues prodding her oysters. They are perforated, but not eaten. Information about Dickens and his family. Information about Thackeray and his family. Trollope . . . "*Please*, Aunty . . . !" implores Rose. "*Do* eat your lunch!"

"These oysters are too big," Aunt Topaz says plaintively. "Rhubarb? Well, eat your rhubarb then. It's good for the blood, doctors say. No, my blood's all right. Whatever does Anna want now? To clear away? Well, then, clear away, Anna! Oh, a cup of tea. Yes, I'd rather have it in the drawing-room. I'll take me cheese with me." Commotion of removal. Aunty. Stick. Bags. Cheese. Tea. Aunty continues in the drawing-room.

"A fire! That's nice. Well, and what have you been doing with yourself? I haven't heard a word of what you've been doing. You must have been doing *something*. You should be more lively, Rose, more interested in everything. Look at me! Always interested, never dull! Not a word have you said all lunch-time –"

"But, Aunty –" breaks in Rose.

"Don't argue," kindly, "it doesn't suit you to argue. The

fact is you smoke too much. Look at you now, lolling in an armchair half naked and smoking a cigar! What your Grandmother would have said!"

This time Rose really exerts herself (and the shade of her Great-Uncle John thunders within her, "Let me speak! Be silent, Topaz! May I not be permitted to express myself in my own house?") "*This*," she says coldly, "is a tennis dress, as worn by everyone who plays tennis, and I warn you I'm going next door to play tennis in a few minutes. And this isn't a cigar, it's a cigarette. You know that very well, you're just being naughty. I am *not* half naked and I am *not* smoking a cigar!"

Wasted, wasted, for Aunty is not listening; she has moved on. "You remember your uncle's old friend Mr. Pontifex with a moustache? I saw him last week at Miranda's. Has a tear duct. Oh, a very handsome man! And he said, 'Is it true that you are still Miss Edgeworth?' Oh, very gallant. He thought I had married, of course. So I told him I was indeed Miss Edgeworth, but I was never very still! How Miranda laughed! You should take more notice, Rose. You're inclined to sit mum as a mouse." Aunty is fond of Rose in a way; but this great-niece whom she has known through childhood has, she feels, defied her and nature by growing up and becoming a married woman and running a house, and this irks Aunty just a little. Rose suggests a nap, a little sleep for Aunty, as she, Rose, is going to play tennis for one hour by the clock.

"Do I want a sleep after me lunch? No, I don't want a sleep. And who have you asked for tea?" Autocratically. "Who? Gray? Gray? What Gray? I don't know any Gray. Oh, GRAHAM. Yes, and a very pretty woman, but her husband is that young man who presumed to speak in that way of Gladstone in this house. I curbed me temper, I curbed me temper, but I told him a few things and I could have said a many more. Oh, several coming in to tea! Good! I brought me birthday-book In Case. It's almost full now. Many's the great name I've got in me birthday-book. There's Lord and Lady Aberdeen and Gladstone himself and Rudyard Kipling and his father and mother, and the Archbishop of Canterbury, and Sir Garnet

Wolseley, and Several Suicides. Oh, I must have at least six suicides now," says Aunty, very proud. "There was that poor young man who . . . what? Well, go, then, go! Charm, charm! Sparkle, sparkle! Scintillate, scintillate! I shall play Beethoven." And she does, resoundingly.

It is half-past nine. The master of the house sits reading by the fire. Dinner is just over, a protracted affair, but shorter than lunch owing to ruthlessness on the part of Rose. Aunty has enjoyed her audience and her dinner. The afternoon tea-party has been discussed in all its implications. Some criticism has been spoken and some praise. Old tales have been retold. Always with Aunty one thing leads to another and everything is new under the sun.

And now this pleasant dinner is over and the master of the house sits reading by the fire. Aunty admires him, the man, the nephew-by-marriage, the surprising husband of the great-niece to whom she has so long been accustomed. "How you came to get such a good husband *I* can't imagine!" He treats Aunty with the right blend of indulgence and authority. He admires her, and she becomes more and more entertaining. She becomes intoxicated with her success and with her own wit and funniness. He teases her. He gives her all his flattering attention, and then he suddenly withdraws into his own mind and into his own books as if she did not exist. What a phenomenon! He sits there reading and note-taking, and she does not exist! She is in the room, racy, amusing, important, but she does not even fret the outside edge of his consciousness! This phenomenon, so unusual in Aunty's experience, does not annoy her. It pleases her; she admires it. Rose has for some reason gone quiet. She is knitting. She is inattentive. Aunty, a reader with taste and discrimination, makes choice from the shelves of books to take home with her. Gibbon, Rabelais. A gap here. A gap there. Book leans upon book. The books will return littered with Aunty's marginal notes ("Yes, I, too, remember that magnificent scene, because Father and I were there in 1874. We . . .")

Elusive, unheard, some significant moment of Time has just struck. She will go home.

Tossing herself into a chair, with books slipping to the floor from her tiny lap, Aunty leans back with the fatigued air of one who is being detained against her will. She closes her eyes, but she continues speaking with gusto, a recapitulation. "Well, a very pleasant day, I'm sure, though I must say that once I got into a fine bad temper with your wife, Charles! But I enjoyed it, I enjoyed it. I *think*," with eyes closed and with the infinitely grand air that she can summon, "I think those young people were all very much interested in all I had to tell them at tea-time, very nice people. But," a little aggrieved, "it's time you took me home, you know. I'm not young, you know. I can't stay up talking till all hours the way you do, you know. Where are me things?" And Aunty, ancient, important, a delight and disturbance to her family, still talking, goes home.

The day is over. The earth turns, and seven times turning brings Friday again. The weeks hasten by. Where are the weeks? They are lost in the years. Aunty's long life inscribes no sweeping curves upon the moving curtain of Time. She inscribes no significant design. Just small bright dots of colour, sparkling dots of life.

Gusto

AUNTY AND Mme Brizard continue to live together in the tall apartment house overlooking the mountains. Great-Aunt Topaz looks frail but she has bursts of unsurpassed energy. Her visits to the family are intermittent now but still she dearly loves a party.

A niece has come to see her. Aunty is sitting up in bed vigorous, vibrating, still talking. She has talked for ninety years. She is no longer John's youngest sister ("*Silence*, Topaz! Let me speak. May I not speak in my own house?") She is the Great-Aunt. She is the Great-Great-Aunt. She is important. She sits up in bed mourning for her King. She wears a black lace cap, crooked; she wears a mauve dressing-jacket and a black woollen shawl; she wears jet bracelets and necklaces and a mourning ring of hair. Mourning mitigates her grief. She enjoys her mourning. She sees herself, pathetic, superb, ancient, historic, suitably mourning for her King. "I am mourning, you see!" she says with dignified satisfaction. She is brilliant and autocratic and her family is important too because it is her Family and has its place in her life like Monday, Tuesday, Wednesday. She is no longer just the beloved Mrs. Hastings' unmarried sister or Rachel's aunt. She is listened to and admired. "Oh, Miss Edgeworth, how wonderful you are!" She knew Rudyard Kipling and his parents (whom she introduced to each other at a "Book-Picnic" at Rudyard Lake). She nearly knew all the Pre-Raphaelite Brotherhood. She still remembers the death of the Duke of

Wellington. ("Pull down the blinds, Topaz, the great Duke is dead.") As she talks she moves her head bowingly and with vigour. She gesticulates with her little hands, the fingers spread, crooked with age, loaded with rings. She has become very small. She closes her eyes as she talks, which conveys a vast importance. She does not flutter her eyelids like Uncle John. She closes them with an air. She can, and does, say what she will. Life is a party and she is at the party. She is the guest of honour. She is sitting up in bed surrounded by books, newspapers, woolwork, apples, and letters. She is recounting an episode to the visiting niece.

"Yes, wasn't it exciting, Georgia? But life *is* very exciting. I'm really in a vortex," says this small being who now spends four-fifths of her life against her pillows. "Something happening all the time . . . look. I found these two old letters today, one from Miss Peacock and one from Miss Pocock."

"What a coincidence!" murmurs the visiting niece.

"Not a coincidence at all. What's coincidence about it?"

"Well, I mean the similarity of the names – Peacock and Pocock," explains the niece.

"They're not similar at all, Miss Peacock was Miss Peacock and Miss Pocock was Miss Pocock. They're not in the least alike," says Aunty, who is not sensitive to the queer tricks played by sound, and does not know that to her nephews and nieces who never saw Miss Peacock or Miss Pocock, Miss Peacock is usually Miss Pocock, and Miss Pocock is Miss Peacock. "Yes . . . Mme Brizard? What is it . . . what is it? She wants something. Whatever does she want? To dinner? Mrs. Forrest? When? When? Tonight? Oh, good, good, I'll wear me black lace. Or shall I wear me crimson velvet? Because, you see, with the crimson velvet I can wear me garnets and – Mme Brizard, Mme Brizard, get out me crimson velvet, I want to have a look at it. And get out me old purple. I can mourn in that very nicely. I want to have a look at that too. Out to dinner and ME ninety-three. You know Mr. Jordan? Well, he's an old rip, that's what he is." "Old rip" is a new word for Aunty, but she likes it. "I was getting into me taxi yesterday with Mme Brizard and he came up. We were going

for a little drive in Stanley Park. Have you been in the Park
lately? Oh, beautiful, beautiful. Such vistas. The flowers are
beautiful and *such* a lot of people. And Mr. Jordan came up
and swept off his hat and was full of admiration at me going
for a drive and not looking me age. And I said, 'Well, I'm over
ninety.' And," says Aunty, flinging her arms wide in mocking
imitation of the admiring Mr. Jordan and tossing her head
with scorn, "he professed to *swoon* with surprise, he professed
to *swoon*, the old rip. Did I tell you that I'm going to have me
miniature painted? Oh yes. Well, I am. Why don't you have
your miniature painted? What? Too expensive! Nonsense,
that's just an excuse. Nose? What's wrong with your nose?
Too big for a miniature you say? Of course it's not too big.
Why, does it feel too big *on*? Oh, here's me crimson dress.
And bring out the purple!"

It is seven o'clock. Rose and Aunty's friend Miss English
sit talking in the drawing-room. Sounds are heard of Aunty
approaching. Commotion. Talking. The front door bursts
open. Aunty enters, supported by the overladen Mme Brizard.

"Well, here we are," announces Aunty agreeably. "Oh, so
there you are, Miss English, in that nice dress too. It *is* a nice
dress. Well, Rose, have I seen that before? What a many
dresses you do have to be sure. I *told* you," addressing Mme
Brizard vehemently, "I *told* you I should have put on me black
lace. Well, where's Charles? Late? He often seems to be late!
What? Gone to Victoria? I made sure Charles would be here.
Whatever did you want to ask us for when Charles isn't here?
Well, then, who *is* coming? What men, I mean? WHAT, NO
MEN? I thought we were going to have a right good time!"

Aunty is escorted to the bedroom still talking. She is not
pleased. Mme Brizard will take off her things. Sounds of
argument are heard from the bedroom.

Aunty hastens back into the drawing-room leaning on her
stick. Mme Brizard follows her. Aunty is not handsome but
she looks very interesting in her purple velvet, her black lace
cap, and a great sparkle of jewelry. Her jewelry makes more
noise than most jewelry. She is still speaking. She has not
ceased speaking.

"Mme Brizard calls this a party. Well, I don't. Very nice, I'm sure," says this ancient and privileged woman, "but not a party. Oh, so here's Anna with something. How are you, Anna? Oh, what a pretty tray! Well, Anna, what's this you've got?"

"Cocktails, Miss Edgeworth," murmurs Anna politely.

"Cocktails indeed!" says Aunty. She looks superbly around the man-less room. She looks lightly upon the three laughing ladies. "Cocktails indeed. *I'd* call them hen-tails. Here, give me one."

TWENTY-FOUR

The 'Thirties

TOPAZ HAS for the last time left Vancouver for her summer holiday, but, of course, she does not know this. We do not know these things. Henceforward she will stay at home.

"Yes, indeed. Victoria is very nice. I always like a cathedral city. But altogether too much bridge. Bridge at that little hotel all day long. No intelligent conversation." Rose pictures the bridge players massed for defence, formed four-square against the prowling Topaz who seethes with conversation. "And tea at the Empress! You know that fine hotel? A very fine foyer; it is called a Rotunda, oh very long, and at each end a portrait, one of the King and one of the Queen. . . ." Rose has heard the story from a friend at the hotel. . . .

Aunt Topaz, weary of waiting for her tea, looks with sparkling green eyes around the rotunda. American visitors sit on chairs and loll back on chesterfields. So do Canadian visitors. No doubt they are all divided into the two classes of persons who sit in hotel lobbies – those unutterably bored persons who detest sitting in hotel lobbies but for some reason have to, and those who enjoy it. The rotunda is quiet, except for a slight busyness of waiters arranging with their peculiar deft swish and grace the afternoon-tea tables. The visitors follow the movement of the waiters with glazed eyes. Aunty does not look glazed; she is spoiling for commotion. She spies the portrait of the King. She spies the portrait of the Queen.

Before Mme Brizard can put out a detaining hand, Aunty is in the middle of the floor, and with her nimble yet pounding gait is hastening down the long expanse between the visitors sitting on chairs, toward the King, all her necklaces dancing. By the time she reaches the portrait of the King, every eye has become unglazed and has turned on Aunty, who drops a deep curtsy to the portrait, wobbling a little, and says for the benefit of those near at hand, "I bow to my King!" Then she turns, and pounds happily down the long distance of the rotunda, dodging and being dodged by waiters. The hotel visitors have come alive, and watch her heavy dancing progress with interest. Will she do it again? Aunty reaches the portrait of the Queen. Again she curtsies, saying in a semi-religious way for the benefit of those near at hand, "I bow to my Queen!" Having stirred up a bit of excitement and brought some action into the rotunda, she returns delighted to the suffused Mme Brizard, who, although the relative of a Cabinet Minister, dares not risk scolding her in public, for Aunty could give back handsomely.

"There, that woke them up a bit," says the aged Topaz, laughing and pleased. "Where's me tea? . . ." Aunty feels sublime for days afterwards and does not very much mind that Mme Brizard refuses to take her to the Empress Hotel again for tea.

That is one of the last sallies of Topaz, whose world now contracts to her apartment and to her pouring flood of memories. Vague news of an outside world comes in. She reads the newspaper, exclaiming. What is this of young men who ride up and down the country on freight cars; who live in jungles; who have no work, no money, no food; who cannot hope to have a wife, nor a home, nor a family; to whom all legitimate ambitions are closed? ("There should be someone like Gladstone!") The young men ride from east to west and west to east on the freight cars, and drop off at cities and walk to people's doors and ask for work or food. Where do they spend the night? They are baffled. They have no past and they certainly have no present, and cannot see a future; neither can the housewives who say regretfully, "I have no work for you, but would you like some lunch?" Yes, the young men would like some lunch, but a lunch does not last long, and they would rather have a job. There are no jobs.

A rehearsal is being arranged in Europe. There will be something to do in Europe and Asia and Africa and on some of the oceans and rivers and in the sky. It appears that things are being planned. The patterns on the curtain of Time are confused, but we are aware of something alarming which is about to begin.

TWENTY-FIVE

The Buried Life

ROSE ENTERED Aunty's bedroom with a guilty feeling. Too long had passed since she had visited Aunt Topaz; but Aunty never showed resentment at this, however much she might, a few minutes later, provoke and enjoy a good tiff with you. She looked up from her book, and her face lighted with the particularly well-mannered winning look which always accompanied her greetings, which were never dull. Aunty was becoming rather attached to Rose, whom she had regarded until lately as still a person of fourteen who had accidentally been married and had no real status. She had suddenly begun to regard Rose as an adult and a genuine married person, indeed as a contemporary, but above all as a surviving symbol of Annie and Rachel. "What a many years of memory we share!" And it was true.

"So *there* you are!" she exclaimed joyously. "You're just in time to hear something. Listen to this! It's poetry. You like poetry, you know," as if this were Rose's odd peculiarity. And she read aloud from the book which she held in her left hand. She read in a very special voice:

> "*The unplumb'd, salt, estranging sea.*"

And again, more slowly:

> "*The unplumb'd, salt, estranging sea.*"

"Mrs. Porter used to say," said Aunty, "that there was

everything that anyone could think, know, or say about the sea in that line. And many's the time I've shaken the hand that wrote that line! He used to come to our house to dinner whenever he came to Ware, and very good he was to me once when he came to dinner. Matthew Arnold, you know. Nobody reads Matthew Arnold now, do they, but they should, they should. Listen to this," and she riffled the pages over until she came to her place. She raised her crooked little gemmed hand (something like a gemmed claw) and, the little crooked hand held up, said, "Listen! Mark this!" and Rose listened.

"How well Aunty reads poetry!" she thought. "With all her love of rattle and bang you'd think she would trumpet it, or read with windy eloquence. But her voice is slow and musical when she reads, and her tone is level and plain. She lets the words and phrases speak for themselves. This must be the training of the classical Mrs. Porter of whom I have heard; eighty years ago and more."

Aunty read, and her hand with its glittering rings remained upraised:

> "Only – but this is rare –
> When a beloved hand is laid in ours,
> When, jaded with the rush and glare
> Of the interminable hours,
> Our eyes can in another's eyes read clear,
> When our world-deafen'd ear
> Is by the tones of a loved voice caress'd –
> A bolt is shot back somewhere in our breast,
> And a lost pulse of feeling stirs again . . ."

She raised her voice and dulcetly she read on:

> "The eye sinks inward, and the heart lies plain,
> And what we mean, we say, and what we would,
>   we know.
> A man becomes aware of his life's flow,
> And hears its winding murmur; and he sees
> The meadows where it glides, the sun, the breeze . . .

> . . . And then he thinks he knows
> The hills where his life rose,
> And the sea where it goes."

There was quiet in the room, and then Aunty descended briskly from poetry. "That's from 'The Buried Life.' Read it. Read it. It's very good, a good man Matthew Arnold. My life rose in Staffordshire and I suppose it's going out into the Pacific Ocean. Well, well! But as for a Buried Life," said Aunty pertly, "I suppose some people have them. Couldn't say, I'm sure. I never did, myself, only for a time I suppose when I loved Unrequited for seven years. It isn't everyone who can love for seven years . . . Unrequited," said Aunty complacently. "Could you do that?"

"No," said Rose honestly, "I don't believe I could."

"There, you see," said Aunty scornfully, "you and your happy marriages! Any simpleton can do that. But to love Unrequited," she continued with satisfaction, "your generation hasn't got the guts to do it. Not a one of you could do it! Have I told you about it before? . . . Oh, I have." (Rose knew the story well.) "Well, here's tea! Good, good! You pour it out. And get down that picture of William Sandbach. That's him. Hasn't he got a handsome nose?"

"I'm always inclined to suspect a handsome nose," said her great-niece.

"What a ridiculous remark! Suspect a nose indeed! He was a widower, the handsomest man in Parliament they used to say. They lost their only son and then she went a little queer before she died. I'm not surprised, I'm sure.

"He gave me that picture. In Court dress with a white ostrich feather along his hat. Oh, I *was* proud when he gave me that picture. No, another lump, I like it sweet. Why don't you take sugar in your tea? You'd be fatter. You'd be a deal better-looking if you were fatter. Well, whenever distinguished people came to the Potteries, Mr. Sandbach gave a dinner-party. And he always asked John and me until John married Annie-John. John and I used to drive there in the brougham and we always Dressed. No one Dressed in Ware except at Mr. Sandbach's dinner-parties. Oh, I met Gladstone there (I worshipped Gladstone) and the Prince and Princess Colonna and Burne-Jones and Sir Garnet Wolseley and Baroness Burdett-Coutts and all the Foreigners. I could always talk, you see, English and French, oh yes. I could always talk and so could John, and so we were always asked. I never could bear to sit mum as a mouse. Very dull I call it. Just like Charles Lamb said, 'A party in a parlour, all silent and all damned!'"

"Wasn't it Wordsworth or wasn't it . . ." interrupted Rose.

"Don't argue so much," said Aunty. "You argue. Very unattractive in a woman, arguing, anyone will tell you. But I'd as lief go to bed as sit mum as a mouse. That young woman here last week. Not a word did she say. I talked to her all afternoon and not a word did she utter."

"Well, Aunty . . ." began Rose, defending.

"A bit more cake. . . .No, that one. And the result was that people said, 'You'll see, William Sandbach will marry Topaz Edgeworth!' Oh, it became very painful to me, very painful." Rose knew what was coming next. If she had not known, it would have shocked her, coming as a disclosure, a secret. But Aunty was enjoying herself. "Oh yes, I fell in love. How I suffered! Driving down with John to dinner and driving home again. My greatest joy and misery too. I loved him for seven years of my life, and it was wasted, wasted. I'm proud of it now, not everybody could do it! But then I said to myself, 'No, it's over,' and it *was* over. And I well remember, in me bedroom I raised me fist to heaven and I CURSED HIM!"

If ever a face flashed, Aunty's face flashes now. If ever a crooked jewelled hand was raised and shaken to heaven, it is hers. She lives through the distant dreadful moment again. Her face is contorted in pleasurable rage. Rose, curled up in the armchair, watches. She has seen this before. She has heard it before. "Wherein is it," she wonders, "that our generation is different? I'd feel a fool, shaking my fist to heaven. Aunty doesn't feel a fool and, moreover, she doesn't look it. She's enjoying herself. Don't we feel as deeply? Yes, we do. But we're different."

"How strange!" thought Rose, looking at Topaz. She marvelled again at the unquenched vitality of the small ancient being who was her Great-Aunt. This vitality had been preserved and untroubled by Aunty's lack of awareness of the human relations which compose the complicated fabric of living. The limitless treasure and absorbing motions of a continuous hidden life had neither enriched nor depleted her. Rose began to admire the candour of Aunt Topaz, who now had passed the zenith of her wrath.

"But," said Aunty, "I'll never forget, when I came back to England in nineteen-twenty, I was driving up Port Hill in John's brougham and I saw William Sandbach walking up alone, and ill he looked, and very very old. And I bade the coachman stop the horse, and I leaned out of the brougham and said, 'Mr. Sandbach, may I offer you a lift home?' And he came up to the brougham and he took off his hat. We looked at each other. It was a strange moment," said Aunty gently, "very strange. And he got in. And as we talked I thought, 'How could I curse him? How could I be so wicked, and how could he make me suffer so?' It was all washed away except that I had cursed him. I regretted it bitterly, bitterly, when I saw him old and ill. We drove him home and I never saw him again, and I could not read his thoughts."

Aunty sat quiet for a moment, but not for long. "Well, and how's Charles? . . . Oh, here's someone. Who is it? Who? Visitors? Oh, good. I like visitors. Now . . . do I know . . .? Oh!" with delight. "Oh-h-h," in a downward ripple of pure joy. "It's Frank, I do declare! *And* Stephen! Well, I do declare!" And with her winning greeting face she offered a fresh welcome.

TWENTY-SIX

Sea-gulls in the City

THERE CAME a day when those who strained their eyes and looked forwards could see the forms of designs blocked out upon the future. These designs took shape and meaning with the present and with the past. Men did not need to be prophets to discern these patterns. Bombs would explode, men would drown, cities would burn, peoples would flee, dissension and faith would prevail, the pattern of suffering was clear. The future ceased to be a peaceful obscurity blocked by a concrete tomorrow which could be reached out to and almost touched as the planet revolved. The future (which was really one with the present and the past) became shockingly discernible. And beyond visibility it was to a point implicit and to be believed. As the planet revolved making day and night against the patterned curtain of Time, men painted daily in violent colours of noise and flame and with an infinite unexpected detail of private living the terrible designs upon the curtain. With the revolving of the planet the painted many-dimensioned curtain slipped slowly by and joined the past while men busied themselves painfully about the present and the future. Or it seemed that as the curtain on which men were painting, with extreme difficulty, slipped backwards, men proceeded forwards against the curtain at a snail's pace into a future already in being. The voice speaking from the field of battle had always, in the nature of things, been prepared to speak. The battle had always been, and was

221

completed before it had begun. The mother sat with the bit of paper not an hour old, and her heart which failed within her told her, "I have always known this, it has always been; when he was so high, this was approved in Time and I sat here with this paper."

While these events were disclosed in the world of Time, there was a timeless and impersonal world to which men turned and in which they found momentary refreshment. The permanence of the fleeting and prodigal joy of this timeless world was without responsibility or question. The unearthly light of morning on the flank of the hill departs and is eternal and no one can prevail against it. The permanence of the impermanent frail flower is for ever. So is the sunshine on clover and the humming bees. The teasing whisper of the little wave on the shingle turns and always creeps in again. The beauty of structure of a tree or of a mountain changes but will never change. In these satisfying things men refreshed themselves painfully yet with delight.

Aunt Topaz had always been too much occupied with living to notice the existence and relation of these two worlds of man. The nature of her world did not change, although it had become constricted, which made it more closely packed with interest. Hence she was never lonely nor anxious. She is cared for diligently. She is visited by the family, but rarely visits the family now. Each night she unfurls the newspaper and rattles it this way and that, and reads, exclaiming to Mme Brizard, the very bad news and all the advertisements with equal attention. She is busy with these things, and seldom turns to observe the dreadful sights which appear upon the great painted moving curtain of Time. Nor does she passionately require the comfort of the sunset or the bird on the wing. She waits for the newspaper with all the beautiful advertisements. "Is it come?"

In the green park opposite the house on the hill where Rose lives there are trees where small birds build and fly and sing. In the late afternoon the ascending songs of evening spiral into the still air. There is a good large space of green there. Legally, it is owned by the city. But actually it is possessed by the people who live around the park, by children who fly kites there, by dogs, and by sea-gulls who have no regard for anybody else. Let us turn and look at these white birds who take no heed of the war.

The sea-gulls walk proudly in this park. They stand still. Then with the air of one taking up the collection they walk away majestically. They then turn and walk back again. The rain pours down and the sea-gulls stand and walk in the rain with indifference. The people who live around the park look through their rainy windows at the sodden park and at the sea-gulls standing there looking fatter than usual, like white sheep on the grass. The people like the sea-gulls to be there. They think it gives the tame and planted park a look of wildness and what-will-happen-next. These sea-gulls fly in from the Pacific Ocean. The people who live around the park always debate when they see the sea-gulls like sheep grazing there. They say, "There must be a dreadful storm at sea or the sea-gulls would not be here." But they can never prove it, because there is not a dreadful storm every time the sea-gulls come. There is some secret reason why they come to the city parks, and indeed further inland, in varying weather. They are not always seeking for food in the grass and furrows.

Sometimes they come in fine breezy weather. Then woe to the sea-gulls, because Rose's two dogs, Johnny and Tuppence, will drive them about the park and give them no peace. Johnny and Tuppence are two wire-haired terriers, but when they see the sea-gulls in the park they become, not two dogs, but a gang, a pack, an army of avenging dogs. They tear from end to end of the little park, driving away the sea-gulls. The sea-gulls wheel about and settle again idly, flapping and folding their great wings. The defeated dogs bear down upon them again, but the sea-gulls elude the dogs and fly away, settling down again, flapping and folding their great wings. This drives the dogs mad. They cannot endure to see the sea-gulls standing and walking in their park. But the big white birds do not seem to notice the frenzied dogs. Simply they rise and fly and settle again.

On a very wet day, however, Johnny and Tuppence, who

love comfort, lie in two compact and similar curves in front of the fire, and the gulls walk in dignity unmolested. Rose looks out of the window. "If I were not a person," she thinks, looking through the streaming window-pane at the devilishly indifferent gulls walking in the rain, "I should like to be a dog in a nice family, or else I should like to be a sea-gull." A dog looks at his own people and his heart is full of love for them. The good smell of his own people fills him with content and often with rapture, and by his soft brown gaze, by his leaping, by his vibrating tail, he tells his love to his dear people. The big white sea-gull has no heart of love. He is beautiful, strong, calculating, and rapacious. He does not love his own kind or humankind. He barely tolerates them. This carnal and lawless bird is slave to nothing but his own insatiable appetite. But just the same, there is something about a sea-gull.

Vancouver runs down to the sea. This way it runs down to the salt inlet. That way it runs down to the salt creek. East to west it runs to the Pacific Ocean. The hungry arrogant sea-gulls possess the water-front. Ships come into the harbour from up the coast, from down the coast, from across the gulf, and again from the Orient, too, they come. The arrogant greedy birds escort the ships to harbour, screaming and wheeling about the stern. Sometimes the sea-gulls fly over the city streets, and their mewing cries disturb the busy or abstracted minds of townspeople going about their business. Something shakes for an instant the calm of a man crossing the street when he hears the cry of a gull above the traffic, something that is not a sound but a disturbing, forgotten, unnamed desire, a memory. Java, Dubrovnik, the Hebrides. What is it?

Rose walks down Granville Street, and the gulls, so scornful of the traffic, swoop between the walls of grey buildings. Their cries sound high above the traffic in the sunlight, like the call of the muezzin in the minaret at the end of the crowded Galata Bridge. Someone, not everyone, hears the voice above the crowd. Rose is going to buy the new hat. She sees the wheeling birds in the sunshine. Then her thoughts fly away as the gulls swoop and cry over the city streets. Land's End, the gusty Channel, the sun on the striped awnings at Ostend. The cry of the wheeling gulls in the city streets.

The gulls know on which side their bread is buttered. For all that they are lawless birds of the sea and shore, they frequent the domestic windows of high buildings, hoping that people will put food out on the window-ledges, and sometimes people do.

Great-Aunt Topaz still lives with Mme Brizard at the top of the seven-storey apartment house, and from her bedroom window she can look out across the salt water of the Inlet to the enchanting mountains north of Vancouver. She has nearly forgotten the mountains (which so enchanted her half a century ago). One does, except when visitors come. "Yes, haven't I a marvellous view!" Then she sees them again. In winter they are white almost to their base, and very glorious against the clear sky. In summer they hold hardly any snow. They lie vaporous, low, unreal, almost dissolving in the warm coloured air. In wet weather no one can see them. No, the mountains are not there. But the sea-gulls come. They fly and turn and fly again past and past the high windows. Great-Aunt Topaz watches for them. She does not like eating crusts, and so she pokes her crusts out onto the window-ledge beside her bed. Down swoop the gulls. Two of them sit on her window-ledge, bowing and flapping and balancing. They look very cruel. They would eat up the little Great-Aunt if she were smaller and inanimate. Aunty laughs with delight and talks to them through the window. She pokes out more and more bread and cake, and the gulls gobble and balance and look at her with their predatory stare.

"Oh, Miss Edgeworth," says Mme Brizard coming in for the tray, "every bit gone! You *have* done well." "Yes, haven't I?" says Aunt Topaz, and the gulls fly past the window and back again.

One gull, however, really settles on the window-ledge. He bows and bows, and presses himself against the pane, staring at the Great-Aunt in his avaricious way. He is not interested that she talks and laughs to him. He is completely interested in food. There is no more food. At last the sea-gull accepts and despises this fact, so he flies away. He looks grey from beneath, but the breaking sunlight from above outlines his strong wings in bright transient silver. He has a fine life, but he is too earnest.

Vancouver people going home from work in the late afternoon who chance to look upwards, see the sea-gulls flying out to sea singly, and in twos, threes, and companies, through the changing skies of evening. On come the gulls, flying steadily westwards and seawards to the places where they will spend the night. If you scatter your pieces now, the gulls will not turn, descend, alight, and devour. Food does not tempt them as they proceed together on their appointed flight. Only a wind disturbs them, and when a west wind blows furiously in from the sea on a bright evening, the sea-gulls, caught in its power, fly high, and higher, wheel, negotiate, gather and disperse. There is an exultation communicated to the evening watcher who lifts his eyes to the mysterious sight.

In the evening while the sea-gulls fly westwards with lazy purposeful flight, and great and terrible events are massed by Time and Plan upon the slow-moving curtain, Aunt Topaz gathers the rattling newspaper together and with her embroidery scissors cuts out a picture of the King and Queen, an account of a wedding, and an advertisement for garlic pearls because they sound so odd. She may send for these pearls some day. She puts the newspaper cuttings into a large overfull box with a red plush cover on which some sea-shells still remain. She is very old. She will soon be a hundred.

TWENTY-SEVEN

Unlike the Saintly Elijah

THE FOURTH day of intense heat came. "Oh, this heat," thought Rose, pushing back her hair. "And I have to meet the train and bring John and Annabel up to the house, and settle them in, and go to the meeting, and take Annabel to the luncheon, and go to the wedding, and here's Mme Brizard away and Aunty's Miss Cox in a state and I must find someone to take her place this afternoon. I'll ring up that Miss Umplethwaite who used to look after old Mrs. Dickenson. Umplethwaite, Umplethwaite. Here it is."

Rose telephoned.

"Oh, Miss Umplethwaite, is that Miss Eleanor Umplethwaite? Oh, Miss Umplethwaite, it's Mrs. Forrest. Do you remember I asked you if you would be able to help with my Great-Aunt Miss Edgeworth some day? Yes, I know, you looked after old Mrs. Dickenson, yes, they told me. Yes, delightful, oh, so nice. Well, so is Miss Edgeworth. Perfectly charming, yes, indeed. Well, we're rather in a fix, her companion Mme Brizard is away on her holidays, and we have little Miss Cox with her, and Miss Cox's sister has just broken her arm and Miss Cox feels she has to go out there but she'll be back this evening, and I'm going to a wedding, I really have to, and so has Mrs. Hastings, in fact we've no one to go in and sit with Miss Edgeworth. Oh no, no trouble. Just to sit with her and get some tea, and be there. Oh no, she's up and dressed today, I really wouldn't ask you if – Yes, it is, isn't it? Really dreadful. Cold I *can* stand, but this heat! No. Really

227

exhausting. I quite agree. *How* kind! You'll find the apartment very cool and pleasant. I envy you I'm sure. I say I quite envy you! Yes, as soon as you can, and I'll drop in later if possible, and, anyway, Miss Cox will be back before six. Oh, thank you, that *is* nice, Miss Umplethwaite, I'm so relieved you can't imagine."

And then she telephoned again.

"Hello, hello. Oh, Miss Cox, it's all right, I've got Miss Umplethwaite, no – Umplethwaite, and she'll be there about two. Yes, I told her. Oh, very nice; she used to be with old Mrs. Dickenson. I told her only tea to get, and just *be* there, and, of course, it's so nice and cool in the flat. I told her Miss Edgeworth would be no trouble. Yes, isn't it hot! Oh, I'm sure you do, oh, really, your poor sister! It *is* too bad . . . above the elbow! . . . such a simple thing too, anyone might . . . yes, I quite understand . . . Yes, you must be . . . terribly . . . in this heat – yes, indeed. It is, isn't it, most exhausting, you could fry an egg on the pavement. I said you could fry – oh, nothing."

"Well," said Aunt Topaz to the agitated Miss Cox, "what's all this fuss about an elbow? Whose elbow? Well, run along, run along. Hot? It's not hot. Very pleasant I call it in this flat with all the windows open. Who? Never heard such a name. Never heard such a name in my life. Umplethwaite? I don't need any Miss Umple to look after me. There's the bell. I suppose it's that young woman with the peculiar name. Oh, how do you do?" with the utmost winningness to the polite Miss Umplethwaite.

Miss Cox and Miss Umplethwaite exchange instructions, lamentations about the heat, and hasty farewells and promises. And as fast as Miss Cox puts on her hat and reaches for her hand-bag Miss Umplethwaite takes off her hat, lays down her hand-bag, and sits down opposite Great-Aunt Topaz ingratiatingly but very much fatigued by her haste and obligingness on this sultry day. Miss Cox departs with lightning speed to her sister.

"Well," says Aunt Topaz, "have I ever seen you before? That's a nice brooch you have on, to be sure, a very nice brooch. Hair in it. I have one with hair in it too. You see! And pearls. This hair belonged to old Mrs. Grimwade; very stingy she was but very kind to me. I have a ring too. Hair in it. What a many things they did put hair in, I do declare. I have some embroidery done with hair. Very sentimental I call it and far from hygienic. Now, let me see, what did you say your name is, Umple-something? Oh, yes, Yorkshire. A very fine county Yorkshire. Oh, the Minster, glorious, glorious" (signs of emotion and desiring to speak on the part of Miss Umplethwaite but she does not succeed), "many's the time I've stayed in York before we came to Canada. My Great-Uncle George Mallet married the daughter of a Canon of York – Canon Tillyard. No!!!" By this time Aunty and Miss Umplethwaite are dewy with the happiness of shared memories of loved places and name. On they go. Suddenly Miss Umplethwaite remembers her duties.

"Wouldn't you like a cup of tea, Miss Edgeworth?" she asks pleasantly.

Great-Aunt Topaz stops short and looks at her. She has thought of something.

"No, I wouldn't like a cup of tea," she says, "but I *would* like a nice bit of ice-cream. Get me me hat and me stick, and me little bag with me purse in, and we'll just walk to the drug-store and sit down and have a nice ice-cream; you can help me, you know."

Now this is very wily of Great-Aunt Topaz, because although it is only one long block it is really much too far for her to walk to the drug-store, and she knows it, especially on this hot day. But Mme Brizard is away, Miss Cox is away, Miranda and Rose, those two lynx-eyed ones, are not here, and innocent Miss Umplethwaite is at Aunty's mercy.

Miss Umplethwaite is dismayed. This is the first time she's been cool to-day. "Oh, Miss Edgeworth!" she exclaims, "you've no idea how hot it is outside! It's so lovely and cool in here. The sidewalk's like a stove, and the sun beating down. It's like an oven! It's most unusual. Exhausting. Everyone complaining. Indeed my sister's husband forbade her absolutely to go out in this heat." Miss Umplethwaite delicately mops her brow and upper lip on which the perspiration starts. She invokes the superior sex.

"If I had a husband and he forbade me to do anything," says Aunty, "I should – well, let me see – I should kick him. I *need* a bit of ice-cream," piteously, "many's the time . . .", and she pounds busily to her bedroom. She reappears with her hat on, with her stick, two hand-bags, and a pair of white cotton gloves. She will go to the ice-cream. It shall not come to her. The already defeated Miss Umplethwaite is still anxious not to go out into the heat; she is anxious not to betray Mrs. Forrest's trust in her; and she really is afraid that Great-Aunt Topaz or she (Miss Umplethwaite) may have a stroke in the street. The heat is intense. She will say the dread word, stroke.

"Aren't you afraid, Miss Edgeworth, that the heat might be too much for you, that you might be overcome by the heat? And um . . .?"

"What do you mean?" says Aunty, who uses plain English. "Do you mean shall I have a stroke? No, I shan't have a stroke. Not one in my family ever had a stroke. It runs in some families. Not in mine. Come along, come along now," rather testily. She is afraid of the return of the preventing Miss Cox.

Leaning heavily upon Miss Umplethwaite, who perspires freely though unwillingly, Aunty pounds in her own peculiar way down the street. She leans thus heavily upon her companion because she uses her stick chiefly for pointing, either at merchandise in the shop-windows, or at people and other objects. She is a menace. People wince as she points. People walk languidly along the hot street; dogs pant in the shade, rise, lie down and pant again. The pavement feels like a stove-top. The heat beats upwards. Aunty indulges a life-long passion of hers.

"Oh," she says, "there's Mrs. Tibbett, I do declare! How do you do, how do you do, there, you see, she's smiling at me. Oh, it's not Mrs. Tibbett. Well, well, it is pleasant out, to be sure. People complaining about a little sun. Oh, there's Mr. Clark, the Rev. Mr. Clark, he comes to see me, how do you do? Oh, it isn't Mr. Clark, he hasn't got his collar on, a very nice man though, I'm sure. Well, *can* that be Mrs. Hogg? Strawberries," she says, pointing dangerously at a shop-window with her stick. "We'll get some strawberries on the way back; I always have a little pepper on me strawberries. And a pineapple! What a treat! Well, I do declare, isn't that old Mrs. Meredith?" And so, smiling, bowing, rejoicing, Aunty goes to the drug-store with the exhausted Miss Umplethwaite.

Their progress back is slower. Miss Umplethwaite, refreshed with ice-cream, turns gratefully homewards. On Aunty the heat and the exercise and all the excitement have begun to tell. Walking becomes difficult. She leans more heavily on her companion.

"You walk very fast," says Aunty who had gaily trampled down to the drug-store almost dragging Miss Umplethwaite with her. "You'll have to go a deal slower. I'm not so young as you, you know. I can't go tearing along the way you do, you know. I'm feeling tired. I don't feel well." Aunty is still expert in accusation.

"Oh, Miss Edgeworth," Miss Umplethwaite says anxiously, "I told you you shouldn't have come, I said –"

"Don't begin saying 'I told you so,'" says Aunty with asperity. "I can't bear being rushed along in the heat. You're rushing me. Me legs don't seem to be functioning. There's something wrong with me legs."

"Oh, Miss Edgeworth," says the alarmed companion (the very first time out!), "lean on me, I'll help you along. I'll put my arm round you!" And so they walk, sweltering, each clutching the other.

"It's paralysis," says Aunty, irritated. "Never before in my family. I can't make it out. I can't feel me legs. I can't use them. OH! Elijah Jones was paralysed, he was a very saintly man was Elijah, handsome too; there were three Elijah Joneses in wheel-chairs, two of them with water on the knee and one paralysed, in three generations. That's why they stopped using the name Elijah in the Jones family. Oh, this is terrible. I can't even use me feet! Miss Umple, Miss Umple! I'm going to fall!"

Miss Umplethwaite is distracted. She seizes Aunt Topaz

more firmly. She glances down. Wreathed around Aunty's feet are her good white calico drawers. Descending, they had impeded her. Descended, they wrap her feet around. She is helpless to move.

"Lift up a foot, Miss Edgeworth, lift up a foot," implores Miss Umplethwaite, hotter than ever. Passers-by rouse from their lethargy and take interest. People turn and smile kindly enough.

"I can't lift a foot. I'm paralyzed! I've had a stroke, I do declare!" says Aunty, shocked.

"Oh yes, you can, Miss Edgeworth. Try. Try. It's only your . . .," murmurs Miss Umplethwaite, wrestling. She bends down and lifts up one of Aunt Topaz's strangely large and heavy feet, and wriggles the garment off; she lifts up the other foot, and wriggles the other part of the garment off; she whips the calico drawers up into a bundle, tucks them under her arm, and faces the world with a flush.

Great-Aunt Topaz is amazed. "Eh, it's me knickers!" she says astonished. She kicks out with one leg, kicks out with the other, and finds them free and active. Distress fades to surprise, to pleasure on her face. She steps out nimbly. She is pleased.

"This is a deal more comfortable," she says. "Well, what people wear all these clothes for, *I* can't think, this weather. This *is* comfortable, I'm sure. No, I won't put them on again. Well, what are you waiting for? I made sure it couldn't be a stroke. Something told me. Well, here we are. Oh, *there* you are, Rose!"

Aunt Topaz prances into the elevator, and up they go to the flat. She laughs merrily, and proceeds with heavy hasty tread to her apartment. Rose and Miss Umplethwaite are nearly fainting, Rose with the heat and Miss Umplethwaite with the heat and Aunty's knickers. Aunty is not fainting. "You see," she says, plucking the bundle from under Miss Umplethwaite's arm, "you see," holding up the calico drawers and flourishing them, "these are me knickers! The button came off, and down they came! And I thought, Rose, I was getting paralysis, just like poor Elijah Jones, a very saintly man and *such* a long beard, and his father and his great-uncle Elijah with water on the knee all in a bath-chair. Miss Umple, Miss Umple, will you get us some tea? And Miss Umple, take these away. I don't want them. A very nice young woman that. Has a brooch with hair in it. Well, that *was* a Do!" She laughs with delight, and, as she talks, Rose is aware that not the least of Aunty's triumph is that she is still one up on the saintly Elijah.

Miss Umplethwaite brings in some tea. She is silent and a little offended. Rose is sure that Miss Umplethwaite feels that she has been deceived, and that she will not come again.

Because Great-Aunt Topaz is a hundred years old and is still little Topaz Edgeworth with a strong infusion of *grande dame*, she is invincible. Small and great lapses from convention do not dismay her. Why should they? They entertain her. She is impatient of illness but not at all dismayed by death, which now can almost be heard approaching, it is so near. She has had a pleasant afternoon. Her enjoyment fills the room and dispels the chagrin of Miss Umplethwaite. "Miss Umple," Topaz says with good humour, "pull up your chair and have a cup. Well, that *was* a bit of a Do, to be sure!"

Miss Umplethwaite begins to smile again and to regard the whole thing as simply a bit of a Do.

TWENTY-EIGHT

A Hundred Years gone, and the 'Forties again

CHOPIN'S RAINDROP Prelude beats heavily through the
room. Those are not drops of rain; they are drops of lead.
Down go the keys, "R UM-ti-too (tum tum tum tum tum). . . ."
A deputy in a white apron rushes in, protesting. Aunty is
sitting on the piano-stool, playing vigorously. She has nipped
out of bed in her cotton nighty and is playing the Raindrop
Prelude. Both feet are firmly down on the pedals of the small
piano. The window is open. No, go away; she will not stop
playing and put her arms in her dressing-gown; no, she will
not go back to bed, and she will not catch cold; go away. This
bit of conflict satisfies her. Soon she is glad to be helped back
to bed, a little tired, after all.

Now her world is bounded by one room. Where are the
mountains which one sees from her windows? They do not
exist in her world; there is no rain driving against the win-
dow-panes; there are no neon lights reflected on Granville
Street, looking so pretty in the rain at night; there are no
sea-gulls; there are no armies and no torpedoed ships. There
is only her room and a friend ("Who is it?") coming in at the
door, to be greeted with tremulous delight. Come to think of
it, she has enjoyed about nine thousand consecutive days of
her apotheosis beside the Pacific Ocean. She has been healthy
and amused for ninety hundred days. Is she not lucky?

Her world continues to shrink. It is a bed; it is a cup of
milk; it is a voice which she essays to greet with customary

234

friendliness. Her memories have flowed away. Wherever can they be? Only habit remains.

Her world has closed down to a point; it is a point of departure. She is restless and ill at ease.

In the middle of the last century, when Topaz was a young girl, at the seasons of the great bird migrations, large areas of the Argentinean plains, "the green floor of the world," were covered by birds as by a carpet, and, when the birds took wing, the sky was invisible. As the time for departure drew near, the vast myriads of birds became nervous and restless to the point of anguish. This spirit of unrest "was marked in the most volatile species, the swiftest of wing and the wildest." One of the greatest of all field naturalists formed the theory that the birds of these migrations – leaving their habitat at a season when food was ample and the climate salubrious, leaving as it were against their will – were drawn in migration by a sense of polarity, that is, by the strong influence of the magnetic poles exerted upon their species at certain times. The birds are uncertain, restless; they are forced to go. One last bird remains alone, restless, nervous, undecided, wishing to go, awaiting something. After pitiful agitation the bird at last rises and follows the flight with confidence. There are certain things about which one can only form a theory.

If there is a sense of polarity which exerts an influence on the winged creatures of the pathless and unpreventing air, it seems reasonable that a polarity should exist, different in kind, to which the unknowing human spirit, through its own atmosphere more tenuous than air itself, responds.

Topaz is dying, there is no doubt of that. She – gay, volatile, one hundred years old, the last of her generation, long delayed – is uneasy. She is very restless. She shows no fear and yet she seems to be in some kind of anguish. Plainly she is awaiting something, an affirmation or release. What is that she is saying? She wants to go, she says. She is being prevented. The poor volatile bird.

"Let me go immediately . . . immediately . . ." she murmurs in her imperious way. "A hundred years . . . I shall be late . . . me, the youngest." Then the small face lightens. "Quick, get me some fresh lace for me head, someone! I'm going to die, I do declare!" Evidently she is pleased and confident. What an adventure, to be sure!

Away she went. Now she is a memory, a gossamer.

After the summing up, after the questions and answers ("O Death, where is thy sting?"), after the fusion of the large family standing together, life again became diffused and urgent; the scene which had bound them together ceased and the family dispersed. Something remained and something was ended.

"Do you want a lift?" asked Ruth. "The men are mostly going back to their offices, and Don's taking Ellen and Aunt Miranda, and Helen's looking after the boys, and Uncle Stephen is taking the others. I'm going up Granville Street." So Georgia and Rose got in and Ruth drove away in her little car. She drove for blocks and they were all three silent. Then they passed a little boy who blew a tin trumpet.

"Did I hear that Allan wants to learn the clarinet?" asked Georgia, suddenly amused.

"Yes," laughed Ruth, "won't it be awful!"

"I don't see why, if you can bear it at first. . . . Oh dear, I never never *never* shall forget the flowers all going to the wrong place. . . ."

" . . . Wasn't it terrible? And we could do nothing at all. There it was . . . I shall never forget . . . the poor little thing . . . I still can't see how it happened . . . and Aunty of all people . . ."

"Yes, *wasn't* it terrible? I felt *awful*, you could feel *everybody* feeling awful all round you," said Ruth driving neatly through the traffic. Her thoughts ran forward to the children and their supper. Should she stop and get ice-cream because they had not wanted to stay at Miss Gam's? Rose and Georgia sat pensive but not sad, thinking backwards. . . . They were away from the shops now and up Granville Street hill.

"Shall I drop you at the corner or will you come on with

me? I have to pick up the children. . . . I can stick them in the back. . . . I didn't like to take them to the funeral. . . ."

They drove along under the trees in the late sunshine. The sunshine was reflected from the leaves of the trees whose branches would soon be grown to touch across the road. First Georgia got out; then Rose. The sea-gulls were flying westwards in their ordained evening flight, in twos, threes, and companies, high overhead on account of the wind; but neither Rose nor Georgia noticed, because of the funeral, and because they were each preoccupied. The customary westward flight of the sea-gulls over the sea, through the evening sky, was, however, as always, a curious and ravishing sight.

(The Bell rings out; the pulse thereof is changed; the tolling was a faint and intermitting pulse, upon one side; this stronger, and argues more and better life. His soule is gone out. . . . His soule is gone; whither? Who saw it come in, or who saw it goe out? No body; yet every body is sure, he had one, and hath none. . . . This soule, this Bell tells me, is gone out; Whither? Who shall tell mee that? . . . mine owne Charity; I aske that; and that tels me, He is gone to everlasting rest, and joy and glory.

. . . We are . . . transported, our dust blowne away with prophane dust, with every wind.

(FROM THE EIGHTEENTH DEVOTION OF JOHN DONNE)

Afterword

BY P.K. PAGE

Twenty-three years after the publication of *The Innocent Traveller*, in a characteristically modest letter to John Gray, her publisher, Ethel Wilson wrote: "it is well written, I like it . . . I value it . . . ."

How different from her doubts in November of 1944 when she first submitted the manuscript to the Macmillan Company:

> Dear Sir – I shall venture to send you a few stories, three of which appeared in the New Statesman and Nation, the fourth in the Canadian Forum, the others not at all . . . I send these, not with expectations of acceptance, but with plain humility, as I am not sure whether they are good, a little good, or no good, or whether they would interest a public at all.

Two days later, even less secure, she wrote again:

> Dear Sir – I sent you lately a bundle of short stories which had suddenly begun to burn a hole in my pocket. I think I told you of my own uncertainty as to whether they are at all good.
>
> Distance has, I think, lent a proper perspective, and also the enormous events which agitate the country now. And my stories have dwindled into their proper size – the matter is so trifling, old fashioned, and of personal interest only, perhaps. One can hardly blame a public that requires "social awareness" in its reading, or something truly funny and entertaining –
>
> So this leads me to say that when you send me these little pieces – *collect* – I will welcome them into obscurity again.

Of such confidence and misgivings are good writers made! And Ethel Wilson was a very good writer indeed – a quirky and sophisticated writer with an individual style, tilting and elliptical. Witty as well as funny. Unique. But as yet unproven.

"If you cannot make something out of that Topaz saga you're not the writer we think you are," read the note accompanying the returned stories. It was not an outright rejection, but for Wilson it might as well have been. "When you definitely refused Topaz for the good reason of being short stories," she wrote in reply, "and I definitely knew that I can't and won't change her form, I sent them to . . . Simon and Schuster." And so began the discussions with Macmillan which were to continue over the succeeding five years.

In today's literary climate, it is difficult to understand why Macmillan took so long to decide to publish. One feels anyone with half an eye would have jumped at such a book. And it is clear from the correspondence that Macmillan *had* half an eye. The trouble lay with the other eye and a half, which could see a book as a book only if it was a novel. Linked stories, however consecutive, would not do. This attitude was not peculiar to Macmillan. In Canada few collections of stories, other than anthologies, had appeared before the sixties.

Then in 1946 Wilson wrote *Hetty Dorval*. Unarguably a novel, it was published by Macmillan in 1947. Two years later, her first-born, *The Innocent Traveller*, appeared. Wilson was sixty-two years old.

The Innocent Traveller is both family chronicle and fiction. "The persons and incidents are true," Wilson said of it in 1957, "or, when I made some up (as I did), they are so truly characteristic of certain persons that they approximate to truth." And she was right. Her characters *are* true – fictionally true. Flesh and blood.

"One day I will write down my stories," she is reported to have said to a friend, "but not until Granny, Aunt Eliza and Aunty Belle are dead." The last of them, Aunt Eliza, died in 1943, aged one hundred. Wilson must have meant "publish," not "write," for it is evident from her papers that she had been writing and revising *The Innocent Traveller* (originally called *Topaz*) for nineteen years. During that time its title was changed and changed again, as was the order of its chapters. What remained unchanged was Eliza herself, the book's central character, and energy. "I called her Topaz," Wilson wrote. "There had to be a 'z' in her name, for she had sudden small dazzles and sparkles, and . . . she was like a semi-precious stone . . . "

Let us have a look at Topaz in the book's opening paragraph as she first appears and makes her presence felt:

> Far away at the end of the table sat Father, the kind, handsome and provident man. At this end sat Mother, her crinoline spread abroad. On Mother's right was Mr. Matthew Arnold. On each side of the table the warned children ate their food gravely, all except Topaz on Mother's left. Topaz, who could not be squelched, was perched there on the top of two cushions, as innocent as a poached egg. Mother sat gracious, fatigued, heavy behind the majestic crinoline with the last and fatal child.

Already we are caught in the spell of the prose, in the pull of the plot. Who cares if this is fiction or memoir, short stories or novel? A world has been created in six sentences. A Victorian world. *Pater familias*, kind, handsome, provident, friend of Mr. Matthew Arnold. Mother about to die. (What a great deal is suggested about men and women of the period. Husbands and wives!) And the warned children – were they indeed not warned in Victorian England, children who should be seen and not heard – gravely eating their food. All, that is, except Topaz, impervious then, impervious always, to the limitations and conventions of her narrow world.

In real life, whatever that is, Topaz would drive one to distraction. She is talkative, trivial, tiresome – overwhelmingly unaware of the feelings of those around her. She is one of those unmarried women who stay "girls" all their lives, who are good sports, game for anything. Chattering and merry. Infuriating. At the same time she is unexpectedly flexible, unwaveringly kind, and, due to an almost total lack of imagination, endlessly surprised by life. She moves uncomplainingly through a hundred years of rapidly accelerating change, from Victorian England to post-Second-World-War Canada, only once raging at her fate.

"I am afraid that if I depart from the life of Topaz as it was," Wilson wrote to her publisher, "and begin to make a *story*, either rather violent or rather psychological out of it, I have to introduce someone who *does* something to Topaz, or to whom Topaz *does* something. But the point about her, I find, is that having no touch with reality below the top layer, she does nothing to anyone! She is incapable of it." She is, indeed, the innocent traveller of the well-chosen title.

With such material to work with, why is Topaz so memorable, so endlessly fascinating, so – lovable? The answer must lie in the fact that Wilson's inscribing eye – her incising, incisive eye – is sufficiently infused with a loving spirit that we catch her love. Literate Ethel Wilson, master of implication, mistress of delicate balances, is incapable of a boring thought. She carries us lightly, as though bearing no weight at all, through a myriad of interweaving mini-stories, deftly skirting the real pain, burning us only a little, but burning us just the same. Letting us touch the flame so we know how it feels. But not dwelling on it anymore than does Topaz herself.

"The drop of water, the bird, the water-glider, the dancer, the wind on the canal, and Topaz, are all different and all the same," she says in the Author's Note. And as this sharp and gentle book unfolds, she shows us their dance – back and forth in time, back and forth again – weaving an intricate fabric into which, while the spell is upon us, we are woven too. We become part of that Victorian community of women – of widows and unmarried aunts; part of that ordered, harmonious world: upper middle-class, reading Greek, travelling abroad, knowing our place. *Knowing our place*. Yet the detached and thoroughly modern mind of the author writes, at the same time, a wry, invisible gloss.

So Topaz, then, is wonderfully drawn, as are the splendid others. And that includes the author herself who appears first, as a disembodied "I" – surprisingly – before she is born. Later, as the orphaned, third-person Rose, she adds a younger voice to the Grandmother's house, even though she is usually off in her bedroom, hidden or half hidden (but observing, observing), while Topaz stamps about centrestage congenitally insensitive to everything – well, almost everything – around her.

But what of the book itself, what of its shape? For it *has* a shape, this collection of stories (or is it a novel, after all?). So delighted are we by its style, by its characters who have become our friends, that we have altogether forgotten shape. We have been carried along – like Topaz herself – absorbed, unthinking, until towards the end, the book gathers itself together, and we see by its circularity and lift that it is, in fact, a spiral. Echoes of its beginning sound once more, altered as echoes have to be. Topaz speaks poetry again not, as in Chapter 1, *to* Mr. Matthew Arnold but *by* Mr. Matthew Arnold. And as the first poem might anticipate Topaz's single life, so the second anticipates her death:

> A man becomes aware of his life's flow,
> And hears its winding murmur; and he sees
> The meadows where it glides, the sun, the breeze . . .
> . . . And then he thinks he knows,
> The hills where his life rose,
> And the sea where it goes.

Three short chapters from the end when, as through a scrim, we glimpse the brutalities of war, Wilson suddenly confronts us with what previously she has repeatedly hinted at – the enigmatic nature of time – and which we now see as the theme of the book. "The future," she tells us, "[is] really one with the present and the past."

And as we confront "a timeless and impersonal world" and are asked to consider "the permanence of the impermanent frail flower," the retreat and return of the little wave on the shingle, we watch the gulls, which have unexpectedly invaded the book, circle and rise and fly off to sea. And we know that it will not be long before Topaz, "poor volatile bird," will follow.

BY ETHEL WILSON

FICTION
Hetty Dorval (1947)
The Innocent Traveller (1949)
The Equations of Love (1952)
Swamp Angel (1954)
Love and Salt Water (1956)
Mrs. Golightly and Other Stories (1961)

SELECTED WRITINGS
Ethel Wilson: Stories, Essays, and Letters
[ed. David Stouck] (1987)